Life is the flower, love is the honey
Victor Hugo

The Middle of Nowhere

Ruth Kipnis

First Edition Design Publishing
Sarasota, Florida USA

The Middle of Nowhere
Copyright ©2022 Ruth Kipnis

ISBN 978-1506-910-43-7 PBK
ISBN 978-1506-910-44-4 EBK

March 2022

Published and Distributed by
First Edition Design Publishing, Inc.
P.O. Box 17646, Sarasota, FL 34276-3217
www.firsteditiondesignpublishing.com

ALL RIGHTS RESERVED. No part of this book publication may be reproduced, stored in a retrieval system, or transmitted in any form or by any means — electronic, mechanical, photocopy, recording, or any other — except brief quotation in reviews, without the prior permission of the author or publisher.

This year I lost a dear friend and my editor when Sue Clark passed away. Her guidance and moral support gave me the courage to publish my first book and now this my fifth book. Thanks, Sue, for inserting the millions of commas and the good-humored critiques. You will be missed.

Previous books by Ruth Kipnis

Lane's End
A French Connection
His Name was David Freeman
The Butterfly.

www.ruthkipnis.com

Chapter 1

It happened in a split second. Headlights heading straight for us, the screech of brakes, the deafening sound of metal on metal. An explosion as the semi hit us head on sending shards of glass flying my way, the air bag hitting my chest causing instant, intense pain. Then nothing but silence.

Like awakening from a deep sleep, I found it hard to find my bearings. I tried to relate the surroundings. My eyes searching for something familiar as the room began to come into focus. Why was my sister Jennifer sitting at my bedside? What was I doing in this semi-dark hospital room? The constant sound of the monitor above my bed echoed in my ears. I noticed a needle taped to a vein at my wrist. What was I doing here? My mind was blank, like an erased blackboard that had been wiped clean except for a few disjointed words left at the edges. Nothing made sense.

My sister leaned over the bedrail and took my hand in hers. "Julia, thank God you're awake."

"Sort of. What am I doing here?"

"You were in an accident, Sis. Don't you remember?"

Nothing registered. I kept drifting in and out of consciousness, hearing disjointed bits of my sister's voice fading in and out, the words sounding as if they came from the depths of a deep tunnel.

I attempted to sit up, hoping to clear my head, but the slightest movement caused intense pain throughout my whole body. God, my head ached.

"What accident? Jennifer?"

"Oh, sweetheart, you and Roger were in a horrific car crash on the way back to the city from the Wagner's party five nights ago."

"Are you saying I've been here for five nights?" I tried to concentrate, feeling Like a traveler lost in a strange world, lost somewhere between dreams and reality. I tried to recall a party, was it another one of the boring family events celebrating Roger and my upcoming wedding.

"Yes, Jennifer, I think I remember, there was a party at Roger's aunt's house in Connecticut, but I don't remember any accident. God, Sis, what's happening to me."

"Let me run and get the nurse. She'll be happy to know you're conscious. We've all been so worried."

No matter how hard I tried I couldn't remember anything about an accident. The doctor called it temporary amnesia, my mind blocking out events too horrible to remember -- things I didn't want to recall like Jennifer telling me Roger had be killed in the collision.

Over the space of this last year, my life has been on hold. My time spent in and out of hospitals and rehab facilities recovering from three surgeries, but that was all coming to an end today. Like a prisoner who'd completed their sentence I was being released for the last time. My body had healed, but my mind was a mess. No matter how hard I tried to push back reality, the time had come to return to civilization. Time for me to try to put my life back together.

I dealt with Roger's death by putting it out of my mind. They told me he died instantly. I'd become used to friends no longer visiting. Once in a while, I'd receive a call asking how I was doing. I was feeling rotten, but that's not what they were interested in hearing. I can't blame my friends for going on with their lives without me. I'd done nothing to suggest I was ready to return to the living. In fact, I'd done everything I could to discourage their invitations.

The gentle tap on the door told me the private nurse my father had hired to watch over me had arrived. She was my warden, my constant companion. I referred to her as Nurse Ratchet. The poor woman meant well, but I had no interest in being any nicer to her than I was to anyone else around me.

"Come in, Ratchet," my inflection dismissive.

She'd never read, *One Flew Over The Cuckoo's Nest*, so she had no idea why I referred to her by that name, or in such a derogatory tone.

"You're not dressed, Julia. Shame. The doctor has already signed your release and we should have been ready to leave by now. Your father will be waiting for us and you know how impatient he can be. Hurry now, put on your clothes, while I call for the wheelchair."

I couldn't explain why I wasn't dressed. I should have been eager to leave, but somehow, I was afraid to abandon the cocoon I'd encased myself in, too afraid to return to the real world. Whoever said, "Life must go on" was an idiot.

A male attendant pushed the wheelchair close to the grey Lincoln Town Car. Sam, my father's driver was holding the rear door open, a broad smile on his face.

"Mornin, Miss Julia. Glad to see you is comin' home. I'm real sorry about Mr. Roger."

I nodded, not wanting to think about Roger. His death was just one of a long list of things I wasn't ready to deal with.

Sam took our cases as Ratchet went around to the other side and got in the car.

"Your father said he was sorry he couldn't take you home his self, Sam said as he started the engine. He had an important meetin' this morning. He said to tell you he'd see you at dinner. Mandy, sure is glad her baby's comin' home. She's been cookin' your favorite food all day long."

"Good to be coming home, Sam." I settled into the back seat ignoring Ratchet as she kept trying to make small talk. I stared out the window as familiar sights came into view. Sam slowed the car as he pulled into the long driveway. The house nestled amid a grouping of shade trees came into view. The manicured flower garden, the lawn freshly mowed, all brought a feeling of comfort, and a sense security from the outside world. I grew up here in the Heathcote section of Scarsdale. We were a happy lot -- Peter and Adam, my older brothers, and my sister, Jennifer. Being the baby of the family, growing up I'd always had someone watching over me, until the last year when I faced almost everything alone. My siblings were now scattered all over the East Coast, busy with their own lives.

My childhood was uneventful. In many ways I'd been too protected. My father, a partner in a successful law firm, worked in New York. My mother stayed at home doing what wives of successful businessmen did in those days. She raised her children, ran the household, and donated her time to various charities. Her life really not much different than what I'd expected my life with Roger to be like. I'd have a career until we decided to have children. Then move into a newly purchased house somewhere in Connecticut suburbs within commute distance of New York I'd raise a family much like my mother did. Was this the life I really wanted or was I being the dutiful daughter doing what was expected?

Sam brought my suitcase in as Ratchet suggested I go upstairs and rest until lunch. I'd reached the point where even the sound of Ratchet's voice set me on edge. The time had come for her to go. I didn't need a nurse or a nursemaid any longer. I just wanted to be left alone.

I climbed the stairs, my hip still painful, and walked down the long hall past the closed doors of bedrooms no longer occupied, and opened the door to my old room. The familiar bedroom with its pale-yellow walls, the grey and white-striped chintz duvet with matching shams held so many memories. The room had been decorated years ago when I was still a teenager. I hadn't lived at home since graduating from college, only coming home for holidays.

My first living arrangement was a walkup with three roommates in Soho. It wasn't much different than the years I lived in the sorority house. Later, as my career advanced with a boost in salary, I moved into a small rented apartment of my own in Manhattan.

I stood in the doorway as a sense of sadness rolled over me like a huge, crashing wave I couldn't escape, dragging me down to the very depths of an ocean floor. I wasn't sure I had the strength to fight my way back to the surface. The room took me back to my happy childhood. I had so many expectations, so many dreams. Would I ever be able to dream again?

I stepped inside and collapsed on the bed, not bothering to turn back the duvet. The room was filled with sunshine from the three dormer windows, but that didn't manage to lift my spirits. I glanced at the built-in window seat, with its peach chintz cushions and pillows, and remembered the hours I spent as a child curled up in that nook with a book and my cat, Ginger nestled beside me. The cat, like everything else in my life, was gone. I fought back the tears.

Chapter 2

While I was hospitalized, my father allowed the lease on my apartment to lapse. He had all my furniture and belongings packed and stored in a warehouse somewhere. The job I loved at Claiborne Advertising was gone as well. I'd been replaced. My career, like my life, was now on hold. Last but not least, Roger had left this world two weeks before our wedding.

Roger and I had been best friends ever since we met my freshman year at Dartmouth. Even though we'd grown up in the same neighborhood, our paths had never crossed. He was a few years older, and we'd gone to different prep schools.

We hit it off at once. We liked the same things, and we got along well. He was almost like one of my brothers, more often than not treating me like his little sister. He quickly became my best friend.

After he graduated two years ahead of me, Roger went to work for his father's insurance brokerage company in New York as was expected. Our relationship grew more serious when I moved to the city after graduation.

It seemed inevitable we'd be married sooner or later. I'd never really dated anyone else on a regular basis. I felt comfortable with Roger. Ours was never a passionate love affair. We were more like two friends comfortable in the prospect of living their lives in the same fashion our parents did. His family, as well as mine, belonged to the same country club. The men played golf there every Saturday, while the wives lunched there every Wednesday. Our families couldn't have been happier with our engagement.

Roger and I agreed I'd keep my job after we were married. We'd make our home in the city, where we had a great group of friends, many of whom we'd grown up with. We all went to the same cocktail parties, had dinners at the best restaurants, and spent summer weekends at somebody's family home in the Hamptons. We were teased good-naturedly by our friends as acting like an old married couple even before our wedding.

I could look ahead then and know exactly how my life would unfold. I knew at a certain point we'd move to the suburbs, have a family, and life would be so simple, but now all that had once been so comfortable and predictable was gone. I felt lonely, alone, and unable to see a future.

I heard Ratchet call me for lunch. I'd speak to dad tonight and have him send her on her way.

Sleeping late became part of the new routine I settled into. There was no reason to get out of bed early, there was nothing I wanted to do, and no place I wanted to go. The therapist I met with in the hospital explained I was experiencing a mild case of depression. Not uncommon considering all I'd been through. He prescribed a medication I never bothered to take.

As the weather grew nicer, I swam laps in our heated pool as part of my rehab, ate a light breakfast on the patio, skipped lunch, and waited for dinner with my dad. The time in between hung heavy. I couldn't concentrate long enough to read a book. I felt on edge, ill tempered. I'd even snapped at Mattie, who I dearly loved, for trying to put a few extra pounds on me.

The days dragged on until one day thinking maybe a change of scenery might help, I asked Sam for the keys to dad's car. He hesitated, offering to drive me any place I wanted to go, but I insisted. The look on his face was one of concern, but he was in no position to refuse me. He reached into his pocket and reluctantly handed me the keys.

I fastened the seatbelt and sat behind the wheel for a long time before I had the courage to start the ignition. I backed out of the garage having no idea where to go, finally deciding that my first outing alone should be to the cemetery to pay my respects.

It felt strange to be driving. I was nervous at first, more cautious than the light traffic demanded. I tried to ignore the honking of an impatient driver behind me. Watching every car approaching from the opposite direction with a sense of fear.

I'd stopped at the florist and purchased a dozen white roses. Now as I drove through the cemetery gates, the flowers wrapped in green tissue paper on the seat beside me, I had an odd feeling. The eerie silence and row after row of grave markers, rather than giving me a sense of peace, made me want to turn and run.

Having missed Roger's funeral, there persisted a sense of detachment. Over a year had passed and my life had gone on without him.

I placed the flowers alongside the granite headstone and read the inscription. He was only thirty years old when he died. Good God, he'd never had a chance to really live life. A cold chill ran down my spine as I thought except for a twist of fate I could have been resting here as well.

The whole experience felt strange, I couldn't explain why I had no tears. Why I felt nothing. I could have been looking at the gravesite of a complete stranger. As I drove home, I knew I'd never visit Roger's gravesite again.

Father's routine was to spend Friday night's having dinner at the country club, so I found it strange he was home. The table set for two. At his suggestion, I joined him for a drink on the patio. My mother died several years ago leaving dad living alone in our large house, alone except for the circumstances that brought me home I think he was enjoying having the company.

Handing me a glass of wine dad sat beside me resting his scotch and soda on the coffee table. "Julia, my dear." He sounded serious. "I'm going to be traveling to Atlanta for an important trial soon. It could take anywhere from a couple of weeks to a month to complete. I'm not happy leaving you here alone."

"I'm not alone, Dad. Mattie and Sam are here. I'll be fine. You really don't have to worry about me. I'm not a child."

"That's the point, my dear. I do worry about you. Besides, Mattie and Sam are going to be away on vacation and I'm uneasy leaving you on your own in the house for an extended period of time without any help."

Picking up his glass and taking a long drink dad continued, "I've spoken to my sister Sarah and she'd be delighted to have you come to Montana for a visit."

"Really, Dad, Tell me you're not serious. That you're idea of a solution is to send me off to visit a woman I don't know even if she is my aunt."

"Sweetheart, I can't help but be concerned. It's time you started putting your life back in order. You can't retreat forever. Mourning time is over. It's time to pick up the pieces of your life and move on."

"I will, Dad. I'm just not ready,"

"My sister Sarah is one of the most level headed people I know. Since your mother's no longer with us, I thought maybe you could use a little feminine help. Spend some time with her, Julia. Maybe she can help you find your way forward."

I went to the bar and refilled my wine glass, realizing my dad was only trying to be of help. I turned toward him with a smile on my face not wanting to seem ungrateful for his concern. "I'll think about it."

Chapter 3

Late Saturday morning, as I walked past the dining room on my way to the pool, I saw my dad sitting at the dining room table with a stack of notebooks in front of him, deep in conversation with a casually dressed young man I didn't recognize.

Spotting me, he called, "Julia, come here for a moment. I'd like you to meet Tim Henderson, one of the bright young attorneys in my office. Tim, this is my daughter, Julia."

Tim stood as I entered. "Hello, Julia. I'm glad to meet you at last. Your father tells me you've completely recovered from the accident." He smiled as he moved to shake my hand, "Your father speaks highly of you."

I felt awkward and embarrassed to be standing there with a beach cover over my bathing suit, my hair tied back in a ponytail, no makeup, and not even a touch of lip-gloss. "Thank you," was all I could think of to say as I attempted to leave.

"Join us for lunch, Julia. I won't be golfing today."

As it seemed there was no way I could avoid joining them, I forced a smiled and walked off to the pool.

Lunch was more than uncomfortable as much of the conversation was directed toward me with a myriad of questions from Tim about my time at the ad agency, the accident, and the operations. I tried to change the subject hoping to turn the attention onto Tim. No matter how sincere Tim sounded I had no interest in discussing personal matters with a complete stranger.

Thank goodness my father was anxious to get back to work on the Atlanta case forgoing his usual leisurely lunch. While lunch was shorter than usual, just not short enough to suit me.

Retreating to my bedroom I mulled over the real reason for Tim's meeting with dad at home and his professed interest in me. I grew madder as the day grew longer. I didn't see my dad again until dinner and by that time I was hopping mad. I sat down at the table, picked up my wine glass as Mattie served the salad, and let the words fly.

"How could you, Dad? Was that your sly way of getting me to move on?"

"What in the hell are you talking about, Julia?" Clearly not understanding what had me so upset.

"You know damn well what I'm talking about, bringing that young lawyer here to meet me. Does he call and ask me out in the next week or two?"

"Whoa. Hold on there. If you mean Tim Henderson, he was here to go over trial strategy. He's part of my Atlanta team."

"I'm sure his is. Since when do you have young lawyers meet you at home? I'm perfectly capable of finding dates on my own when I'm ready. I don't need help from you or anyone else."

"I'm sure you are, my dear, but you're all wrong." Dad reached across the table resting his hand on mine. "Tim's happily married with a couple of kids. Today had nothing to do with you."

I felt my cheeks redden. I took a long drink from my wine glass before I said I was sorry.

"Julia, you're spending too much time at home. Too much time isolated in your bedroom. Can't you see this isn't healthy?"

I felt the tears begin to run down my cheeks. "I'm so sorry, Dad. One part of me knows what I should do, another part is just plain scared. It means rebuilding my entire life and I don't know where to start."

"Dry your tears, my dear. I know you'll find a way to get through this."

Sunday, around noon, the telephone rang. Father was having brunch at the club. I'd been invited to join him, but I opted out. Mattie and Sam had the day off so I answered.

"Is that you, Julia? It's your Aunt Sarah here. You're just the person I wanted to speak with. I've had several conversations with your father in the past few days and we've agreed it might do you some good to come to Montana for a short visit while he's away. I admit I don't have much of a social life anymore, but I think you'll find this part of the country a refreshing change from the East Coast.

"Thank you for the invitation, but I don't need babysitting. I'm fine here."

"Who said anything about babysitting? It would seem you are as stubborn as your father says you are, but I won't take no for an answer. Pack casually. We don't fuss much out here. Oh, yes, if you still have riding clothes, nothing fancy, just boots and jeans, you might find them useful."

"Well, let's just say I'll think about it."

"You'll do no such thing. I can be as stubborn as you and I'm not taking no for an answer, besides it's time I got to know you. Tell me your flight time and I'll be there to welcome you to Big Sky Country. I'm looking forward to our spending some time together. You were just a toddler the last time I saw you."

As I hung up the phone, I thought good God, how do you say no to someone like that? It would seem my aunt won the argument and I guessed I was heading to Montana after all.

Two weeks later on a Monday morning, Sam dropped me off at Delta's check-in section at JFK for an eleven o'clock flight, scheduled to arrive at Billings Logan International Airport by early evening. With the pressure I was getting from both Aunt Sarah and my father I found it easier to agree than fight with both of them.

I'd seen old family photos of my aunt, but I must admit I was taken aback by what I saw as she walked toward me. The tall angular, grey-haired woman with piercing green eyes looked like something out of a Ralph Lauren advertisement. Her ankle length squaw skirt, silver Conch belt, tan suede jacket and boots set her apart from the conservative county club women back home.

With perfect posture and an easy stride, she approached and reached out her hand. "I'd know you anywhere, Julia. You resemble your mother, the same blond hair and blue eyes. I hope your flight wasn't too onerous. I hate what flying has become, which is why I never travel anymore.

We retrieved my luggage and walked out to the parking lot. I wasn't prepared for the dusty Range Rover we approached. I would have expected something more conservative, considering her age, and certainly a lot cleaner.

Noticing my surprise my aunt smiled. "Sorry about the car, dear. I've been doing some landscape painting in Yellowstone National Park and the roads are dusty this time of the year."

"Painting? My father never mentioned that you were an artist."

"Put your suitcase in the rear and we'll be on our way." Unlocking the car doors, she settled into the driver's seat

"I'd hardly call myself an artist. I haven't really painted anything since my college days. My life here was too full. I had so many commitments there were never enough hours in the day, but the last few years I've had nothing but time on my hands. It seemed opportune to pick up my paint brushes again. I understand you've quite an artistic bent yourself. Maybe it's somewhere buried in our genes."

Aunt Sarah was not at all what I had expected. Maybe this wouldn't be too bad after all. Besides I wasn't planning on staying all that long. A few days at the most and then I'd head for home.

After a short drive we turned down a long driveway alongside a tall hedge separating my aunt's house from the one next door, then stopped in front of an old two story, beige-colored, stone house. A vast expanse of lawn, shrubbery and tall trees surrounded the dwelling on a street full of large older well-maintained houses. My aunt noticed my look of surprise at the size of her home.

"This house has been in the Senator's family since the turn of the century, my dear. I do rattle around in the old place and common sense says sell it, but it would have broken the Senator's heart to see it either torn down or fall into disrepair."

"The Senator?" I grabbed my luggage and followed my aunt to the front door.

"My late husband, John Ridgemont. Everybody called him Senator. He was first elected decades ago."

We walked into what might be called a great room. It looked more like a hunting lodge than a home. Dark wood paneled walls, a massive stone fireplace, exposed beams and an enormous moose head that dominated one wall. The final touch was a large black bearskin that served as a rug in front of the oversized brown leather sofa. I'd never seen anything like this before.

Noticing the startled look, my aunt smiled, "The room looked like this the day I arrived here as a bride. I've never bothered to change a thing, as we really didn't spend much time here. The Senator preferred to stay at our ranch when we were in Montana. With regret, I sold the ranch a few years ago. I loved the place, but it became too difficult to manage, and too costly to maintain on my own. "Come let me show you to your bedroom. I guarantee you'll find no stuffed animals mounted on the walls."

I was relieved to find a warm comfortable looking bedroom. An old-fashioned ornate iron bed complete with a down comforter, a hand-stitched quilt folded at the end of the bed. White tieback curtains hung from the windows and Native American throw rugs covered the stone floor.

"This is charming, Aunt Sarah. I'm sure I'll be very comfortable here."

"Freshen up if you like. The bathroom is down the hall. I'll wait for you on the back patio. Oh, by the way, call me Sassy. Everyone does. Aunt Sarah sounds like a sweet old lady, not who I am, despite my years." She was right. Sassy suited her to a T.

My aunt proved to be a charming hostess. Over a quiet dinner and several glasses of wine she dominated the conversation with what seemed like innocuous questions. I had a strange feeling she was sizing me up. I offered to help with the clean-up, but was instructed to go to bed as we had a busy day ahead of us. Taking her at her word, my body still on Eastern Time, I was happy to head for bed.

Hearing a gentle tap on the bedroom door, I awoke with a start thinking it was Ratchet. Sassy's voice brought me back to reality. Following her suggestion, I had opened the windows wide in order to capture, as she put it, the aroma of sweet-smelling air as it drifted in and slept like a baby.

"Rise and shine. We're off to Yellowstone after breakfast."

After taking a quick shower I put on jeans and a white linen shirt and hurried downstairs, following the smell of freshly brewed coffee. A bowl of fresh fruit sat on the counter along with a tray of muffins and scones. I poured a cup of coffee and filled a plate. The small table that sat in the corner of the large, rather dated kitchen had been set with a mat and silverware. I took my plate and coffee cup, and sat down to enjoy the view from the floor to ceiling windows. The mountains in the distance, still snowcapped, were breathtaking. This didn't look anything like New York or even Connecticut.

By the time I'd finished the last drop of coffee, Sassy entered the kitchen, her hair pulled back fastened with a rubber band and tucked into a baseball cap. She wore an oversized sweatshirt, form fitting tights, and running shoes. Her face glowed, there were beads of sweat on her forehead.

I looked at her with surprise.

"You can come running with me tomorrow if you like. Exercise is good for the body as well as the soul."

No wonder she looked to be in such good shape. "I'll pass. I'm hardly fit enough to run."

"Then start slowly. You'll never be fit if you keep making excuses. I'll grab a shower and then we'll be on our way." She turned and left me alone.

We left for Yellowstone taking the Beartooth Highway, which Sassy described as "the most beautiful drive in the whole country." The plan was to stay overnight.

We had little time for conversation, the steep zigzags and switchbacks took all of Sassy's attention, while the splendor of the scenery was absorbing all of mine. Everywhere I looked was a sight more beautiful than any I'd seen before, snowcapped mountains, glacier lakes, alpine plateaus, and the bluest of blue skies.

We stopped for lunch at the Old Faithful Inn then proceeded on to a cabin where we were to spend the night.

Sassy turned off the engine in front of a small log cabin resting in a cleared area of the woods. Not another structure anywhere within sight. She told me the cabin belonged to friends who allowed her to use it whenever she wished. I was told to take the cooler and sleeping bags into the cabin while she checked to be sure we had everything we needed before dark.

Sassy retrieved a red five-gallon gas can from the back of the vehicle. I watched in amazement as she twisted open a cap and poured in the gas. Recapping the opening and started the generator. She went about removing logs from the woodpile stacked alongside the cabin and laid a fire in the fireplace. She'd grown up in the same house with the same family as my dad, but they were as different as night and day. Even thought she was university educated and married into a wealthy Montana family, Sassy prepared for a night in the wilderness like an outdoorsman. I was impressed.

At Sassy's suggestion, I brought a couple of chairs from the cabin and placed them outside on the small patio, its stone surface covered with a thick blanket of pine needles. She opened the cooler and took out a couple of bottles of beer.

"Julia, you're about to sample one of our Montana Brewing Company's best brew. This isn't the place for wine." Sassy twisted off the cap and handed the bottle to me. No need for glasses I was told.

"Look around, have you ever seen anything more beautiful? Take a deep breath and smell the fresh mountain air. I come here often when the weather is right to paint and think."

"Don't tell me you come here all by yourself?"

"I find its good sometimes to be alone, it gives one time to sort things out. I too, have suffered losses in my life, so I'm not without sympathy as to how you must feel. I spent one spring and summer here by myself. Six months spent brooding, and feeling very sorry for myself."

For a moment or two Sassy seemed to be in another place. I waited for her go on having nothing to add to the conversation. My aunt intrigued me. What an amazing woman.

"Sorry dear, I was lost in thought." She took a long drink of her beer and continued, "I needed to get away from everything. The job of staying alive up here all alone, away from all the comforts I'd known was enough to put me on the path to healing. That's sort of what I have in mind for you. But we all have to find our own path."

"What exactly do you mean?" I began to panic. "Good God, you're not planning on leaving me here by myself?"

Sassy laughed at my concern. "Oh, no my dear, of course not. Sorry if I scared you. I have another path in mind. Finish your beer, and go grab us another. You may need it when you hear what I have in mind."

Chapter 4

I reached into the cooler and as I started to head back outside, Sassy called, "There're chips in the paper bag on the table."

I sat down and waited for Sassy to speak, still feeling as if I'd been under a microscope ever since I arrived, but she seemed more interested in a group of deer at the edge of the forest.

"Please, Sassy, you can't just leave me hanging. I agreed to come for a visit. I didn't agree to anything else."

She must have sensed the tension in my voice because she smiled before saying, "I know my dear, but maybe you'd be wise to listen to what I have to say before you get your back up."

I swallowed a gulp of beer waiting to hear what she had in mind.

"I know I've asked a lot of questions and I've watched you carefully. I wanted to get a handle on what you're made of and who you are underneath the façade you hid behind. I think the plan I have in mind might be just the answer to helping you find yourself."

"I'm listening." I held my breath as I waited for her to begin.

"I have a dear friend, Julia, who owns a large cattle ranch on the plains some distance outside of Billings. The couple that work for him are leaving on vacation for a month, and he's agreed to let you come and stay at the ranch in exchange for some simple cooking and a few chores. It's a beautiful place, though quite remote. You can swim and ride. It's the perfect place to concentrate on what you want to do with the rest of your life."

"You must be kidding. You're thinking of sending me off to be cook and housekeeper on some cattle ranch in the middle of nowhere?" Hard as I tried, I couldn't imagine myself spending a month on some remote ranch.

"Trust me, I'm not kidding. By the time the month is over you'll be well on your way to finding yourself. You'll have the roadmap leading to your final destination, wherever you decide that might be."

"No way. I appreciate what you're attempting to do, but I have my own plans. Coming here was a mistake. I'll be going home on the first plane out of here."

"Before you stop listening and opt out, remember there is a pot of gold at the end of every rainbow. I have your father's promise that if you stick it out for a month, he will agree to making the down payment and a year's mortgage payments on a condo for you in the city."

I was speechless. The tradeoff for the month would be my own condo in New York, a year without any payments, time enough to find a job. I was tempted. "I need time to think it over, Sassy."

"Of course, you do. Now let's reheat the take-out from the Inn, then turn in early. I've lots to show you tomorrow and it's also a long drive home. We don't want to arrive home too late. You'll be picked up in the morning. That is if you agree to a stay at the ranch."

I don't remember eating dinner, but I do remember packing up all the garbage to take with us so there'd be nothing left to attract the bears. I lay awake in a down sleeping bag on an upper bunk, Sassy sound asleep in the bunk below. The only sound was a screech owl off in the distance. My mind was going off in a million different directions. What was I doing zipped into a sleeping bag in this remote cabin? How could I even consider Sassy's ridiculous plan, I was a city girl? A month was a long time to be stuck on some cattle ranch with nothing to do. Did I really need more time alone to think? That's what I've been doing for the last year without any answers. After what seemed like ages, I drifted off to sleep.

I awoke when I heard Sassy moving about in the cabin. She fixed a light breakfast for us and announced we were going for a hike in the woods. She suggested long sleeves, as the woods were full of ticks. Jeans, she advised, should be tucked into my boots as a precaution as well. I wasn't sure if I was really interested in either a walk in the woods or a month on a ranch.

We walked along a narrow path for a considerable time when Sassy stopped, turned toward me, and asked, "Well Julia, tell me what you see?"

I looked at her not quite understanding the question. "Trees and a trail through the woods. Why?"

"Just curious, my dear."

I detected a sense of disappointment in my answer, but I couldn't fathom why. Nor her saying, "I'll explain later." What was there to explain?

We'd hiked some distance before I began to take in the magnitude of my surroundings, so different from the manicured landscape and concrete sidewalks of suburban Connecticut.

Bugs or no bugs it was absolutely beautiful here. The only sounds were the birds or an occasional rustling of the leaves as a deer or rabbits moved beneath the trees. I'd never been on a hike in the woods before and marveled at Sassy's knowledge of our surroundings. She pointed out the various trees by name as well as identifying the birds. We waded across small creeks, climbed rises, and never saw another human being. Once I relaxed, I began to appreciate that there was something so peaceful so spiritual about the remoteness.

Early in the afternoon, after closing up the cabin, we left for the long drive home. Sassy concentrated on the road and had little to say.

When she stopped the car in front the Billings house, Sassy turned toward me and asked if I'd made up my mind. "You can accept the offer of a month at the ranch or if you wish, take the next flight home. Your choice."

I'd thought about nothing else on the drive. Sassy hadn't given me much time to make my decision. Do I stay or fly home to an empty house? After all, a month wasn't a very long time and her proposal sounded like an interesting trade off.

"I've decided." I laughed. "Sassy, it's sort of like the old TV show Mattie loved to watch. I'll take the prize behind door number one. It's the condo for a month at the ranch."

"You've made a wise choice, my dear. You won't regret it in the end. I'll call Cole and tell him you'll be ready in the morning. I know you packed for a few days and not a month so If you need to shop for extra jeans or anything, we'd better do it now. Your options will be limited once you're on the ranch."

Chapter 5

Thinking I'd sleep in and take my time getting packed to leave I was surprised when I heard a tap on the door. I knew it must be early as the morning light was just beginning to creep over the horizon.

It was Sassy. I sat up half awake as I heard her say, "Julia, Cole is here and he's anxious to get back on the road."

"I'm still in bed and not even packed. Alright, tell him I'll be down as soon as I can." I looked at the clock on the nightstand -- it was only six-thirty.

I rushed through my shower, dressed as fast as I could and threw everything into the suitcase. Thank God I'd never really unpacked. I had just enough room for all the new things Sassy helped me pick out although I had to sit on the suitcase to get it to close. I shoved everything else into my cosmetic case.

Hurrying down the stairs, still half asleep and longing for a cup of coffee, I walked into the kitchen to see Sassy talking with a tall, well-built dark-haired man, with his back to me. His faded Levi's, scuffed western boots, well-worn jean jacket, and battered old straw hat was just what I'd expected a cattle rancher would look like.

"Good morning, Julia. I'd like you to meet Cole Clayton, a suspicious smile on her face as she continued, "Cole this is my niece, Julia Johnston."

I was shocked as the tall stranger turned around to meet me. He was young, probably in his mid-thirties and quite handsome, not the grizzled old rancher I was expecting.

"Well, you sure took your sweet time, Miss Julia. Come on, let's get this show on the road. I have a ranch to run and we have a long drive ahead of us."

"Have I time for a cup of coffee, at least?"

"I brought a thermos full of coffee. I'll share it with you."

"Well then, could you bring my suitcases downstairs? I left them in the upstairs hall."

He turned and left without a word, though I heard him mumble, "Suitcases. Where the hell does she think she's going?"

Once he was out of earshot I gave Sassy a troubled look, "You didn't say he was young."

"What difference does it make? You each have a job. Age has nothing to do with it."

"But I'll be living in his house. Alone."

"So?"

"So, it just doesn't feel right."

"It's as right as you want it to be. I've known Cole practically since the day he was born and I trust him completely. You're safe in his hands."

Cole appeared with my cases in hand. "If you're ready, let's hit the road."

I walked outside with Sassy as Cole put my cases in the tailgate of a beat up, dusty, old Ford pickup truck.

"You have a truck."

"I do, Miss Julia. What did you expect? A limo? Climb aboard. I'm in a hurry to get back to the ranch."

I hugged Sassy as she gave me a big smile. "Put your time to good use, Julia. We'll talk soon."

I began to regret my decision as I struggled to climb into the truck. It had no running board and seemed bigger and higher than most trucks I'd seen. The hinges of the passenger door creaked as I pulled on the handle and tried to shut it. I assumed the Indian blanket thrown over the seat was to hide the worn upholstery.

What had I gotten myself into? As I fastened my seatbelt, Cole started the engine and turned on the radio to a country western station. "There's coffee in the thermos on the floor behind you. Help yourself."

We'd been on the road about an hour when Cole turned off the freeway onto a two-lane country road. So far, we hadn't exchanged one word. By now the scenery had changed leaving the urban and suburban far behind.

"How much longer before we get to your ranch?"

"About another hour and a half. Why? You in a hurry to get someplace?"

His voice was anything but friendly. "No, it's just this seat is a little uncomfortable. The springs seem to be gone."

"They've been gone for a long time. You'll get used to it after a while."

"I've had some recent hip surgery and I find the seat most uncomfortable." I tried to find a comfortable spot.

"Well, Ma'am, you'll probably find the ranch," he paused. "How did you put it? Most uncomfortable as well."

This had to be the most disagreeable person I'd met in a long time. He must be getting something out of this besides a cook and a housekeeper, maybe just not enough."

After another hour we left the paved road for a gravel road that turned into a dirt road, creating a cloud of dust as we arrived at a gate blocking our entrance.

After opening the gate, Cole drove across parallel metal bars over a shallow ditch, which in answer to my question, he said was a cattle guard. If cattle get loose the guard prevents them from getting out onto the road."

"So, I assume this your ranch?"

"Yes, ma'am. This is as good as it gets."

I looked around. There was nothing but open space as far as my eye could see. "But it's in the middle of nowhere."

"No, ma'am. You're mistaken. It's in the middle of God's country."

We drove quite a ways down the road to the ranch house that looked nothing like I'd imagined. The two story, white stucco and stone building had a large porch surrounding the house. The green shutters at every window looked as if they could be closed against the weather. When the truck stopped, I stepped out and stretched before walking through an opening in a low stonewall surrounding the garden and followed a path made of large stepping stones cut into patches of grass. Thank God, the drive was over

I started to climb the three steps to the front door when I saw a large growling dog approaching. Cole was behind me bringing my suitcases. "His name's Bear. He won't hurt you. The door's unlocked. Go right in."

I watched as Cole bent down, scratching the dog behind his ears. The huge dog wagged his tail so hard his whole-body shook.

"Hi, big guy. Did you do your job? Is everything okay here?"

I thought he was sure a hell of a lot nicer to the dog than he'd been to me. I opened the door only to have the dog bound in ahead of me. I didn't know what to do. I was concerned. We'd never had a dog when I was growing up and this dog was huge.

"Make yourself at home. Your bedroom's upstairs at the end of the hall. It used to be my sister's," Cole said before he turned and headed for the door, Bear followed close behind him. "I've chores to do. I'll be back in time for dinner. I'll be doing the cooking tonight. Don't worry about anything. Old Bear will be sure you're safe."

"Do you want me to lock the door after you leave?"

"Hell, no. It's been unlocked for so long I wouldn't know where to find the key."

With that, he was gone and I was alone in a strange house with a huge dog close by my heels. I peeked into the living room before going upstairs. Like the entrance, the floors were wide planked pine with paths worn between different areas. The first thing I noticed was a large stone fireplace with an antlered deer head mounted on the wall above. What is it with these people and their fondness for dead animal heads as decoration?

I took one suitcase and climbed the stairs. From what I could see of the house it appeared to be clean. The bedroom was more than acceptable if a little dated, with an oversized twin bed, highboy dresser, and a high-backed wooden chair. Indian throw rugs covered the wood floor.

I walked down the hall to the bathroom. An old cast iron tub sat on the white octagonal tile floor. The showerhead was attached to the back wall. A metal rod held a flowered shower curtain encircling the tub. A pedestal sink with a mirror above was on the opposite wall. The toilet sat hidden in a corner. The room was a throwback to another era. Way before my time.

Having unpacked I went downstairs to check out the rest of the house, walking through the dining room into the large kitchen and the mudroom beyond.

I hadn't taken two steps outside Bear by my side, his tail wagging, prepared to follow me. The first thing I saw were row after row of vegetables growing in raised beds surrounded by at least a dozen mature fruit trees. I decided to explore further down the dirt path. I'd gone some distance from the house, when I came across a small structure with chickens wandering around outside. Having absolutely no interest in chickens, I decided to go no further and returned to the house.

My stomach was growling. Checking my watch both hands were pointing to noon and I was hungry. Cole hadn't given me time for breakfast. I guessed it would be all right if I fixed something to eat. I opened the refrigerator and found an open package of bologna and a bowl filled with apples, plums, and apricots. It felt uncomfortable wandering around in a strange house, but I decided I might as well figure out where everything was if I was to be the cook and housekeeper for a month.

I fixed a sandwich, adding an apple to my plate and walked out onto the patio plopping down into one of the comfortable chairs surrounding a cast iron table. The patio was more modern and tasteful than the rest of the furnishings in the house. The quiet that surrounded me was eerie, as if I were all alone in the world. The only sound came from the birds perched high in the trees.

After finishing my lunch, I began to feel unnerved. The uncertainty was catching up with me. Was I going to spend the entire month all by myself looking for ways to occupy my time? I stretched out on one of the two matching chaises and fell asleep.

I awoke to the sound of a truck backfiring as it drove up the driveway. I glanced at my watch surprised that it was five o'clock. I hurried into the kitchen just as the back door slammed shut. Cole walked into the kitchen and without a word reached into the refrigerator and grabbed a beer. "I'm going outside. Grab a beer if you like. I'll be on the patio." I found him resting one of the chaises.

"I'm not much of a beer drinker."

"Of course not. I'll bet vintage wine is your thing."

I thought his sarcastic remark was uncalled for. It looked like my month's stay was going to be a very long thirty-one days.

"You find everything? Get yourself settled?"

"Yes, no problem. It's a nice old house."

"It's been the family's home for generations. I grew up here."

"And never left home?"

"Not exactly, but that's a long story. I'll finish my beer and clean up. I'm barbequing tonight. Got a couple of steaks marinating in the frig. Whoa, wait a minute, don't tell me you're a vegan?"

"No, I eat real people food."

"Good. Had me scared there for a minute. I'm going to town tomorrow afternoon. If you need anything, make a list. I can pick up whatever you need." Finishing his beer, Cole stood. "We'll eat out here. You'll find the mats and silverware in the kitchen. There's salad stuff in the frig. Make yourself useful." I didn't like being treated like the hired help and really didn't like his whole attitude

A half-hour later Cole reappeared, his dark hair still wet from the shower. Clean-shaven, he wore clean jeans and a bright blue, starched, short-sleeved cotton shirt. The color highlighted the deep blue of his eyes, and went well with his tanned face and arms. He was good looking in a disgusting sort of way.

"I see you found everything," Cole said as he walked out onto the patio. "Want to grab me another beer while I start the fire? It'll take a bit before the coals are hot."

Walking back to the kitchen I wondered why he couldn't get his own beer on his way outside. Was this going to be some sort of power struggle?

When I returned to the patio, I found Cole sitting at the table, a sheet of paper in front of him, motioning me to join him.

"I've made a list of your responsibilities so there won't be any misunderstandings. If you have any questions, we can settle them up front."

Cole handed me the computer printout of a PowerPoint presentation of my duties. What was a cowboy doing handing me an executive type memo? I got no further than item one.

"You really mean you expect me to fix your breakfast at six-thirty in the morning?"

"Absolutely. I've given you a thirty-minute break. Juanita fixes my breakfast at six on the dot. You'll note I eat a good-sized breakfast...bacon, eggs, toast or muffins. Waffles, or pancakes will do, as well as orange juice and coffee."

"You're kidding, of course. You're expecting me to be a short order cook."

"Trust me, Julia, I never kid."

I couldn't believe what I was reading. Second item on the list was tidy the house with the exception of his bedroom, which was off limits. Gather eggs from the hen house, pick vegetables from the garden before they were overripe, and prepare dinner to be ready by six. "Think you can manage?"

Obviously, I had no real understanding of what my responsibilities would be when I agreed to Sassy's proposition. Nor was I expecting the cool reception I was getting. I couldn't believe this was what Sassy had in mind, but what would have normally reduced me to tears, had the exact opposite effect. Come hell or high water I'd show this arrogant S.O.B. I was tougher than I looked. I smiled and told Cole I was sure I could easily accomplish the items on his list.

"Looks like the fire's ready. You'll find the steaks in the frig, as well as some beans in a plastic container. They need to go in the microwave for five minutes. Hope the salad's ready as the steaks won't take long."

I bit my lip and marched into the kitchen. I found the beans and started the microwave. I took the steaks outside and came back to put the dressing on the salad, fuming with every motion.

We ate the entire meal in silence. I must admit the steak was done to perfection. The beans were really good, too, and I got no complaints about the salad. For dessert I put apples, plums, and peaches on a plate along with the homemade looking oatmeal raisin cookies I found in a tin, and brewed a fresh pot of coffee.

After downing the last of the coffee, Cole got up from the table. "I'll see you later. Gotta' feed the dog and do one last check on the horses."

Kitchen clean up wasn't one of my strong suits. Mattie was in charge of the kitchen at home and the whole time I lived in New York I seldom ate in. If I did, I ate Chinese take out right out of the cartons. By the time I finished cleaning the kitchen, I was ready for bed. The day had been long and I had to be up early to fix the lord and master his breakfast.

Chapter 6

I slept like a log, and only awoke when the alarm went off. Jumping out of bed, I turned on the bedside lamp. It was way too early for the sun to be up. The last thing I wanted was to be late. I put on a pair of jeans and a pale blue polo shirt, brushed my teeth, and tied my hair back in a ponytail. I didn't bother with makeup. I had no interest in making myself attractive for Cole.

By the time Cole appeared, I'd set the table in the kitchen, the bacon was cooked, and I was ready to turn over the omelet.

"Morning, Julia. I see you made it up in time. Sleep well?"

"Yes, thank you." I poured the juice and coffee, placing the omelet and bacon in front of him. I'd already put toast, butter, and jam on the table. The surprised look on his face was annoying.

"This looks good. You're not eating?"

"I haven't had time."

"Well, you better grab something as we're riding out to check a line of fence this morning."

"Riding?"

"Yes, according to Sassy, you like horses. I'm obliged to provide a horse for you and make sure you have time to ride. First, I need to see how well you handle a horse before I decide which of our animals to give you to use while you're here. Don't want any problems."

I poured myself a cup of coffee and made more toast.

"So you're going to see if I know on which side to mount."

"Among other things. I'd hate to see one of my horses get hurt."

Day two wasn't starting out any better than day one had ended. Thirty more days to go. I took a deep breath and remembering the condo that was promised I knew I could do this.

"This omelet is good. Sassy didn't say you knew how to cook."

"For your information, three friends and I took a college course 'A Summer of Cooking' in France. I learned enough to get by."

"In France. Wow. That is impressive. The poor girls around here learn to cook in their mother's kitchens, but lucky you, you got to take a cooking course abroad."

I bit my tongue again. The less I said, the less opportunity for another snide remark.

Cole had a second cup of coffee and excused himself after telling me to meet him at the barn in an hour.

I had just enough time to do the dishes, clean the bathroom, put on my boots, and head for the barn. I closed the door to my room leaving the bed unmade.

During the short walk to the barn, I tried to relax, promising myself no matter what Cole said I'd keep my cool. It didn't take long before the barn came into view. The old wooden structure seemed well maintained. As I walked through the open barn doors everything looked organized. The center aisle was raked, the tack room door stood open. I glanced in to see saddles resting on racks, bridles neatly hung, blankets folded and stored on shelves, and against the back wall, three green metal tack trunks with the monogram C/C.

Two saddled horses were in the cross ties, one a good-looking roan Quarter horse gelding, the other a common looking smallish Appaloosa mare. There was no question which one was meant for me.

Cole came out of the feed room wearing half chaps, western boots, and a straw cowboy hat asking, "Are you ready?"

I nodded and walked toward the mare, noticing the saddle. "Cole, I don't ride western. Do you have an English saddle I could use?"

"This is a working ranch, Your Highness, not a show barn or a riding academy. Stock saddles are all I have. Take it or leave it."

"Really. That was uncalled for." So much for keeping my cool.

"Look, I'm not any happier about your being here than you are, but I promised Sassy and damn it, I'll try my best. Now do you want to ride or don't you? I don't really care one way or the other."

"Yes I'd like to go for a ride." I started toward the tack room. "Just give me a minute to get a helmet."

"You're kidding, of course. A helmet? Were you planning on falling off on your head? Grab one of the baseball caps on the back of the tack room door. You'll need something to keep the sun out of your eyes."

Grabbing a cap off the hook and adjusting the back strap I wondered why I always seem to come off sounding like a spoiled child? Why does he seem to bring out the worst in me?

I untied the mare and stood on a bale of hay to mount.

The saddle was really uncomfortable, way too big. Obviously meant for a large man. When I rested my feet in the stirrups, it felt like too much leather between the mare and me and the saddle horn was in the way.

Cole rode up alongside me as we left the barn. "The mare's name is Beetle. She's a little stubborn and a lot barn sour, so you'll have to get after her to get her to go, but try and keep up, I don't have time to come back and look for you."

I took the reins in each hand, taking light contact with the bit.

Cole looked at me with disdain. "We hold the reins in one hand not two. The mare neck reins, like this." He showed me how with the rein in one hand, he crossed it over his horse's neck to make him turn. "We need one hand free to swing a rope. If you're ready, lets go. By the way, you look pretty cute in that baseball cap."

Cole was right about Beetle. I had to keep kicking the mare to make her keep up with Cole's big striding gelding. Spurs would have helped. I was getting more exercise than the mare.

We rode along until we came to a wide metal gate. Cole placed his horse alongside, reaching down and unlocking the gate he held it open for me to ride through. The horse turned as Cole never let go of the gate, side-stepping to allow Cole to close and fasten the gate shut without dismounting. I was impressed. We were now in an enormous meadow knee deep in spring grass with hundreds of black-coated cattle in the distance.

We rode beside the fence as Cole looked for breaks in the barbed wire. I watched as he gave the horse a gentle touch with his spurs and he did what I would call a slow sitting trot. Beetle decided she wanted to keep up and once I got into the rhythm, it felt almost comfortable.

We rode for almost an hour without exchanging a word until we came to a large group of trees that provided a shady area. Cole dismounted and at his suggestion, I did the same. I wasn't sure I could stand, my legs seemed wobbly, and my hip was beginning to ache. I hadn't had this much exercise since long before the accident. Roger didn't care much for the out-of-doors as he had problems with allergies.

"You all right?" Cole took Beetle and tied her to a tree alongside his horse. "Sit down and rest a bit."

He seemed concerned, almost pleasant as he handed me a bottle of water he'd taken from his saddlebags.

"You did okay for a city girl. We'll gallop for a stretch on the way home. If you feel okay riding alone, I'll bring my sister's horse up from pasture. He's a nice old Thoroughbred she used to show."

"Your sister doesn't ride anymore?"

"No, she lives in Boise now, married with a house full of kids."

"Do you have any other siblings?"

"Yeah, a brother in the construction business in St. Helena. Why?"

"Just curious. So, it seems you're the only one who never left the ranch."

"Not exactly. Let's just say I left the ranch for a while, but I chose to come back." There was sharpness to his tone. "It's a long story and not really any of your business."

Cole pulled a power bar from his suede vest and handed it to me. "This should keep you till we get home. We'll have to hurry if I'm going to get to the village and get back before dinner.

Thinking I should change the subject I said, "Could I ask you a question?"

"Ask away."

"Why do all the cows look alike?"

"Cole gave me a condescending look and laughed at me. "They're supposed to look alike. They're all registered Angus. Technically speaking, they're called cattle. The herds made up of cows, heifers, calves, and bulls."

We rested for a few more minutes. Then Cole said it was time to go. I untied the mare and put the reins over her head trying to put my foot in the stirrup. I heard Cole behind me.

"Grab hold of the horn and then you can ease your way up into the saddle."

He mounted and headed off at a gallop, which I thought was rude. I kicked the old mare as hard as I could and was surprised to feel her take off. She knew she was headed for home. I hadn't ridden in years, but one doesn't forget. I was enjoying every minute being back in the saddle, smelling the distinctive aroma of horse sweat, enjoying feeling the sheer power in the horse underneath me.

We returned to the barn about noon. Needing to unsaddle the mare and realizing it was lot more complicated than removing an English saddle, I watched how Cole went about it. The first thing I had to do it seemed was to unbuckle the rear girth. Then looking over my shoulder to follow Cole's action, I loosened the leather strap that fed through a ring and freed the main girth. I watched as Cole put the stirrup over the saddle horn and I did the same, though I hadn't realized how heavy the saddle was until I let it almost drop to the ground as I slid it off the mare's back. The last thing I wanted was to look like a complete green horn. I rested the saddle against a stall door and removed the saddle blanket.

After Cole put away the saddles, bridles, and saddle blankets, I followed him the mare's braided rope lead line in hand, as he led his horse back to the pasture. I felt very accomplished.

"I'll bring Charger up to the barn tomorrow. If you like him, he's yours to use as long as you're here."

We turned the horses loose. Cole closed the gate and fastened the chain around the post tied his lead rope to the gate and strode off toward the house leaving me behind. I couldn't begin to match his long stride. He had to be the rudest individual I'd ever met.

Chapter 7

Cole grabbed a quick sandwich, and said he was ready to leave. I handed him my shopping list, which he scanned and began to cross off all the salad items I had on my list.

"If you haven't noticed, we grow all the lettuce, tomatoes, cucumbers, and vegetables we need right here." Addressing me in his usual condescending tone. "I don't go to the village often, so are you sure you've got everything you want or will need on the list?"

I watched Cole leave and went upstairs to make my bed. It looked so inviting I deciding to lie down for a few minutes, every bone in my body ached and I was dead tired. I awoke with a start. The clock said three and none of my chores were done. Knowing I'd be on the receiving end of an uncomfortable lecture if I failed to accomplish everything on Cole's checklist. I grabbed a quick shower, washed my hair and changed into clean clothes.

Retrieving the eggs was the first item on his damn list. As I approached the henhouse, at least a dozen chickens were milling around, pecking at the ground. What was I supposed to do now? I was a city girl. I had no idea what to expect so I took each step with caution trying to stay out of their way.

I opened the door to the henhouse, and the smell just about knocked me over. A few chickens were still inside. I went about gathering eggs from empty nests, but one chicken, still sitting on her eggs, refused to give them up. After I made a vain attempt to get her to move, I figured fine with me. I'd be damned if I was going to start a fight with a damn chicken. As far as I was concerned, she could keep her damn eggs. I walked back to the house thinking only thirty days left until my return to New York where, thank God, dealing with chickens would never again be part of my life. I placed the basket full of eggs on the counter and hurried back outside.

Next, I picked lettuce, a few tomatoes, a cucumber, and a large red bell pepper for tonight's salad. I found an unopened box of pasta in the cupboard and decided to make my own version of spaghetti carbonara. Having prepared the salad, I put the bowl in the refrigerator. I'd add the dressing later. I fried the bacon and cut it into small pieces the tomatoes simmering on the stove. It wouldn't take long to boil the pasta. Dinner would be ready no matter what time Cole came back. I'd show him I wasn't incompetent.

I couldn't miss Cole's return. The muffler wasn't the only thing badly in need of repair on his old truck, but for sure it was the loudest.

Cole opened the back door and placed a large box of groceries on the kitchen counter. "I've already fed the horses. I'll wash up and be ready for dinner in a jiff."

I started to put things away -- coffee, bread, beer, and several bottles of red wine. Maybe he wasn't a total ass after all.

By the time I'd stowed everything Cole returned, beer in hand and offered to open the wine. I did the honorable thing and thanked him.

Dinner was a success, at least I passed one test. We even had a limited, almost civil, conversation and lingered over coffee.

Cole stood, pushed his empty coffee mug aside, "Good meal. I'm going to feed the dog. If you want to take a walk, I'll show you where the riding ring is."

The sun had gone down, but it wasn't dark as yet. Bear was waiting by his feed bowl, his tail wagging as Cole filled it full of kibble. The big dog dove in inhaling his meal. We left Bear to finish his dinner and walked down a long lane separating the horse's pastures, until we came upon the really nice sand ring.

"My sister was into showing horses, so my father built this for her years ago. Nobody's used it for a while, but the footing looked fine when I checked it out yesterday. Might be a good place to get the feel of Charger. He hasn't been ridden in a long time."

Looking off in the distance, I was amazed to see nothing but green pasture in all directions. "How large is your ranch, Cole?"

"About forty-five thousand acres. The adjoining ranch is about fifty thousand acres, so if you don't know what you're looking at it might seem like it's all one big piece."

"That's a lot of land for just cattle. I'd think you'd want to make improvements. Build houses or something."

"Your right. I guess a guy could build houses, only one problem, there wouldn't be anybody to buy them. Montana has a lot of land and not a lot of people. Here cattle outnumber people by better than two to one. Besides, cattle eat a lot of pasture in a season and you need to cut a large amount of pasture grass to store for winter feed. In case you didn't know, we get a lot of snow and the cattle still have to be fed"

Our house in Connecticut sat on an acre of land, which I thought was sizable. I couldn't imagine forty-five thousand acres. Bear had joined us as we started to walk back toward the house. Outside of the horses milling around, there wasn't a sound to be heard. I couldn't believe how peaceful it seemed. Of course, there wasn't much here in the middle of nowhere to make a sound.

When we returned to the house, Cole said goodnight. "I have some book work to do. See you in the morning."

Up again before dawn, I turned on the kitchen light and opened the pantry door. I checked every shelf, but couldn't find a box of pancake mix. Plan A was out the window. I'd have to revert to plan B -- bacon and eggs.

I asked Cole as he poured coffee into his mug, if he was out of pancake mix, but I should have known better. Of course, Juanita made her pancakes and waffles from scratch. Didn't everybody.

"To bad you can't get a taste of Juanita's pancakes. She makes them with beer and buttermilk. They're the damn lightest pancakes you've ever eaten."

I had no idea how to make pancakes or waffles. I'd have to find advice somewhere. "I'd like to call my sister for a few of her recipes, Cole, only I'm having trouble with my cell phone. Is there some secret to getting service out here?"

"No lady, no secret. We don't have much in the way of cell phone service. It's spotty to non-existent. I need a satellite dish just to get the internet, but if you need to call your sister or anybody else, we do have that old fashioned instrument called a telephone. It's in the hall. Feel free to use it. Just don't try to call a taxi. We don't have those, either."

Jesus, one minute the guy can seem so reasonable, and in the next he's dripping with sarcasm.

"When you're finished with your housework, come down to the barn. I'll bring Charger in from the pasture and put him in one of the stalls. Oh, by the way, I borrowed a flat saddle for you. It's in the tack room. His bridle is the one with the snaffle bit." With that Cole finished his coffee and headed out the back door.

I walked by every stall until I found the one with the door closed, an old nylon halter with a cotton rope attached hung on a hook outside as a tall, bay gelding with a white blaze was munching hay. My expectations turned to despair, one look at the horse was enough to turn anyone off. His coat so dirty I'd bet he hadn't been groomed in years. His mane was a mess, long and uneven, it looked as though something had been chewing on it. His forelock had grown so long it covered half his face and his tail a knotted mess full of debris. .

I reached for his halter just as Cole walked into the barn.

"I found Charger, but he's filthy. When will you have time to clean him up?"

Cole stared at me as if I was crazy. "Sorry, Your Highness, like I told you this isn't a dude ranch. Groom him or leave him as he is, I really don't give a damn what you do. He's yours while you're here, but if the old horse is too much trouble, leave him in his stall. I'll take him back to his pasture later."

I could feel my face turning red. Your highness was the last straw. I couldn't contain myself.

"Is it just me you dislike or is it all women?"

"No, Ma'am, I don't dislike all women, only snooty upper class New York women."

He pulled his horse out of one of the other stalls, mounted up and rode off.

All I could think of as I picked up a metal bucket and threw it against the barn wall was I hate him. I hate him. I hate Him.

I slipped the halter on Charger and led him out of the stall and put him in the cross ties. "Well, old boy, we won't be going for a ride today."

My work was cut out for me, I picked up the groom box and started to curry and brush, but all I was doing was raising the dust and dirt imbedded in his coat. I took a razor to his mane, making it as short as possible. I'd work on thinning it, little by little. I pulled his forelock and tried to comb the knots from his tail with little success. The old horse seemed to be enjoying the attention but this was a waste of time a good soap bath was what was needed.

I retrieved the bucket I'd thrown against the wall wondering how I was going to explain the huge dent in its side and looked for a wash rack. I found a long hose and a tie ring on the side of the building. A shelf held soap, a sponge, and a scraper.

It took all morning to get Charger halfway clean. I put him back in his stall to dry, giving him another flake of hay. The horse seemed quite happy, but I was wet, filthy dirty, and exhausted and I still had a full days chores ahead of me. If I was supposed to be spending my time thinking about my future, the experiment was failing. I had little time to think about anything, but my next chore.

While we were both good about using the boot scraper outside the back door, careful to leave our boots in the mudroom, we still tracked in a lot of dirt and dust. I found the vacuum cleaner in the hall closet. Was I really about to clean somebody else's house? I'd never once used the vacuum at home, and a cleaning lady came every other week to at my apartment in New York. This whole thing was ridiculous.

With the house clean I was about to check out the garden, thinking I might find inspiration for dinner, when I heard Cole's footsteps behind me.

"It's Saturday, Julia. A bunch of us usually hang out in the village most Saturday nights. We have a few beers, chow down, and finish off the evening with a few rounds of pool. They're nice people, nothing fancy like your New York City friends, but you're welcome to come along."

"Thank you, but I didn't bring anything to wear."

"These are my friends, Julia, they don't give a damn what you wear. Clean Jeans will do just fine. Like I said, it ain't fancy. If you're game, I think you could use a night out. I'll flip you to see who's first in the shower."

Chapter 8

We met in the front hall at seven. Cole looked quite handsome in his starched Levi's and a blue-checkered shirt, the western kind with snaps instead of buttons, fancy dress cowboy boots and an expensive looking leather jacket. I didn't have much choice, a pair of tight, slim legged designer jeans, a long-sleeved white silk blouse, and espadrilles were all the nice clothes I'd packed. It made a great looking outfit when I viewed myself in the mirror on the back of the closet door. My hair was loose and I'd put on makeup.

"Well, well. Look at you, Miss Julia, you clean up real nice. You're quite a stunner when you put yourself together."

"I might add you look quite nice as well."

"If the mutual admiration society is finished, let's get going."

It took about forty minutes to reach Silverton. The village was the only commercial area for miles around. The main streets consisted of a modest number of houses, a bank and a post office, as well as the kind of stores one would expect in a small town. The buildings themselves appeared dated. It would appear nothing new had been built in years.

We drove to the outskirts and stopped in front of the pine log building with a neon sign perched on the roof that read, Longhorn Bar and Grill, except the G didn't light up so I read Longhorn Bar and rill. The parking lot was full, a mix of large SUV's, trucks, and a few motorcycles. I could hear music and laughter coming from inside as Cole led the way. It took a moment for my eyes to accustom to the dim lighting before I could get a good look at the Longhorn Bar and 'rill. Good God, I thought, we drove forty minutes for this. The place looked like a throwback to another era. It could have been an old western movie set complete with a bunch of cowboys leaning against the bar. Worn wooden floors and knotty pine paneling throughout. Half the large room was taken up by the long bar, the rest consisted of booths and tables. A small bandstand and dance floor against the back wall, and a large jukebox in one corner of the room. The place was a smoke-filled dump.

The bar's floor was thick with peanut shells, and the place reeked of beer and cigarettes, but from the sound of laughter, everyone was having a good time.

A male voice shouted, "Hey, Cole, over here."

I followed Cole to the end of the bar as a tall, rugged looking man of about forty reached out his hand, "Good to see you 'ole buddy. Wasn't sure you were comin'." He proceeded to look me up and down. "How about introducing me to the pretty lady."

"Boone, this is Julia, my house guest from New York."

"Well, you sweet thing, how about a drink?"

Cole looked at me. "Wine?"

"No, thanks. I'll have a beer."

He gave me a big smile. "Good choice. "Bartender," he shouted. "Two local brews on tap."

"You here alone, Boone? Where's Mary Jane?"

"The 'ole lady's here somewhere gossiping with her friends. So tell me, sweet thing, how long are you going to be, what did Cole call you, oh yeah, a house guest?" The inference wasn't lost on me.

"Knock it off, Boone, Julia's Sassy's niece. She's just visiting."

"Well, that's a whole different story. Sorry if I was off base. Your aunt is a real fine lady. Glad to meet you."

Cole handed me a beer in a frosted glass as he asked Boone if the gang was there.

"I seen Pete and Charlie, and Big Billy is down at the other end of the bar, don't know if Johnny's here, yet?"

"Excuse us for a minute, Boone. I want to introduce Julia to the rest of the gang."

Drinks in hand, we walked to the area where Cole's male friends were standing behind their wives seated on bar stools. The men looked like they'd been chosen by central casting to represent ranchers -- tanned, muscled, most like Cole, without an ounce of extra fat, except for the one they called Big Billy. His belly hung over his belt buckle and his grin was as big as his gut.

They seemed a friendly, happy bunch. I was introduced to the wives as a man sitting next to them got up and gave me his seat. Not something you'd expect would ever happen in New York.

The women seemed very interested in me, a stranger in their midst. I was Cole's date. I got the impression Cole came alone on Saturday evenings, so there was a great deal of curiosity concerning our relationship. I tried to make it clear that I was only here for a short stay and we were barely friends. Nothing else.

I hadn't realized I'd finished my beer until Cole handed me another. I could hear the guys kidding him about me. Saying I was to good lookin' for the likes of him. The conversations went on for a while longer, all in good fun, until the men began to head for the eating area. A couple of them pushed two tables together making room for all of us to sit together.

By the time we were seated the waitress, a buxom female with every bit of cleavage showing, began to hand out menus. She fit right in with the atmosphere. She smiled at Cole in a knowing manner as she brushed up against him. "Drinks anyone?"

The guys ordered pitchers of beer. I went along with the women and asked for water. Two beers were my limit. I starred at the menu. Buffalo burgers caught my eye. That was a first. Looking past the long list of burgers and steaks, I noticed rocky mountain oysters and asked what they were. The women began to snicker as Charlene, big Billy's wife suggested I play it safe and order a burger and fries.

I turned toward Cole who had a silly grin on his face. "Really? What did I just say that's so funny?"

"It's not funny, Julia, it's just everyone who grew up in cattle country knows what rocky mountain oysters are?"

"Well, seeing as I didn't have the benefit of growing up on a ranch, please educate me."

Everyone's eyes were on Cole, broad smiles on their faces as they leaned forward awaiting his explanation."

"Well Miss Julia, it's like this. Every spring when the young calves are castrated their testicles are saved and renamed Rocky

Mountain Oysters. Some folks consider them a treat you might say a real delicacy."

I could feel my checks redden as everyone had a good laugh at my expense. I ordered a burger and fries.

Despite the room being noisy, the acoustics awful, the rowdy crowd was having a good time. No one seemed out of line.

"Cole leaned over. "You doin' okay?"

"I'm fine."

"Good. I feel sorta' responsible for you."

"I noticed the special smile you got from the waitress. Are you friends?"

"Not exactly." Cole glanced at me with that same silly grin. "Not since high school anyway, but then she was friends with all the guys on the football team, if you know what I mean."

Reaching for the pitcher of beer in the middle of the table, Cole filled my glass. "Enjoy yourself, Miss Julia, tonight's a night to have fun. Tomorrow's Sunday, so I'll be a sport and let you sleep in till seven."

The waitress arrived and placed a huge hamburger smothered in barbeque sauce and a basket full of French fries and onion rings in front of me. More food than I could eat. She proceeded to serve everyone else leaning over the men as she put the food in front of them, giving them a glimpse at her enormous boobs. Placing another pitcher of beer in the middle of the table, she giggled and left swinging her wide hips in a very sexy manner.

The conversation among Cole's friends was different from my New York evenings out. The men's conversation was about cattle futures and the weather. Here the wives talked about their kids, the PTA, and their church. I had nothing to add so I just listened. Unlike Saturday nights in New York, I heard no gossip no back stabbing, and no discussion of the latest fashions.

About ten, somebody turned off the jukebox as a small group of musicians took the stage. I counted two guitars, a fiddle, a bass, and a harmonica. Not a typical New York dance band. As they started to play, the crowd began to clap in approval. The music was a lot different as well, but it had a good beat and much to my surprise the band sounded great.

Cole stood and asked if I wanted to dance. Before I could answer he took my hand and led the way to the dance floor.

He put his arm around my waist. "You're sure a skinny little thing." As he pulled me closer, I caught a whiff of his aftershave. I could feel his muscles. Even though the espadrilles added to my height, Cole still stood a lot taller.

I listened as the guitarist sang something about a cowboy hurrying to spend time with his girlfriend in his truck. I didn't catch all the words.

"I don't recognize the song."

"It's called Runnin' Out of Moonlight."

"It sounds very depressing."

"Yeah, that's how a lot of cowboy songs sound. They're all about hard-drinking cowboys, lonesome creatures either taking up with the wrong women or not recognizing a good woman until she's gone."

"Does that describe you?"

He didn't answer.

I guessed the music takes getting used to. As we moved across the floor I was impressed. "You're a really good dancer, Cole."

"Well, Miss Julia, I do have my finer points and a few hidden talents. I'm not all rough edges."

I felt a strange sensation being in a man's arms again. I loved dancing, but Roger and I never danced. He hated dancing probably because he had no sense of rhythm. After more than two beers, I was beginning to enjoy myself a little too much. My usual reserve and need to be in control was disappearing.

We started back to the table just as the lead guitarist called out, "Up on your feet everybody. Let's have a little fun. Are you ready for a line dance?"

I turned to Cole. "What's a line dance?"

"You're kidding. Man, you have led a sheltered life, way too much time in fancy clubs. Come on I'll show you."

It took a bit of doing to catch on, but Cole was a great teacher. The dance floor was crowded everyone was dancing and singing the words to "Achy Breaky Heart." By the time the song was over I was out of breath, laughing at having had such a good time doing something I'd never imagined I'd agree to. Forgetting how tacky the place was.

"I didn't know you were so talented, Cole."

"And I didn't know you could be such a good sport, especially when you come off your high horse, New York attitude."

The party broke up after midnight. I said goodbye and was surprised at the hugs and heartfelt hopes I'd come again.

I easily climbed into the truck. I'd begun to get the hang of it. It'd been a fun evening, but I was ready to call it a night.

"Have a good time tonight, Miss Julia?"

"It was great. I haven't had that much fun or laughed so hard in a long time. Your friends are really nice people."

"They're the salt of the earth. They were there for me when I needed them the most, and I'd do anything for them. You might be surprised to know they're as well educated as your snooty New York society friends. The only difference is their degrees are in Animal Husbandry, or Agronomy instead of MBA's."

"We rode a long way in silence until Cole asked if I'd ever been to a rodeo."

"No. They're not big in New York City."

"There's a rodeo tomorrow at the county fairgrounds. Would you like to go?" I didn't hesitate. "Yes. Sounds like fun."

The radio played as Cole drove along the highway. I must have dozed off, because all of a suddenly I awakened with a start, in a panic. I saw bright headlights heading toward us and screamed, "Look out," at the top of my lungs. A scream louder than I thought I was capable of.

"Look out. My God, Cole, look out. He's going to hit us." I screamed again. By then I was shaking all over with tears running down my cheeks, huddled against the truck's door, my arms wrapped tight around me waiting for the impact. Cole pulled off to the side of the road.

"Are you alright?"

It only took a moment for me to realize what had just happened. "I'm sorry. I'll be fine. Just give me a minute."

"Nothing to be sorry about. Is that how the accident happened? You were struck head on?"

"Yes." I was still shaking. "Coming home from a party. They said the driver tried to stop, but it was too late." I wiped away my tears and sat up straight. "I'm okay now. I don't know what got into me."

Cole started the engine and drove back onto the road. "What you saw was a big cattle truck. His headlights were on high, but he was clearly on his side of the road. Sassy told me you were in an accident. She never said how it happened."

The rest of the ride home was uneventful as I tried not to think about any of the events leading up to the crash.

Bear jumped off the porch as we walked toward the front door. Cole reached down to pet him, greeting him as he always did with a "Good boy, you did your job?" He opened the door and before I started up the stairs to my bedroom I stopped and turned toward him.

"Goodnight, Cole. Thanks again for a very nice evening. I'm sorry about the outburst."

"You're welcome. I'm glad you had fun. I promised Sassy I wouldn't leave you here alone at night. See you in the morning. Sleep in. I'll make my own breakfast. I should be through with I need to do by ten. We need be on our way by eleven if we want to be at the fairgrounds in time to get seats in the grandstand."

I closed the door and leaned against it thinking Cole could be really nice if he wanted to be. I wondered what he was all about. So much about him remained a mystery.

Chapter 9

We went our separate ways all morning. Cole called from the front hall just before eleven asking if I was ready.

"I'll be right down."

Cole took a baseball cap off the coat rack handing it to me. "It can get hot in the afternoon and the grandstands aren't covered. The cap will do until we can buy you an appropriate straw hat."

It took about an hour to reach the fairgrounds. The whole area was a buzz with activity, people and animals everywhere. We parked on a grassy field alongside a sea of trucks, horse trailers of all sizes and descriptions, many with horses tied to the trailers eating hay filled nets. A large number of stock trailers were parked at the far end of the field.

"Come on. I'll show you around."

We passed by the back of a row of what Cole called chutes. A bunch of cowboys some participants in today's events according to Cole. I surveyed the group milling around. I'd never seen anything like this before anywhere but in the movies. Some seemed very young, the rest older and scruffier, a rough looking lot for the most part. Chaps over their jeans, rowel spurs on their boots, cowboy hats pulled low over their foreheads. A few with ponytails, most unshaven, some sporting beards. Cole pointed out the safety vests some were wearing as protection. They were smoking, laughing, seeming to have a good time. I noticed a bottle in a brown paper bag being passed around. My curiosity was drawn to two men some distance away.

"Those two olive skinned men, Cole, the ones with the long pony tails, leaning against the fence. Are they Indians?"

Cole glanced at the two men standing apart from the rest. "Yeah, but I'm not sure what tribe they're from. The Blackfeet, Chippewa Cree, and Crow all have reservations in Montana. Indians are first class horsemen and tough competitors."

I'd never seen cattle chutes before or holding pens. Nothing about the area or the crowd resembled the fancy horse shows I remembered.

We passed a number of vendors selling hot dogs, hamburgers, beer, and soft drinks to the large crowd wandering about. Cole pointed out a trailer with the sign that read Hardy's Tack and Apparel, painted on its side.

"Come on, Miss Julia. Let's find you a summer hat. The kind a pretty lady should wear."

The trailer was packed full of merchandise, everything from one-eared western bridles, fancy silver bits and buckles, saddles, blankets, boots, brushes, liniments, anything you could imagine for horses and horse people. An assortment of straw hats both men's and women's hung on pegs along one wall. Cody picked a beige colored straw hat off a peg, one that was lacey with an intricate cut-out pattern and a large brim.

"Try this one on. It's pretty fancy, just like you."

"What do you think," I asked, as I tucked my hair behind my ears."

He studied me for a moment. "Hold still. It needs a bit of an adjustment." Cole bent the sides up a little and tried to crease the top. "There that's better. Perfect. Now nobody would guess you're from New York."

I reached into my purse for my wallet only to be told, "No way. It's my treat. Now that you look the part, let's go find something to eat and get settled in the grandstand. The afternoon events should be getting underway any time now."

The stands were filling as we carried our hot dogs up the steps and found our way to a row of seats up high enough to get a good view of the arena, much larger than I'd expected. The crowd was laughing at a couple of guys in clown costumes rolling around in barrels on the arena floor. I asked what they were doing.

"Those guys might look silly screwing around out there in the dirt, but they're the toughest cowboys in the rodeo. Their job is to protect the bull riders. When the horn signals the ride is over and the rider jumps off, or when he gets bucked off, the clown is supposed to distract the bull until the rider can scramble to safety."

"Isn't that dangerous?"

"Damn right it is. It takes a special kind of guy to be a rodeo clown. A lot of those guys get hurt every year. A few have been killed. Usually, you see two clowns working together. Some of the bulls can be real mean."

Before I had a chance to ask more questions, I heard the music. As I didn't see a band anywhere, I guessed the music was recorded. The crowd jumped to their feet, hats off, hands over their hearts, as a young girl in pink chaps and a pink cowboy hat started to sing, The Star Spangled Banner, the crowd singing along with her. When she finished, they rewarded her with a round of hoots, hollers and applause. I watched with same excitement as the rest of the crowd, as the back gates opened and mounted teams rode into the arena at a full gallop, carrying the American flag, a bunch of banners, and what Cole said was the state flag. The stands went wild with cheering, clapping, and foot stomping. When the riders left, and the crowd settled down, I waited with heightened anticipation just like everyone else as the rodeo begin. This was a whole different world.

"The steer wrestling and team roping competition was this morning, Miss Julia. I didn't figure you'd find that too interesting. My older brother and I competed years ago. We were pretty good. We got a lot of trophies and nice silver belt buckles the year we were junior champions in our district."

The voice on the loudspeaker welcomed everybody, laid out some ground rules, and announced Saddle Bronc riding would be the first attraction of the afternoon.

"What's going to happen, Cole?"

"See the wooden chute over to your right? When the cowboy says he's ready, they'll open the chute and he'll have to stay on the horse for eight seconds. He has a saddle without a horn and free-swinging stirrups, no bridle just a simple cotton braided rein attached to a leather halter.

I watched as the horse leaped out of the chute and started twisting and bucking.

"Now watch, Julia. The rider can't touch the horse with his free hand and he has to spur him the whole ride. The score depends a lot on how hard the horse's bucks are to ride and how hard the rider spurs him on."

"How do they train the horses to buck like that?"

"Well, look closely at the next horse out of the chute and you'll see a flank strap. The stall man tightens that strap just as the gate opens. The horse is bucking to get rid of the strap, though they have to have a good buck in them to begin with. They've never been broken to be saddle horses."

There must have been fifteen riders bucking their way across the arena, one at a time. A few cowboys fell off, but most stayed with the horse for the eight seconds. They announced the winner with the best score. The crowd cheered.

The next event was the bareback bronc riders. Cole explained the rider had no rein only a rigging that consisted of a leather and rawhide piece kind of like a suitcase handle attached to a surcingle and placed behind the horse's withers. I couldn't imagine myself staying on a bucking horse for eight seconds, let alone a horse with no saddle or bridle. By the time they finished, I'd seen enough bucking horses to last a lifetime. But the crowd loved it, calling out the names of their favorite cowboy and rooting them on. I noticed as soon as the flank strap was removed, the horse settled down and headed toward the "out" gate. As if the horse knew he had a job to do and once the strap was removed, he could go home his work over for the day.

The announcer called for a fifteen-minute break before the bull riding began. "Want a beer, or a cold drink?" Cole asked.

"A cold lemonade would be great."

"Stay put and save my seat I'll be right back. Don't give it to one of the good-looking cowboys over there that have been eyeing you, and for God's sake don't run off with one of them. I could never explain your disappearance to Sassy."

Cole returned with two Styrofoam cups in hand just as bull riding, the main attraction, was about to begin. I could feel the crowd's excitement building. Surprised to find myself excited as well.

I noticed the clowns had rolled a barrel close to the chute resting an oversized broom against its side. A hush grew over the crowd as the gate to the bucking chute opened and the first rider entered the arena. He hadn't gotten more than three steps from the chute when the bull turned, giving one huge quick twisting buck and the rider hit the ground landing alongside the bull. He attempted to get to his feet as the bull, head down, began to charge. I turned toward Cole. "My God, the bull's going after that poor guy."

Before I could say another word, the clown stepped between the cowboy and the bull, pushing the broom in the bull's face. He began to wave a huge, oversized red handkerchief he pulled from his pocket. The bull turned his attention toward the clown who ran for the barrel, the bull behind him, the crowd cheering. The "out" gate opened as the clown jumped into the barrel. With the sound of the gate opening the bull turned and left the arena.

I watched in horror as rider after rider was subjected to bulls spinning, rearing, and bucking so high their hind feet were at least five feet off the ground. One bull, which they announced had never been successfully ridden, with all four feet off the ground easily dropped his rider to the ground. The crowd loved it as rider after rider hit the dirt before the eight seconds necessary to score. I began to think bull riders must have a death wish.

Only two riders had managed, so far, to last eight seconds. I asked Cole how the judge came up with their score.

"They're usually two judges. One scores the bull and the other the rider. One hundred percent is the perfect ride, so each judge can award fifty points. These guys are probably in the sixty to seventy points range."

"Are they crazy, Cole? They could get seriously injured or even killed out there."

"It happens, but there's an adrenaline rush, a real high when you try to ride a bull. A lot of aches and pain if you hit the ground, and real problems if the bull stomps on you."

"Please, don't tell me you've ridden bulls."

"I tried it a couple of times, but I wasn't very good."

Only two riders were yet to compete when the accident happened. The bull rider was bucked off after two or three seconds, but the long rope that was wrapped around his hand and looped around the bull didn't come loose. The bull was dragging him across the arena tossing him in the air like a sack of potatoes and then slamming him to the ground. Both clowns were doing their best to free him. While it only lasted a few seconds, it seemed like an eternity. I closed my eyes. I couldn't watch the horrifying sight. The crowd was silent. When I heard a loud cheer erupt from the crowd, I opened my eyes to see the bull leaving the arena while the rider lay motionless on the ground, face down, a clown on his knees leaning over him.

The gate to the arena opened and an ambulance drove in. Two paramedics hovered over the motionless cowboy. One pulled a stretcher from the back of the ambulance while the other turned the cowboy over after secured his neck in a brace. They slid a board underneath him and after placing him on the stretcher they carried him to their vehicle. Then, with the siren wailing, they drove out of the arena to the applause of the crowd.

"My God, Cole, how awful. Do you think he's dead?"

"No, I don't think so. If he was dead, they wouldn't have left with the siren blaring, but I'm damn sure he's pretty seriously banged up."

The last rider chose not to compete and the event was over except for the closing ceremony.

Cole grabbed my arm. "Let's get out of here before the traffic jam."

I followed Cole as he raced down the grandstand steps. I was still shaking from what I'd just seen.

"I'm sorry about what just happened. I didn't mean for this to end on a downer."

"It's not your fault. I was having fun up until then. Do you think he'll be okay?"

"Don't know, but I do know I need a drink. That scene brings back a few bad memories. There's a roadhouse about a mile from here it's not fancy, but the food's good. Are you game?"

"More than game. A drink sounds great."

Chapter 10

By Monday, we were back to our normal schedule. I fixed Cole's breakfast. He cleaned his plate, re-filled his coffee mug and left for the day with no more than two words spoken between us. The friendly really nice guy I spent time with on the weekend had disappeared into the aloof, sarcastic, Jekyll and Hyde creature of the previous week.

I went about my chores. When the house was cleaned, the eggs gathered, the vegetables picked, it was time to see what Charger was all about.

With halter in hand, I opened the pasture gate. He nickered as he walked toward me. He seemed glad to see me as he dropped his head into the halter and walk back to the barn like a perfect gentleman. I put him in the cross ties and went to find the groom box and the English saddle Cole had mentioned.

I enjoyed grooming the old horse as much as he was enjoying the company. Saddled and bridled I led him to the bale of hay I used as a mounting block, put one foot in the stirrup and eased myself onto the saddle.

We walked down to the ring and after a few turns around at a walk, I reached down and tightened the girth. Time to see what Charger knew. His fluid trot was more than comfortable, his canter like sitting on a rocking chair. The old boy hadn't forgotten his training. He'd been well schooled.

It must have been close to one o'clock by the time I walked Charger back to his pasture. If Cole had come home for lunch and I wasn't there, I'd never hear the end of it.

Bear was stretched out his full length sleeping in the sun on the grass by the back door. He picked up his head as I came into view and thumped his tail. He seemed disinclined to get up and went back to sleep.

No sign of Cole anywhere. I'm sure I'd have heard the truck. Seemed like a good time to shower and change into something cooler.

Feeling refreshed after the shower, I grabbed my book and headed for the kitchen. So far, I'd been too busy to read during the day and too tired to read at night. I sliced an apple and a peach putting them on a plate alongside a couple of cookies from the tin, and went outside on the patio to enjoy the sun. Despite everything I was beginning to feel quite comfortable here. I settled on the chaise and opened the book. Bear joined me. For the first time, even though I was alone, I didn't feel as if I was hiding from the world. A feeling of peace came over me. Something I hadn't felt before.

About four in the afternoon, I thought I'd better start dinner. I'd picked some large zucchini and tomatoes earlier thinking I could use them to make lasagna. In a strange way I was enjoying the challenge of preparing meals. There was something creative about the whole task.

I washed the salad greens and assembled the lasagna. All I had to do was pop it in the oven. Earlier I'd noticed some wild flowers growing along the stone wall in front of the house. I decided to pick a few for the table. Then removing the candlesticks from the dining room table I placed them on either side of the vase full of flowers. I thought the kitchen table looked very festive. No longer was I fighting being here. The days were passing by so fast and I was beginning to feel more confident in the future and myself as the days went by.

Cole came home a little past five. "How was your day," I asked. He didn't look happy. "Have a problem?"

"A big problem. I found a dead calf in one of the pastures. It hadn't been dead very long by the looks of it, probably the work of a small pack of coyotes or a couple of wolves. Could have been a mountain lion. That one calf was probably worth a thousand at the very least. We'll probably lose a few more if I don't catch whatever attacked the herd."

All I heard was coyotes, wolves and mountain lions. I had no idea those sorts of animals were so close by. I thought of all the days I rode through the pastures alone. What would I do if I met one? The thought scared me to death. As far as I was concerned coyotes, wolves and lions belonged in a zoo.

"What are you going to do?"

"For a start, I'm taking my rifle and spending the night out with the herd." I heard him say as he left the room, "I'll be down for dinner after I clean up."

We finished dinner and split the last of a bottle of wine. Cole was in his Dr. Jekyll mood this evening. Had it been Mr. Hyde at the table I would have kept my head down and my mouth shut.

"Great dinner, Julia. I'll give you a break and barbeque tomorrow." He got up from the table and walked toward the hall. "I'm going to try to get a few hours of shut eye. No use going predator hunting before dark."

I called after him feeling confused. "You're not going to leave me here alone, are you? Remember I'm a city girl. I don't know how to deal with wild animals."

"Believe me, there's nothing for you to be concerned about, you're safe here. I'll leave Bear to keep you company. He likes coming in the house."

"No way. I'm not staying here alone, Bear or no Bear. I'm coming with you."

"Suit yourself, but trust me, you'll be a lot more comfortable here. In any case, it would help if you made a pot of coffee, filled the thermos, and made a couple of sandwiches. This could take the better part of the night."

By ten o'clock, having changed back into my jeans, I was trailing after Cole, headed for the truck. I carried the thermos and the sandwiches while he carried two large rifles, placing them in the trucks gun racks.

Cole closed the truck door and started the engine. "Last chance lady. I think you're crazy to come along, but if you're sure that's what you want to do, hold on. It's going to be a slow and bumpy ride. There's no road where we're going."

We drove down the driveway to a large gate near the entrance to the ranch. Cole got out, unlocked the gate and drove through, locking the gate behind us. We bumped along for several miles with only the moonlight guiding the way. Cole had turned the headlights off. Spotting a large number of cattle grazing, Cole brought the truck to a stop.

"With luck I might catch sight of whatever killed the calf. The herd is spread out over so many acres it's hard to tell where the predator might be."

"How many animals do you own?"

"None. I lease the grazing rights. The herd's owner pays so much per head to graze on my land and a fee for management. I had to sell off all our cattle to settle my dad's debts after he died."

What seemed like hours passed by as we sat motionless in the truck not saying a word. Cole warned me to keep quiet telling me wild animals are very sensitive to noise. The only sounds I heard were cattle moving about.

Twenty or thirty minutes passed before Cole started the engine, telling me the herd seemed too quiet for anything to be prowling among them. "I'm going to drive to a spot closer to where I found the dead calf. Hold on, it might be rougher going now that the moon is hidden behind the clouds."

When we finally came to a stop by the creek Cole whispered, "I'm gona' wait here for a while. The cattle come here to drink. Maybe I'll get lucky."

We were so close to the creek I could hear the cattle as they drank, but no other sound. Cole poured himself some coffee handing me the thermos. I was about to ask if he wanted a sandwich when Cole put his fingers to his lips, indicating keep still. The truck door was already ajar, Cole slowly opened it wider, reaching behind him for his rifle and a pair of strange looking glasses. He'd taped over the interior light so the interior remained dark even with the door open.

Feeling a sense of stark terror, I watched as Cole slowly eased himself out of the truck, taking a few steps in the direction of the herd, leaving me alone with the door wide open. I zipped up my jacket against the cold night air and began to worry. What if some animal tried to attach me? I had no way to protect myself. I was all alone with the truck door wide open. My sense of fear grew as I realized I couldn't see or hear Cole. The moon was still hidden behind a bank of clouds and it was pitch black outside. What in the hell was I doing out here. I must be crazy.

I sat frozen, not knowing what was happening, or what to do. How would I know if some animal had attacked Cole? Did I just sit here until dawn and hope he returned? I suddenly realized I had no idea what I would do if he didn't return? I'd never felt so helpless. I had no idea how to find my way back to the house. There wasn't any cell phone service for me to call for help. Did they even have 911 in this God forsaken place.?

The only sound was cattle moving about. Tense minutes passed before I heard the crack of a rifle being fired, followed by the sound of cattle running off, then nothing. I didn't dare get out of the truck. Maybe if I turned on the headlights, I could see something.

Before I could do anything, I saw Cole approaching as the moon's rays peaked out from under the clouds. He was dragging what appeared to be a dead animal behind him.

As he came closer into view, I noticed to the large bloodstain on Cole's pant leg. My nerves on edge I pointed to his leg and asked if he was okay.

"I'm fine, it's the wolf's blood not mine.

"God you scared the living daylights out of me." No hiding the panic in my voice. "I didn't know what to do. You could have been killed."

"Hey, slow down, Miss Julia. Take a deep breath. I'm fine. There wasn't anything for you to do except to be quiet and stay put. Remember you're the one who wanted to come along. I'll throw the carcass in the tailgate and we can head for home."

Cole placed the rifle back in the gun rack and put the glasses in their case.

"Those are odd looking things."

"Yeah, they're military gear...night vision glasses. They're great, they let you see things in the dark through an eerie green haze. I'd never have spotted the wolf without them."

"How can you seem so calm? Aren't wolves dangerous?"

"They sure as hell can be, but like most predators if they're alone, they'll run off rather than attack a human. If they're in a pack, yeah, you could be in big trouble. This one almost got away. She probably caught my scent and started to move off. I got lucky and nailed her with one shot. At least she won't be killing any more steers.

I couldn't believe how at ease he seemed about wolf hunting in the dead of night. "Weren't you even the least bit concerned?"

"Hell, no. I've been doin' this ever since I was a kid trailing after my dad, but enough for one night. Ready to go home?"

"Yes, I've had more than enough excitement for a whole lot of nights."

I wrapped my jacket close around me. "Could you please turn on some heat? It's cold in here."

As we started the long slow drive back to the house I was curious, realizing I knew next to nothing about this man. He rarely talked about himself.

"Tell me about yourself Cole. The only thing Sassy said about you was she'd know you since you were a kid.

"Nothing to tell. What you see is what you get."

It dawned on me by some of the things he did and said that he hadn't spent his whole life ranching in the middle of nowhere.

"I don't believe that. My guess is there's a lot more to your story. Did you go to College?"

"Yeah, but I don't know why that would interest you."

"Let's say just because I'm curious."

"Well, Miss Curious, for what it's worth, undergraduate degree from the University of Montana, MBA from Columbia University. Does that satisfy your curiosity?"

"No, it only makes me want to hear more. What do you need an MBA for if you're going to be a rancher?"

"You don't, but I never wanted to be what you call a rancher, what I prefer to call a cattleman. My idea was to get off the ranch as soon as I could and never come back. I'd set my heart on being a big wheel in the big city."

"That's interesting. Which city, Billings or Helena?"

"Neither, I meant the big city, New York, of course."

That really caught me by surprise. The truck bumped along at a snail's pace as I tried to digest what I'd just heard.

"You're kidding. You're proving me wrong about how I perceived you. It seems you're a man of many mysteries."

"What you mean is, because I live on a ranch and wear Levis I couldn't possibly be anything more than a simple cowboy. Maybe you should learn not to judge people too quickly."

"I never meant I was judging you, Cole, but I'm dying to hear about your time in New York."

"Another time, maybe. It's a long story. For now, I just want to get home. It's been a long day."

I climbed the stairs to my room, undressed and crawled into bed wanting to know a lot more about Cole Clayton, but how could I get him to talk about himself. He seemed reluctant to let his guard down. He could be fun to be with one minute then be aloof, and sarcastic the next. I found him impossible to understand. I glanced at the clock it was three in the morning, almost time to get up. Figuring out Cole would have to wait for another day.

Chapter 11

The days began to fall into a pattern, I made breakfast, tided up the house, and rode Charger. Cole had assured me I was safe from predators riding alone. The old horse and I had formed quite a bond. I'd found so many beautiful areas to explore, acres and acres with nothing but green pasture and black cattle. I never quite mastered Cole's art of opening and closing gates on horseback, but I managed. I tried to give a wide berth to the cattle finding them a little intimidating. Sort of the same system I used with the chickens.

All the open space was a far cry from my life in New York. No traffic or noise, just meadows, creeks, trees, and the bluest, clearest sky I'd ever seen. Even the air smelled sweeter. I was regaining my health and my sense of well-being. I'd even put on a few pounds. My time on the ranch was proving to be worthwhile after all. I'd begun to look forward rather than backward. It would seem Sassy knew what she was doing.

Cole stopped picking on me, but he seemed even more remote. On Friday during dinner, he mentioned the local cattlemen's association was holding a fund-raising dinner Saturday at the Armory in Silverton. Would I like to go with him?

I knew Cole considered it part of his responsibility to see I wasn't left alone at night.

"I'd like that, but if you remember my telling you, at Sassy's suggestion, I didn't bring anything but jeans with me. I have nothing to wear."

It took a minute or two before Cole smiled. "You know what. I think I might just have a solution. Your mentioning Sassy reminded me there's a suitcase full of her things upstairs on the shelf in my bedroom. You're about the same size. There might be something there you could use."

How strange. Why would Sassy leave a suitcase full of her things here? I followed Cole into his bedroom, the place that had been off limits since my arrival. The room was much larger than the other bedrooms. The décor was as dated as the rest of the house. He opened the closet to reveal what looked like business suits, shirts and jeans all neatly hung. Shoes lined like soldiers at attention all in a row on the closet floor. I watched as he took down a rather large brown leather case from the shelf and placed it on the bed. Inside were folded skirts, blouses, belts, an assortment of undergarments, and a small satin pouch containing jewelry.

"Wow, this is quite a surprise." I pulled out several quite lovely squaw skirts similar to the one Sassy wore the day she picked me up at the airport.

Cole picked out one skirt in shades of black and brown and handed it to me. "Try this one on."

I took the garment back to my bedroom, slipped out of my jeans and stepped into the skirt. I checked it out on the closet mirror thinking, with the right blouse it might just do. I walked back to show Cole, loving the way the full skirt swirled around my ankles as I moved. The material was the softest cotton I'd ever felt.

"Well, what do you think?"

"I think it's perfect. You'll turn every head. You remind me of the Sassy I remember as a kid."

After searching through the blouses, I found one I thought would be perfect. I opened the small satin pouch. A pair of silver earrings caught my eye.

"I'll be back after I change back into my jeans."

By the time I'd returned Cole had put the case back on the shelf, leaving a spectacular silver trimmed wide black leather belt on the bed.

"The belt should be the finishing touch. Nobody'll guess there's a stranger in our midst. Not one from New York, for sure."

I picked up the belt. Large silver conches were attached every few inches to the wide black leather, ending with an oversized ornate silver buckle. I'd never seen anything quite like it, but the whole thing seemed strange.

"I have a question. What's a suitcase full of Sassy's things doing here?"

"Another long story."

"You seem to have a lot of untold long stories." I sat down on the bed. "This is one story I'm damned curious to hear about, so I'm not going anywhere until I do."

Cole sat next to me. Hesitating before he started the explanation by saying the Senator used to own the adjoining ranch. "The ranch had been in his family longer than Dad's family owned ours. We're talking generations. The Senator and Sassy's main house was the one you stayed at in Billings, but whenever they were in Montana, he preferred to spend his time at the ranch.

"Sassy was friendly, always bringing something with her as gifts for us kids. The Senator was sort of austere, a scary kind of guy we kids steered clear of. Sassy would invite us over to their ranch for treats, she was fun to be with. Sometimes, when the Senator was traveling, she'd come and stay at the ranch alone. She'd ride over on her horse and we'd take her along to check on the cattle. She and my dad got along real well."

"So far this doesn't explain the suitcase,"

Cole took a deep breath seeming to be taking great care with what he was about to say.

"My mom died about a month after the Senator had a heart attack and died. She'd been suffering with cancer and all that entailed for a long time. My mom and dad had been married almost thirty years when she died. They'd married right after they graduated from high school."

I listened not wanting to say a word for fear Cole would stop. For a moment he seemed so deep in thought he forget I was there. When he looked up and saw me, he took a deep breath and went on.

"My mom must have been a pretty young girl from what I've seen of their wedding pictures, but she didn't age very well. She didn't take much interest in her looks. Don't get me wrong, she was the perfect mother, she baked cookies, cleaned our rooms, saw to it we had clean clothes, tended to our wounds, and was always a sort of buffer to dad who could be tough on us kids. Mom was always available if someone in our community needed help. A really good church going woman who everybody liked."

"You and your siblings were grown when she died, right?"

"Yeah, my sister and brother were married and I was starting college."

"That still doesn't explain the suitcase."

Cole looked rather ill at ease. "Well, I'm coming to that."

He stood up and walked toward the window, his back to me as he spoke.

"Sassy moved to the ranch after the Senator died and my dad helped her run the place. She had hired hands, but Dad took over the responsibility for both ranches. The two of them were as different as night and day. Dad was as handsome as Sassy was gorgeous, but she came from a sophisticated, educated world while Dad's education stopped with high school. She was a world traveler, and Dad had never been any further than Billings. I guess opposites attract. Sassy was forty-five at the time and Dad was almost fifty. He couldn't believe that someone as beautiful and worldly as Sassy could be interested in him. She was attracted, I guess, to his masculine, rugged, sort of down to earth manner. Dad was as different from the Senator as dark is to light.

"They fell in love. Dad adored her and I saw him change almost overnight. She was fun to be with and he began to laugh and enjoy life in a way I'd never seen before."

Cole stopped talking. He seemed miles away.

"That can't be the end of the story?"

"No," he said. "I just don't know how much I should tell you."

"Come, sit back down. You can't stop now. I want to hear everything."

Cole gathered his thoughts for a moment before he spoke. "Well, Sassy moved in here with Dad. He wanted to marry her, but she said no. The Senator's estate was complicated as was his will. If she remarried, it might mean her financial circumstances could take a dramatic shift downward. Dad was old fashioned in so many ways. I know he worried what people might think about their living together. He worried about Sassy's reputation.

"Sassy told him she wasn't worried about anything as silly as her reputation. She'd never been happier in her life and didn't give a damn what people thought. Her life was with him."

"Wow, I'm beginning to get a whole new take on my aunt. I'm sure my dad has no idea about any of this, but what did you think about their arrangement?"

"I could have cared less. They were happy together. At times, damn right embarrassing to be around. They acted like two teenagers most of the time, holding hands, kissing. They couldn't keep their hands off one another. He taught her to fish and shoot, and she taught him to drink wine and eat sushi."

"I'm not sure I'm going to like the end of the story."

"Well, they had more than ten happy years together before Dad had a stroke. Sassy would travel on her own sometimes, or stay alone at the house in Billings if she had some social obligation, but that all came to an end after dad's stroke. As soon as he came home from the hospital, Sassy never left the ranch. She took care of him, nursed him back to health."

"She must have loved him deeply."

"She did, and he really tested that love, fought her tooth and nail over the exercise routine she laid out. He was ready to give up, but in large part due to her persistence, and being smart enough to understand that it was his manhood, his pride that was causing the problems, he recovered. He was left with only a slight limp on his left side and a loss of some strength in his left hand. He lived two more years doing almost everything he'd done before. When he had a second major stoke and lay dying, she stayed at his bedside night and day until the end."

I tried to wipe away the flow of tears as I let the whole sad, but beautiful story sink in.

"Now you understand, Julia, why I would do anything Sassy asked of me. Why I agreed to let you come and stay here. Not only did Sassy tend to Dad when he needed help, she gave him the kind of love few find in their lives. They never counted their time together in years. To them, each day was a lifetime."

It took a few moments for me to get my emotions under control before I said, "Thanks, Cole for telling me their story. It gives me a different perspective on a lot of things. Wouldn't we all like to find the kind of love those two had?"

We stood, neither of us saying a word until I broke the silence. "I'm going downstairs. I need a breath of fresh air. You want anything?"

"Wait I'll come with you."

Chapter 12

I walked out onto the patio. The night sky was filled with thousands of stars, and a crescent moon. The only sounds were the soothing songs of the crickets. I could never find the quiet I needed at the moment, or a peaceful setting like this in the city.

Cole stood in the doorway. "I could use a beer. You want anything, Julia?"

"A glass of wine would be nice. I'm not ready to call it a night."

Cole returned, drinks in hand, and settled on the chaise next to mine.

"Finding out how intertwined our families are I think it's time you told me more about yourself."

"Like what?"

"About your time in New York for one. Did you ever get your wish and make it big in the big city?"

Cole twisted of the bottle cap and took a long drink before he answered.

"Believe it or not, I did get my wish. I became a big wheel for quite a while. I worked for a large brokerage house on Wall Street, one of the glamour boys, with thousand-dollar suits, a fancy apartment, and a big fat bonus at the end of the year. One of the guys who hit the bar scene every night, my life was about nothing beyond money, booze, and broads."

"Sorry, Cole, I just don't see you as the outgoing, fun loving, bar scene kind of guy. As it is, I can hardly get more than a sentence at a time out of you."

Cole laughed. "Does seem out of character doesn't it. Well, I arrived in New York the shy ranch kid who'd never learned how to make small talk, but I soon learned the ropes from the guys I worked with. Alcohol goes a long way to overcoming inhabitations and the lows in the morning after a big drunk the night before were easily transformed by uppers."

I looked at Cole in disbelief. "You're kidding me?"

"Look at it this way, the world is a volatile place. If something good happens the markets go up and if something goes wrong the markets go down. You better be ready to act in either circumstance. It was kinda' like riding on a merry-go-ground, except I wasn't on the horse that doesn't move. I was aboard the one that goes up and down until the music stops. Only for me the music never stopped. I couldn't get off the merry-go-round, it was drinking all night and popping pills all day."

Wow. This was a side of Cole I never would have imagined. I drank from my wine glass in slow sips before I spoke again. Trying to get my head around what Cole had just told me.

"You never married?"

"Wrong again. My wife was a lot like you. Well she didn't look like you, but she was upper-class, society born, Ivy league educated, who knew which fork to pick up, who'd never been denied a thing in her life. Spoiled rotten,"

"Hey, wait a minute. I resent that. Don't make me out to be some spoiled rich kid. I may have been overly protected, but I wasn't spoiled."

"Maybe that was a little rough, but most of it is true, isn't it?" I decided to let that go by for now. I didn't want the conversation to be about me

"But what happened to you in New York that you became Montana all over again."

"You really want to hear more?"

"Absolutely." I drained what was left in my glass and stretched out on the chaise waiting for Cole to continue.

"What happened was my dad died. Cynthia, my wife and I came back here for the funeral. I needed to stay on for a week or so, after Dad was buried, to clear up his affairs and make some decisions regarding the ranch. Both my brother and sister dumped the whole responsibility in my lap.

Cynthia wasn't willing to stay. She hated the ranch almost as much as she hated Montana."

"So, she left you here alone?"

"At the time I thought it was no big deal. A week at the most and I'd be back in New York, but then I had a come-to-Jesus moment. I remember walking into Dad's lawyer's office thinking this was all going to be routine."

"And that's not what happened?"

"Not by a long shot. I shouldn't have been shocked dad didn't have a will, but I wasn't expecting what he did have, which was a stack of unpaid bills. He had no health insurance so his illness left a pile of hospital and doctors' bills that were long overdue with demands for payment. His cash assets consisted of a small life insurance policy with my mother as the beneficiary, even though she'd been dead for years, and what was left in his checking account."

"What a mess."

"That was the easy part." Cole stood and tossed the empty beer bottle into the garbage can. "The real mess was yet to come. Dad had received a notice from the IRS, which he'd turned over to his lawyer. It seems he'd never filed an income tax return. According to the attorney, Dad claimed because he never paid himself a salary, he didn't owe any taxes."

I guess the expression on my face said it all.

"I know, don't say it. Dad wasn't ignorant. He wasn't intending to cheat the Government, it made perfect sense to him. He only paid bills with the money the ranch earned. He never wrote himself a check. Whatever money, if any, was left over at the end of the year, stayed in the ranch bank account to pay next year's bills.

"Dad's attorney pointed to a large number of boxes stacked in the corner of his office, saying those were his records. If I could make heads or tails of them, he'd try to cut a deal with the Feds. If not the Government would come after the estate for what they considered he owed."

"My God, what did you do."

"The only thing I could, I left the lawyers office with boxes of records piled high in the back of my dad's old truck and headed home. The fate of the ranch was now in my hands. My brother and sister agreed that if I could save the ranch, it would be mine as long as I didn't put it up for sale. They too wanted the ranch to stay in the family, but in the event the ranch was sold, we'd split the proceeds three ways."

I was beginning to get a glimmer into the real Cole.

"It's getting late. Let's call it a night, Julia."

"No way. You can't just leave the story hanging in the air without an ending. Not now."

"Come on. You don't really want to hear more."

"But I do."

Cole stood and started back toward the kitchen.

"Boy, you're a real glutton for punishment. I need another beer if I'm going to relive the whole damn mess again. Want another glass of wine?"

"No, thanks."

I watched Cole go inside thinking something was missing. So far his story doesn't explain why he's here and not in New York.

Cole pulled his chaise closer to mine, uncapped the beer bottle and began to speak. "It felt strange to be back in the old house. I stacked the boxes on the floor next to the dining room table, prepared to try and make sense of the mess. If I couldn't put together some sort of record of profit and loss, for almost forty years, the ranch my great grandfather founded would probably be gone. If my dad hadn't paid the IRS, I was damn sure he hadn't paid the State of Montana either.

"From the look of things, it was going to take a while to put his affairs in order. I telephone my boss and he agreed to let me use my vacation time to stay in Montana and straighten things out. I called Cynthia to tell her I would be stuck on the ranch for at least three or four weeks, maybe longer. I asked her to catch a flight as soon as she could. I needed help, but more than anything I needed company.

"Cynthia laughed, telling me there was no way she was going to be stuck on the ranch for weeks on end. She was sorry about the mess I'd inherited, she missed me, and hoped I be back soon."

I couldn't believe what I was hearing. He was only asking his wife for her company. Weren't married people supposed to support one another? Was this what was wrong with a lot of marriages today?

Cole said he put in long hours going over bank statements and other records. He spent a few Saturday evenings with his old buddies at the Longhorn having only a beer or two, but otherwise he stayed close to home. No drinking and no pills.

"I slept in my old bedroom, Julia, full of trophies, ribbons, and awards from years gone by, and spent a lot of time accessing my life and where I thought I was headed. To make a long story short, I turned the data over to the attorney hoping he could make a deal with the IRS. I hired an extra hand to help the foreman look after the cattle until they were sold and headed back to New York. I tried to settle into the life I'd left behind only a few weeks before, but sober things seemed different."

Cole's expression seemed so far away. I wanted to reach out to him, hold his hand, but I didn't dare. I waited for him to go on. It wasn't the time for me to break his silence.

Cole said in the light of day, his feelings toward Cynthia had changed. He began to examine their relationship and found it wanting. She couldn't have missed him very much as she continued to party with her friends. He guessed if he had a financial downturn or got sick, she'd bail.

"I was making mega bucks, but had nothing to show for it outside of a BMW convertible and a closet full of expensive clothes. Cynthia and I spent every nickel I made on fancy restaurants, weekends away, and my wife's expensive tastes. That woman could spend money faster than I could make it. For the first time, since I'd arrived in New York, I'd found the time and the solitude at the ranch to examine what I'd become and I didn't like what I saw. All the booze and uppers had changed my life. Pushed aside my values. If I was to find the person I'd been raised to be, to look in a mirror without disgust, I knew I had to come back to the ranch. I had to find a way to preserve what my great grandfather had started.

"I gave Cynthia the opportunity to join me. There'd never been a divorce in our family, but it was hopeless. She filed for divorce and I came back alone."

Cole stood. "It's almost two a.m., Julia. I've nothing more to say except goodnight."

As he turned and left, I could only imagine how difficult it must have been to recall what had happened, and in many ways how uncomfortable it must have been to let his guard down. I saw him in a whole new light. There was a vulnerability to the tough guy exterior.

I yawned. Time for me to go to bed as well.

Chapter 13

Saturday's chores didn't take long as we'd be out for the evening, meaning I could spend more time with Charger. I heard him nicker as I approached his pasture. He walked toward the gate waiting for me. I'd miss the old horse. Our long rides gave me the time I needed to think about a lot of things in my life. I'm sure that is what Sassy had in mind. Hearing about her love affair with Cole's father would give me a lot more to think about as would last night's conversation.

One thing I hadn't given any thought to was Roger. Somehow, sadly, he was gone and forgotten. He would have hated the ranch, hated Montana. The big surprise was I hadn't given any thought to New York, either, until Cole brought it up last night.

The excitement I felt about my father's promise of a condo had been pushed aside in the last weeks. But as my departure grew closer the time had come to plan for the future, to pick up the pieces of the life I had before the accident. Getting back into the routine of a nine-to-five job.

I promised to be dressed and ready by five. Cole didn't want to be late arriving for happy hour. He'd mentioned he had a few things he wanted to explore with one of the men before dinner and it was a good forty-five-minute drive. Nothing was nearby.

Dressed in Sassy's clothes, wearing her long silver earrings and silver belt, the whole outfit unlike anything I'd imagined I'd ever be caught dead wearing, I left my room. Cole was waiting at the foot of the staircase.

"Stop right there, Julia," he said as he stared at me. "Wow, you look amazing. Like something out of a fashion magazine. You'll have every male salivating and every woman envious before the evening's over."

I eyed Cole, his grey slacks, starched white shirt and bolo tie, the ostrich-skinned boots, leather jacket and Stetson thinking Cole really did fit Hollywood's depiction of a rugged handsome cattleman. I imagined that was what attracted Sassy to Cole's father who must have had the same sexy, very masculine look.

By the time we arrived the Armory was crowded with cattleman. I noticed every man was wearing boots. Not a single pair of shoes to be seen.

"Look around, Julia. These aren't the Texas, all-hat-and-no-cattle boys. These men are the backbone of Montana's cattle industry. For the most part, their families have been ranching here long before Montana became a state."

The bar set up along the back wall seemed to be catering to men, only. The women were gathered in the middle of the room. The crowd seemed older than our last outing, a lot more grey hair than I'd seen at the Longhorn.

"I'll try to push my way through the mob and get you a drink. What would you like?" Cole gave me that boyish smile.

"It's okay to order wine or any mixed drink as long as it's not some fancy New York cocktail these guys have never heard of."

"White wine will be fine."

He must have found a way to the bar, returning with a beer in one hand, a glass of wine in the other.

"I see Big Billy's wife, Charlene over there. I know she'll be happy to keep you company for a few minutes. There's someone I need to talk to. Come on. Let's go meet her."

Charlene turned and smiled. "Well, hello Cole, Julia. My don't you two make a handsome pair."

"I'll leave you ladies on your own." Cole started to walk away, "I'll be back soon, Julia. Don't talk about me when I'm gone."

"What makes you think we'd be interested in talking about you, Cole Clayton? Julia and I have better things on our minds."

Charlene turned toward me. "So, Julia, how long much longer are you staying?"

"I leave next Saturday, I'll be sorry to go. It's been a wonderful visit."

"Will you be coming back? You and Cole seem like such a perfect couple."

"I haven't any plans to return. I'm going back to New York to look for a job. Cole's just a friend."

"From the way he looks at you, I'd say he doesn't see it that way. Pity, I haven't seen him give a second look to any woman since his divorce." Charlene shrugged her shoulders. "Oh, well, what can I say? Here, let me introduce you to the rest of the ladies."

I met three women, who asked all the polite questions, when a fourth, with her back to us, turned around. She gasped as she saw me, a look of surprise on her face.

Charlene introduced me, saying I was visiting from New York.

"I'm so sorry young lady, what did you say your name was again."

"Julia."

"Julia, I didn't mean to be rude, but I was shocked when I caught a glimpse of you. You reminded me of Senator Ridgemont's beautiful wife when I first met her a lot of year ago."

"I'm delighted to hear that, She's my aunt."

"Well, that explains it. I thought I'd seen a ghost."

"My aunts very much alive."

"She sort of dropped out of sight. No one's seen her in these parts since her affair ended when Hank Clayton passed."

All conversation stopped. After a long, uncomfortable moment, Charlene spoke, "Come along, Julia. I need to find Billy. I'd like another drink. See you ladies later."

"Well, that was embarrassing. Pay no attention to her. She doesn't know what she's talking about."

"It's all right, Charlene. I know the whole story."

"Well, whatever. None of it's important. Let's find the men. I wasn't kidding about wanting another drink. Most of these women are really nice if a little old fashioned, but there are always one or two gossip mongers. Your aunt is a very special lady and most of these women not only admired her, they envied her."

We found the guys and joined them for another drink. Billy was in rare form as we waited in the long line at the buffet. He joked about this being the only meeting the wives were invited to, which was why he was on his very best behavior.

We found places at a table and the other couples were pleasant company. A few speeches were made during dinner followed by an awards ceremony. After the officers for the following year were announced, everyone was invited back to the bar.

Cole and I stayed around for a little while longer, then, said goodbye to Billy and Charlene, and left. I thought we were on our way home. Instead, Cole stopped in front of the Longhorn.

"As this is your last Saturday and our last night out, I thought we should celebrate with a drink and a dance or two."

Cole pointed to a seat at the bar and stood behind me. "What'll you have?"

"I'm thirsty. I've had my fill of wine. A vodka and tonic sounds about right."

When the drinks were placed in front of us on the bar, Cole smiled. "You were the prettiest lady at the affair. I hope you've had a good time and you'll come back for another visit someday soon."

"That's very sweet Cole. I just might return one day."

It was all I could think of to say although I knew deep down it would never happen. "I appreciate your letting me spend time at the ranch. It's been a wonderful experience and I've learned a lot about myself. I'm grateful to you for allowing me to invade your time and your space."

It had been wonderful, I thought, as I sipped my drink and listened to the music, but I was getting more anxious as the day grew closer to return to New York. Wanting to see my friends again, have my family nearby. I had no reason to come back.

"The music sounds too good to waste. May I have this dance, pretty lady?"

The floor was crowded. After all it was Saturday night, probably the only going out place around.

Cole put his arm around me and pulled me close to him, so close I could sense his warm breath on the back of my neck, feel the beat of is heart. I fit well in his arms, my cheek resting against his.

As we moved across the floor, I began to feel flush all over. Probably too much to drinks I thought, but I'd never felt like this before. Being in his arms, the closeness of his body aroused feelings I was having a hard time controlling. We danced through a slow tune before a guy dressed in faded jeans, a guitar in hand, a ponytail visible under his well-worn Stetson stepped up to the microphone. He began to strum a few bars before he spoke. "Good to see y'all having such a good time. I'd like to add a few numbers I hope you enjoy. What say I begin with a favorite of mine and I hope yours, Merie Haggard's Silver Wings". After a few more cords he began to sing.

"Silver wings, shining in the sunlight.

Roaring engines headed somewhere in flight."

Cole began to sing the words as well, but at a whisper that only I could hear.

"They're taking you away and leaving me lonely.

Silver wings slowly fading out of sight.

Silver wings, shining in the sunlight.

Roaring engines headed somewhere in flight."

By the time music stopped I found myself in a different place, imaging all sorts of unrealistic happenings, confused by the way Cole was looking at me. Though seconds had passed since the music stopped, I remained in his arms.

"That will be you soon flying out of sight." His hand slowly lifted my chin upward as he bent down and kissed me. A long passionate kiss that caught me by surprise, so much so that without thinking I kissed him back, clinging to him until the cat calls and clapping brought me back to earth.

Embarrassed by my response, and the response by the crowd, I stepped back, all the while feeling chills run down my spine. I'd never been kissed like that before. No, I can't let this happen. This isn't what I bargained for.

Cole took a step forward, "Forget the drinks. Let's get out of here."

We drove home in silence. I had nothing to say. I think we both knew what just happened was a mistake. I was leaving at the end of the week.

Cole held the front door open, pulling me close as I walked by him, kicking the door shut behind him, while holding me tight in his arms. He kissed me again and again, each kiss more passionate than the last. My head was spinning, my heart pounding.

"I've wanted to do that since almost the first time I laid eyes on you," Cole whispered in my ear.

"We can't do this. I'm leaving. It's foolish to let this go any further."

"Maybe I can convince you otherwise."

Cole picked me up in his arms and carried me upstairs to his bedroom closing the door behind him. I could have resisted, but I didn't.

"More than anything in the world, I want to make love to you, Julia. I've been fighting the urge for weeks."

He reached under my blouse undoing my bra, cupping his hand under my breast. My head was saying no, but my heart was saying otherwise. The liquor made the decision easier. I slipped off my blouse and bra and unbuttoned my skirt letting it fall to the ground. This was so unlike me. I'd never behaved this way before, but then I'd never wanted a man to make love to me before either.

We walked toward the bed as Cole removed his shirt and slacks.

He lay down beside me in the moonlit room and stared at me. "You're even more beautiful than I Imagined. He began to caress my body showering me with kisses, as I lay motionless. After a minute or two he sat up, looking at me. "Julia, I don't understand. I thought this is what you wanted. Surely this isn't your first time."

"I'm scared. I've never felt this way before. I'm confused."

"You just need to let your guard down, you can't always be in control. Go where your body wants to go. Love me back. This isn't about having sex. I want this to be about love and that takes two. I'll stop now if that's what you want."

"Don't stop. I want you to make love to me." I might regret it in the morning, but this is what I wanted now.

Cole wrapped his arms around me, whispering in my ear. "I know we both want this and I want making love to you to be perfect, Julia. Now close your eyes, shut off your brain, stop trying to be in control, enjoy the moment."

I did as he said and began to feel a sense of ecstasy. His every move brought a sense of pleasure reaching a peak I'd never felt before. I discovered the joy of sex for the first time.

Cole rolled over on his side and held me close. "You know I've fallen in love with you."

I had nothing to say. I just clung to him with mixed emotions. Trying to forget I was going home in a week.

Chapter 14

We awoke in the morning, still wrapped in each other's arms. I was beginning to feel uncomfortable. In the daylight the situation had changed. The effects of the alcohol had long since passed. I sat up pulling the sheet up to my chin. Wondering how I was going to retrieve my clothes, which were lying in a heap on the floor, embarrassed to find Cole staring at me.

"Good morning. You're every bit as beautiful asleep as awake."

"Close your eyes, please. I need to put on some clothes."

"No way. I had my first glimpse of your beautiful body in the dark last night. I'm eager for a second look in the light of day."

"Please Cole. You're embarrassing me."

"Hey, that's the last thing I want to do. There's nothing to be embarrassed about. We made love. We both enjoyed ourselves. Two consenting adults reacting to their normal instincts."

He smiled that boyish grin I found so likable.

"Okay. You win. I'll close my eyes if you insist. How about a swim before breakfast?"

"A swim sounds great. Now close your eyes and I'll meet you downstairs in a few minutes."

I grabbed my clothes off the floor and scurried back to my bedroom, staring at the bed I hadn't slept in. Searching the bottom of my suitcase for the bikini I'd packed, I thought about last night and its consequences. I knew it had to stop. I couldn't allow myself to have feelings for Cole. I pulled a t-shirt over my swimsuit and headed downstairs. Cole was waiting, bare-chested, in swim trunks, holding two large towels. He did have a great body. The only other man I'd seen naked was Roger and there was no comparison. The artist in me thought, Adonis, as I looked at Cole.

Walking out the door I asked which way to the pool. I thought I'd seen everything on the ranch, wondering how I could have missed the swimming pool.

"You New Yorkers are all alike. You do realize it's possible, even enjoyable, to swim in places other than a pool? Hop into the truck."

"Where are we going?"

"To the best swimming spot in the world."

About ten minutes later, we stopped near the bluest lake I'd ever seen, so large I could barely make out the trees on the far side.

"This is where my dad taught us kids to swim. The water's a bit cool, but it's so clear you can see the bottom and the fish swimming by. Come on, bet I beat you in."

I started to laugh. Of course, they didn't have a pool. This wasn't Connecticut. This was rural Montana, the middle of nowhere. I ran behind Cole, trying to catch up with him as he stood at the water's edge and dove in.

The water was so cold it took my breath away. I swam alongside Cole, trying to get accustomed to the temperature. As I expected, Cole was a strong, confident swimmer. After a bit, he floated on his back and told me stories about swimming in the lake as a kid. When we'd had enough, he raced me back to shore, grabbing the towels and spreading them out on a grassy area by the edge of the lake. I stretched out enjoying the sun's warm rays on my cold body.

Cole lay beside me. "Ever been swimming in a lake before?"

"No, never, I tried the ocean at the Hamptons, once, but the water was too damn cold. This was fun once I got used to it."

"A first time for everything, right?"

I noticed a large scar on Cole's back just below his rib cage. "That's an ugly scar. What happened?"

"I tried my hand at bull riding."

"You're kidding. Why would you do such a crazy thing?"

"Just to prove I could, I guess, but I learned my lesson the hard way." Cole rolled over close to me and eased down the straps of the top of bathing suit.

"What are you doing?"

"Getting rid of one more of your inhibitions. Let's pretend we're Adam and Eve, and this is our very own Garden of Eden."

"You're kidding, of course. Somebody might see us."

"If they did, they'd only think how lucky we were. But there's nobody for miles around. This part of the lake is on my property. It's just you and me, and my mad desire to make love."

I couldn't believe I was lying on the ground atop a damp swim towel in the heart of Montana making love in broad daylight and enjoying every minute of it.

I lay in Cole's arms feeling free. I'd never felt like this before. For the moment, all my inhibitions were gone. I'd let my guard down. I didn't care what tomorrow brought.

Sometime passed before Cole spoke.

"That was better than wonderful. See what can happen when you abandon your fears and let your heart be in control, but I think it's about time we head back home. I promised to cook breakfast and I'm famished. You about ready, Your Highness, or would you like to make love again?"

"Not at the moment. I think breakfast sound marvelous."

"Good. I doubt I could make love like that again right now, but if you want, I'm willing to give it a try."

"Lets try for breakfast."

Cole kissed me again. "I shall be eternally grateful to Sassy for sending you to me."

I thought that was an odd thing to say. The idea that this might have been part of Sassy's plan began to sink in, but no, that wasn't possible.

I rushed upstairs, changed out of my damp suit, and was back in the kitchen ready to set the table, feeling a glow unlike anything I'd ever felt before. I looked at Cole and my heart skipped a beat. All I wanted was to feel his arms around me. His body close to mine.

"Let's eat on the patio and enjoy the sunshine."

Cole had the barbeque going. A frying pan filled with hash browns cooking on the grill alongside pork sausages. A bowl of fresh farm eggs waited to be scrambled.

"How about making the coffee and toast while I finish the rest?"

I watched as Cole dropped the eggs into a pan. I got stare at him all day. I'd never felt this inner glow before.

I sat down to breakfast and ate as if I'd never seen food before.

"Happy?" Cole said.

"Yes. Confused, but very happy."

"I'm glad, because I've never been happier in my life."

"You know Julia, I wonder if this is how married people spend their Sundays, making love before sitting down to a quiet breakfast together."

The word "married" brought me back to reality. We weren't married, nor would we ever be. In all likelihood, we'd never see each other again after this week.

"Weren't you and Cynthia happily married?"

"You know, I don't think so. I was never sober enough to look at what we meant to each other outside of a drinking partner. Ours was never what I expected married life to be. Certainly not how my parents lived their lives. But the last thing I want to talk about is Cynthia."

We both pitched in and cleaned the kitchen, then settled down on the chaises in the warm sun, enjoying being together with no plans for the day. After a while I broke the silence.

"Tell me, Cole, do you ever miss New York?"

"Sure, in a way. Lots of things to do and see, there's nothing like it anywhere else in the world."

"Any thought of going back?"

"Not a chance. I'm here to stay. New York brought out the worst in me. I didn't like what I'd become. Didn't like going against all I'd been taught about right and wrong. No, once I came back to the ranch, I knew I was here to stay. I'd come to believe I was rich. I cashed a big fat paycheck every month. I had to come back home to discover what rich was all about. Somehow I had it confused with money."

"So, you're happy here alone in the middle of nowhere."

"Maybe not happy, Julia, more like content."

Bear appeared wagging his tail and stretched out on the patio between us. "A man, a dog, and his old pickup truck," Cole said. "The makings of a great cowboy song."

Cole said he was working on a plan to put the ranch on a paying basis. That's what he wanted to speak about with the man at the dinner last night.

"I respect his business sense. I wanted his opinion on the plan's merit,"

"I think this would be a perfect spot for one of those so-called Dude Ranches. The countryside is beautiful and there are miles and miles of places to ride. I understand they're quite a profit-making venture."

From the look on Cole's face, I knew I'd struck a nerve.

"What makes you think I'd be interested in a dude ranch?"

"I don't know, Cole. I thought that's what brings people to places like Montana."

"That's the last thing I'd ever consider." Cole rose from his chaise and began to pace. Bear picked up his head sensing a change in Cole's voice.

"Julia, you don't understand. I respect the ranch and what it's meant to my family. I couldn't imagine building a Disney like western themed resort here, because that's all they are, nothing more than Disney Land for city folks to play cowboy for a week. Like living in a rustic log cabin instead of a hotel room makes you feel like a cowhand."

Cole seemed to be getting madder as he spoke. I seemed to have hit a sore spot.

He turned toward me. "Catering to a bunch of green horns all decked out in their new boots, fancy belt buckles, and cowboy hats. No way. Sitting around a campfire at night singing songs Gene Autry or Roy Rogers made famous isn't for me. Putting wannabes on horses some ranch hand curried and saddled, taking them for a trail ride. No, the whole thing is a joke. I'm a cattleman, not a fantasy salesman."

"Please sit down, Cole. I'm sorry. I didn't mean to upset you. I never looked at it that way. I thought people were flocking to Wyoming and Montana. Sort of the 'in' thing to do."

"Nothing to be sorry about. It's kind of a sore spot, but you're right. A lot of cattle ranches have turned themselves into baby sitters. It just gets my back up to think that people have so little understanding of what it means to be a cowboy, or how much hard work and financial risk is involved in running a cattle ranch."

"So, if you have something different in mind, I'd like to hear all about it."

"Not yet. It's still just a concept. A lot has to go into the idea first. Trying to get financing could be a major hurdle. The plan might never get off the ground. I'll share it with you when the time's right. The day's young, Julia. Let's go for a ride. There's a beautiful meadow I want to show you. My favorite spot on the ranch."

Chapter 15

We saddled the horses and rode for about thirty minutes in a direction I'd never gone before. After climbing a steep hill, we rode down into the lush meadow below -- a breathtaking sight. The pasture grass knee deep, a stand of mature trees nearby, a narrow creek meandering through, and the sound of water as it spilled over rocks. The meadow was devoid of cattle.

"The pasture is ready to be cut for winter feed. Cattle are never allowed in this meadow."

"It's truly beautiful, Cole. No wonder it's your favorite spot."

"Let's ride over to the trees and tie the horses. I want to show you something."

Cole looped a rope over a branch of a large tree and tied the horses in its shade. He motioned for me to follow. We walked a short distance through the knee-high grass to a small picket-fenced plot of land on the far side of the trees. As we drew closer, I could see a granite marker in the ground.

"This is where my grandpa is buried, his wish was to rest here in his favorite spot. Maybe this will help you understand why this land is so important to me. From the time I was six or seven, I remember riding alongside my dad and Gramps, checking fences, bringing salt to the cattle in the summer, branding cattle, and bringing orphan babies home to bottle feed. All the while learning by example not only the care of the stock, but the responsibility for tending the land. Gramps was the one that taught me to rope and told me stories of what life was like when he was a kid. It was always Gramps, who if I got tired, would put me in front of him on his saddle while dad ponied my old mare. Gramps and my dad were my heroes when I was growing up, but somewhere along the way, I thought this love of the land stuff was all nonsense, nothing but hard work. Success was to be found in big cities."

I stood without saying a word and read the inscription of the headstone. Unlike viewing Roger's grave, for some reason I felt tears forming in my eyes. I didn't even know the man, but what he represented to his family and somehow to the pioneering spirit was more than touching.

"Thank you for bringing me here. I think I'm beginning to better understand your love for the ranch and maybe even a deeper understanding of what you're all about."

"I've never brought anyone else out here, but I wanted to share my heritage with you, hoping maybe someday you could love this place as much as I do. I hope, one day, to have a son I can pass all this on to."

In a way I was sorry he'd shared so much with me. I knew I could never be part of what he was suggesting.

We put the horses away and walked back to the house. "How does a gin and tonic sound?"

"It sounds like a great idea."

Cole brought the drinks outside and we settled down once again.

"It feels good to spend a day relaxing, enjoying the time with you."

"Don't you ever take a day off, Cole?"

"Not much reason to. There's always plenty of work that needs to be done, and sitting alone on your ass all day can prove to be very lonely."

We sat outside until dusk, fixed dinner together, lingering over coffee. In some ways I didn't want the day to end, but by the time we'd finished the dishes, it was late, time for bed. I turned down Cole's suggestion we sleep together, even though he promised sleep only. I needed to put an end to that part of our relationship before it went any further, no matter how attractive I found him, or how much I enjoyed his company. He presented more problems than I was ready to deal with.

Chapter 16

Even though I wasn't in a hurry for the week to end, the days seemed to fly by. All of a sudden Friday had arrived. I hadn't seen much of Cole. I think he was keeping his distance on purpose. He began to fix his own breakfast in the morning and was gone by the time I came downstairs. We'd have dinner, then he'd excuse himself saying he had bookwork to do. He'd hurry upstairs and close the door to his bedroom. The invitation to his bed didn't occur again. I think he was waiting for me to make the first move.

I rode Charger, for the last time, taking extra care to see he looked like the champion he was. I'd miss him and our rides. I'd miss so much I'd taken for granite during my time at the ranch. I packed everything except what I'd need for the morning, showered, and washed my hair. I took a little extra care with my appearance -- makeup and clothes. I wore the white silk blouse that set off the tan I'd acquired, and my only pair of clean jeans.

I thought our last evening should be as festive as possible. I fixed a nice dinner paying extra attention to the table, setting it with fresh flowers, candles and the last bottle of red wine.

I heard Cole's truck coming down the road at five and waited for him to open the back door.

"Well, Your Highness, you look more attractive than ever this evening. And look at the table. Are we celebrating your leaving?"

"No, not a celebration. I just wanted tonight to be a special thank you for a wonderful experience."

"Interesting. So, in your way of thinking I've been nothing more than a wonderful experience."

"No, Cole, you know that's not what I meant."

"I'm not so sure. I'm going to clean up."

I served the beef stew prepared the way I'd been taught in France. I'd picked everything for the salad fresh from the garden. I wanted it all to be perfect.

Conversation was difficult at best. Finishing the whole bottle of wine didn't seem to change the mood. When I returned to the table with the coffee pot, a small package wrapped in silver foil sat at my place.

"What's this?"

"It's a little something to take home with you. Something I hope will remind you of me. I was going to give it to you tomorrow, but I thought under the circumstances tonight would be more appropriate. Open it."

I removed the wrapping with care revealing a small jewelry box. Lifting the lid, I removed an exquisite pair of silver and turquoise earrings. "These are spectacular, Cole. They're unlike anything I've ever seen before."

"Do you like them?"

"Like them? I love them."

"When I saw how fabulous you looked in Sassy's earrings the other night. I designed these for you. I had a friend make them. They're one of a kind. He cannibalized an old broken piece of jewelry in order to use the real Indian turquoise. The new stuff comes from Italy and the color's not the same."

"You designed these?"

"Yes."

"That makes them even more special. I don't know how to thank you."

"That's easy, Julia. Don't go. Say you'll stay."

I got up from the table, taking dishes to the sink. "I can't."

I put the last of the plates in the dishwasher as Cole watched my every move. I placed the leftovers in the refrigerator, trying to keep busy. The moment was awkward. What more could I say.

As I stood at the sink Cole walked up behind me, running his fingers through my hair, kissing me on the nape of my neck, sending shivers down my spine.

"Julia, you know as well as I do, we have something special happening between us. Stay just a little longer. You can if you want to. There's nothing holding you back. Let's see what develops. If it doesn't work out, you can always go back to New York."

I turned toward him, but before I could say a word, his lips touched mine. I could have stopped what was about to happen, but I followed Cole upstairs to his bedroom. I could always blame it on the wine.

I hurried to shed my clothes. God, I wanted him. I knew that was foolish, but I couldn't stop the desire any more than he could.

I awoke with a start, alone in Cole's bed, ashamed and horrified by what I had allowed to happen, knowing nothing could change my mind about leaving. I got up. My plane left at three in the afternoon.

Cole had coffee brewing by the time I came downstairs with my suitcases in hand. I didn't know what to say. Hadn't I just left his bed? Our relationship was a series of contradictions, but last night was unfair to him.

I poured coffee for myself. I couldn't think of food. Most of all I wanted to be on our way. A tug of war was going on in my head. One I wasn't in the mood to deal with it. I just wanted to get on the plane and go home, put this all behind me. Staying on for a little while longer might have been tempting, but it wouldn't prove anything. In the end I'd still go home. New York was where I belonged.

"Let's get going, Julia. If you're going to leave, I can't stop you, even though I think you're making a big mistake. What we have between us happens only once in a lifetime. But the last thing I want is to face Sassy if we're late."

I started walking toward the truck, and then turned to take one last look at the old ranch house. The place had become a part of me. A part I had to admit I was sad to leave behind.

The long drive to Billings was uncomfortable. Neither one of us had anything to say. When we reached my aunt's house, Cole stopped the truck in the driveway, jumped out and left my suitcases at the front door. He was about to go when Sassy opened the door.

"You're back. Come in, Cole. It's a while before Julia has to leave for the airport."

"Sorry, Sassy, I can't stay."

He turned toward me, "Well, Your Highness, I hope you find what you're looking for." He held me close for a second or two. "Be safe."

"Thanks for everything, Cole. I mean it. I'll write."

"No, you won't."

Cole started walking toward the truck, giving me a thumbs up as he climbed in and drove down the driveway, the old truck belching smoke.

"So, tell me what was that all about?"

"Nothing Sassy, really nothing."

"Please. I saw the way he looked at you. Come inside. We need to talk." Sassy closed the door behind her and asked if she could get me anything? Coffee, tea?"

"No, I'm fine. There's nothing to talk about."

"Of course, there is. From the moment I met you, I knew you two were meant for each other. It would seem I was right, even if you haven't quite figured it out as yet."

"You mean you planned this?"

"Well, it wasn't my original plan, but I must confess, after spending a little time with you, I thought if I threw you two together, you'd figure it out."

I walked toward the windows. I didn't want to face her as I asked my next question.

"Why didn't you tell me you and Cole's father were lovers."

"Well, at first I didn't think it was important. I would have told you when the time was right. Why, does it upset your New England upbringing that I'd have an affair at my age?"

"Of course not. Among my friends, living together is more like the norm."

"What about you, Julia. Were you and your fiancé, what was his name, living together?"

"Roger? No, we lived apart."

"Come, sit down. If you have questions, you don't have to be afraid of offending me. I loved Cole's father with all my heart. He brought me more happiness in the few short years we had together than any other time in my life. Remember the cabin we visited in Yellowstone?"

"Yes."

"If you recall, I told you I'd spent six months living there all alone. I was mourning Hank's death. I didn't want to see anyone, talk to anyone. I wasn't sure I could go on without him. He was the love of my life. Cole's a lot like his father. Even looks like him, the handsome devil."

"What about the Senator? Didn't you love him?"

"In a way, yes, but not with the kind of passion I had for Hank. I met the Senator when I was very young. I'd just celebrated my nineteenth birthday. You can guess what I was like in those days. After all, I'm your father's sister. We were raised in the same house by the same parents."

"That's funny. I can't picture you being as uptight and strait laced as my father."

"Come on. Let's have a cup of tea and a sandwich before it's time to leave for the airport and I'll tell you all about the Senator and me."

I watched as Sassy went about making Brie and smoked sausage sandwiches, and brewing a pot of herbal tea. I followed her to the living room as she put the tray full of food on the coffee table. We sat together on the sofa.

"The Senator was thirty-four at the time we met, fifteen years older than I was. I guess he was taken with my good looks and my naiveté. I was quite pretty in those days. And I, in turn, was impressed with him. In many ways he was more like a father figure than a romantic partner.

"He treated me like a prized possession, expecting little in return, only that I be the perfect hostess, and be at his side at the many social affairs his position required."

"That must have been a difficult relationship."

"Oh, no, I found it quite easy. We traveled a lot. I saw much of the world, met exciting people, and of course, boring people as well. He made almost all my decisions and for the better part of our marriage we slept in separate bedrooms. Oh, I had plenty of opportunity for affairs and or lovers, but I was never tempted. It would have destroyed him. My one regret was that I had no children."

"So, you didn't take up with Cole's father until after the Senator died."

As Sassy poured more tea, I could see her face light up as she began to tell me about Cole's father.

"With adjoining ranches, I met Hank Clayton long before the Senator died. No question a powerful attraction developed between the two of us, but he was married as well. We kept our feelings in check until both our partners had died."

"I find it hard to believe that after traveling the world, living in luxury, socializing with famous people, you'd be content somewhere as remote as the ranch."

"Oh, my dear, you have so much to learn. Where you live is of no importance. The only thing that matters is who you live with."

All Sassy was doing was confusing me, putting thoughts in my head I thought I'd already dealt with.

"Julia, my dear, it's obvious that you've changed so much since you arrived here a month ago. Looking back on the Julia I met the few days we spent together I bet I can describe Roger. Describe the kind of man you'd have been comfortable with."

"No way."

"So let me try. He was nice looking, but not what you would call handsome like Cole, well groomed, and a perfectionist. Right?"

"Right."

Sassy seemed quite pleased with herself as she went on.

"Roger was never late, he suggested what you should eat at a restaurant, then ordered for you. Mentioned what he would like you to wear for evenings out with business associates. He was several years older than you, a generational republican, and probably a vice president in some fortune five hundred company. The successful, but boring man your father approved of."

I had to laugh. "Sassy, you're amazing. You make Roger seem maybe a little too boring, but you described him to a tee."

"I left out one important fact, my dear. When he kissed you, did it elicit a sense of passion? I bet his kisses never sent a chill down your spine like Cole's." She paused for a second, smiling at me. "You don't have to answer that."

Of course, I didn't have to answer, with my cheeks turning bright red Sassy knew the answer.

"Don't you think it strange you never once mentioned Roger the whole time we spent together. Well, that's enough for now. Would you like another cup of tea, Julia?"

I nodded no as I stood and settled into a comfortable chair facing Sassy.

"Did you ever meet Cole's ex-wife?"

"You mean the lovely Cynthia? Only once."

"What was she like?"

Sassy paused, "Cynthia was beautiful in a superficial way. You're as different as night and day. She was blond, with the help of her beauty parlor. It took lots of artistically applied makeup to create her glamorous appearance, where your beauty is natural. She's the type who'll become buxom with the years, while I guarantee you'll be slim your whole life.

"But glamour was all there was to her. She came with Cole to attend Hank's funeral and let everybody know by her actions as well as her words, she didn't want to be here. Cole was devastated, filled with guilt by his absence during Hank's illness. The whole event was difficult for him to face. Cynthia's attitude didn't help.

"Cole was his father's pride and joy, the son he pinned his hopes on. Hoping Cole would be the one to continue the family's ranching tradition, the next generation of Clayton's in Montana, but Cole left home and never looked back."

"What was Cynthia really like?"

Sassy stood, taking the dishes to the sink as she began to clean up. "Cole had no experience with a woman like Cynthia. But, my dear, all that glitters is not gold. When Cole needed her most, she wasn't there," Sassy paused, as she seemed to gather her thoughts.

"Cole and I had a long conversation months after his return. He needed someone to talk to, someone he trusted, and I was there. Don't forget, I've known Cole since he was a youngster. Anyway," she continued as she placed the dishes in the dishwasher. "He was shaken by the way everything turned out. When Cynthia refused to move to the ranch, they agreed to go their separate ways. She managed, with the help of a clever lawyer, to take almost everything Cole had worked so hard to obtain. What made it hard for him to deal with was she didn't need his money she was just getting even. Afraid she'd be embarrassed if her friends thought she couldn't hold on to her man. It left him with a sour feeling about Cynthia and women in general. Though I could never see the two of them as a fit."

"Well, that explains the animosity he had toward me in the beginning." I glanced at my watch. "How much time before we have to leave for the airport."

"About a half hour. Why?"

"I need to know more about Cole and Cynthia."

"Why, my dear? As someone who, as you profess, has no interest in Cole, why are you so interested in his marriage?"

"I'm just curious, Sassy. After all we did spend a month together."

"All right, if you insist, but I'm not sure I believe your reason. Cole told me he'd been drinking pretty heavily. The business tactics he was employing, while making him rich, were going against everything he'd been taught and it was taking a toll on him. Cynthia, as best I can tell, wasn't anything more than a gal he'd dated on and off for some time. She was part of the crowd Cole hung out with. As he tells the story, after a night of partying with friends, they'd both had way too much to drink, when on the spur of the moment, they decided to run off and get married. As I remember, Cole told me marriage was Cynthia's idea. She thought it would be a blast to shock all her friends and relatives."

"Somehow that doesn't seem like the Cole I know. How long were they married?"

Sassy dropped the tea leaves in the garbage and put the teapot in the cupboard.

"Less than six months I think, but it was a rocky relationship from the beginning. I could never understand any of his story, like you, it just didn't seem like the Cole I knew."

With the sound of the grandfather clock in the hall, Sassy suggested it might be wise to start for the airport.

I put my cases in the trunk of Sassy's car and climbed in beside her. I couldn't leave the story there. I had to know more. We'd been driving for a few minutes when I asked what happened next.

"You are dammed determined, I must admit."

"Please, you have to finish the story."

"There's not much more to tell, Julia. Cole came home, got Juanita to come back and take care of the house. He'd stopped drinking. Having sold his car, he spent almost a month rebuilding the engine on his dad's old truck. Hank loved that beat up old Ford. Cole began to recapture his roots and little by little he began to put his life back together. He was fortunate to have close friends he'd grown up with as his support system. Nothing changed until you came along. End of story."

"I do have one question."

"Ask away my dear,"

"I had a hard time understanding why you never called to see how I was. It was as if you shoved me out the door and then never gave me another thought."

"Oh, Julia, you are so wrong. While I thought about you every day my reaching out to you, giving you a shoulder to cry on would have destroyed what you were learning about yourself. You've been way to protected and had too many easing the way for you to ever know who you are and what you're capable of."

We had nothing more to say. Sassy concentrated on driving, and I remained lost in thought. As we pulled up to the terminal, I thanked my aunt for her hospitality. "It's been wonderful getting to know you. I'll always be grateful to you for my time in Montana."

"Keep in touch, my dear. Enjoy your new condo and spending time with your friends. But before you leave, do you remember the question I asked as we started our walk in the woods? Do you remember your answer?"

"In a vague sense, yes. You asked what I saw and I said trees and a trail."

"Exactly. But by the time we'd finished our walk you'd looked beyond the obvious and discovered the wonders of what was hidden just out of sight. You saw the beauty that was there, all around you, if only you were willing to open your eyes and see it.

"Julia, my dear, life in so many ways is like that walk in the woods. If you look only at what is in front of you and not at the joys waiting to be discovered, the wonders hidden just out of view, you'll miss the beauty to be found in life. The joy is there only if you don't lose sight of the forest for the trees."

I started to reach for the door handle. I'd mull over Sassy's remarks some other time, for now I just wanted to leave.

"If being back in New York in your old familiar surroundings, you find something or someone missing in your life, don't let your pride get in the way of your coming back. I can assure you Cole will be waiting."

I gave Sassy a big hug, wheeled my suitcases behind me and walked into the terminal. Leaving Montana would put an end to the mixed emotions I wasn't ready to confront.

Chapter 17

With my baggage checked, I boarded the flight and slid into a window seat and buckled my seat belt. Watching every passenger who approached, anxious to see who I'd be sharing the long flight home with. An older gentleman settled into the aisle seat, his wife occupying the aisle seat across from him. That left the middle seat in question.

The last few stragglers came aboard. A bizarre looking young girl wearing black lipstick, heavy black eye makeup, torn jeans, and a blue denim jacket took the middle seat. She shoved her backpack under the seat in front of her and settled in. The musty scent of her perfume was overwhelming. She plugged in her earphones as the pilot prepared for take-off. I breathed a sigh of relief. Conversation wouldn't be a problem. The last thing I wanted was a gabby seatmate.

Sassy's comments were still replaying in my head. I couldn't seem to settle down. I had so much to think about, there were too many snippets of past events running through my brain. I looked out the window as the plane continued down the taxiway. Turning onto the runway the pilot began to gather speed until we lifted off. Gaining altitude, I watched the ground disappear, hearing the sound of the wheels retracting as the plane continued climbing into a bank of white clouds that reminded me of the meringue on top of Mattie's lemon pies. We leveled off. I closed my eyes and tried to sleep, but I couldn't turn off my brain. I couldn't stop thinking about Cole, the hurt look on his face when we said goodbye. Was it all my fault? He'd offered me love. Had I led him on?

The damn music wouldn't stop replaying over and over again in my head. I could hear Cole's voice as he whispered "Silver wings shining in the sunlight taking you away and leaving me lonely."

Nonsense. Ours was nothing more than a summer romance. They happen all the time. For two weeks you can't live without one another and then, the vacation is over and you return to reality. I vowed to put Cole and the damn song out of my mind and chalk it all up to a summer fling, nothing more.

Sam met me at the airport. "My, my, Miss Julia, your vacation sure done you good. You look just fine, tan and all. Your daddy gonna' be real glad to see you. He's playing golf, but he be home early. He said to remind you it's the first Saturday of the month so you is expected at the family dinner night at the club."

He opened the rear door of the family sedan, a welcome sign of being home. With millions of confusing thoughts still just below the surface I wasn't paying much attention to the drive, surprised when the car stopped in front of the house. I stepped out resolved that Montana was yesterday. Today I'm home.

Sam took my suitcases upstairs. I followed glancing at my watch. I had just enough time to change for dinner.

I hung my jeans on a hanger, thinking I'd have little use for jeans any longer and took a yellow silk sheath out of the closet. I realized how good it felt to put on a dress again. I waited downstairs for father. The wait wasn't long.

"Welcome home, my dear." My father smiled at my appearance. "You look wonderful. Spending a month with my sister proved to be a good idea after all. What did you two do with yourselves out in the Montana wilderness?"

"Really Dad, I'd hardly call Billings the wilderness."

"Well, as far as I'm concerned, any place outside the immediate vicinity of New York City is wilderness. At any rate, how did you two spend your time? From the color in your cheeks, I'd guess a great deal was out of doors."

"Actually, I only spent a few days with Sassy. She arranged for my stay at a ranch several hours away. I spent the month there. You mean you didn't know? I thought you spoke with her."

I noticed the frown as Dad said. "Her name is Sarah, who ever gave her that awful nickname ought to be shot. So you spent the month at a dude ranch. That must have been a pleasant change for you, horses and all. It certainly had a remarkable effect on how trim and healthy you look."

"It wasn't a dude ranch, it was a working cattle ranch. I was the only one there besides the owner."

Father seemed satisfied with my answer as he opened the front door, took my arm, and walked toward the car. I settled into the front seat beside him. He drove down the driveway mentioning we didn't want to be late for dinner.

We'd gone several blocks before he spoke. "Sarah and I talked several times, odd she never mentioned you weren't with her. She assured me you were doing well."

"Let's forget it, Dad. My time at the ranch was well spent. It helped to be off by myself. While I was busy every minute it gave me time to sort things out. I'm looking forward to moving to the city and going back to work."

"It's so good to hear you speaking in a positive manner about your future. On Monday, my dear, we have an appointment with a realtor to see about the condo, just as I promised."

Father and I took the early train to New York Monday morning. I was excited at the prospect of searching for a place to call my own. I knew exactly what I was looking for. I'd put the past behind me. The accident, all the surgeries, Roger, Cole, they were only dim memories now.

The taxi stopped in front of an older building in mid-town Manhattan. Dad spoke to the doorman as he helped me out of the car, holding the door open for my father.

"We have an appointment to meet with George Ryan from Ryan Associates. Has he arrived?"

"Yes, sir. He's waiting for you in the lobby."

"Come along, Julia. Do you like the appearance of the building? This location can't be beat. Wait until you see how nice the lobby is."

I thought it was easier to check out the building, and placate my father, even though the building was a far cry from what would interest me. My first glimpse of the lobby was pleasant enough. A lot of wood and mirrors, hardwood floors with oriental rugs scattered about. An oversized round table in the middle of the entry held a large floral arrangement. The elevators were against the back wall.

"George." Father reached out his hand as a middle-aged man arose from the lobby bench. "This is my daughter, Julia. Shall we show her the condo?"

"I'm happy to meet you, Julia. I've shown your father a great many condo's these last few weeks. This is the one he liked the best. I'm sure you'll find it satisfactory."

The elevator stopped at the tenth floor. The hall carpet looked new, the area smelled of fresh paint. Mr. Ryan led us to an apartment near the end of the hall, putting his key in the lock and holding the door open for us.

"The building has been completely renovated, Julia. The work was completed just a few months ago, so as you will see, everything in the building is fresh and new. Come in. I know you'll like the view."

The condo had lots of windows and a great view, all very nice if a little sterile. I preferred the converted brownstones. They had more character. I explored every room with Mr. Ryan leading the way while Dad pointed out all the attributes. A large living room with an alcove that could hold my desk and computer, a small dining area next to an even smaller modern kitchen, stainless steel appliances, granite countertops, and designer cabinets.

A short hallway led to an ample-sized bedroom with an en-suite bathroom -- granite counter tops with two large sinks, a soaking tub, a huge tiled shower with multiple rain shower heads, and an enclosed toilet and bidet.

"Well, dear, what do you think?"

"It's nice, Dad."

"I told you she'd like it, George. Hand her the keys."

Mr. Ryan put a ring of keys in my hand. Congratulations, I'll show you around the rest of the building. There're storage areas in the garage and a gym on the second floor.

I looked at my father questioning what was happening.

"It's yours, my dear. I always live up to my promises."

"But, I thought you were going to let me find the condo."

"Now, now. You've always respected my judgment. You know I only have your best interests at heart. The developer is a client of our law firm and he offered me a very good deal. I know you'll be happy here. It's a wonderful location, so close to everything."

Dumbfounded, I didn't want to seem ungrateful, but I was devastated. I thought the choice would be mine.

I smiled and gave my father a big hug. "Thank you. Yes, I know I'll be happy here, Dad."

"Good. Then leave everything to me. I'll arrange to have the movers bring your things from storage as soon as possible." Looking at his watch he said, "I'd better be on my way. I'm late getting to the office already. Stay as long as you like, then I suggest you take the train home, time to start packing. I'm sure if I apply a little pressure, you'll be moved in before the end of the week. See you at home this evening."

Mr. Ryan showed me the gym. I nodded in approval, "It's nice."

"Pardon me for saying so, Julia, but you don't seem too pleased with the condo. You know, once you get your furniture in place, the unit will seem larger. Empty rooms have a tendency to look smaller. But if you're not happy with your father's choice you could sell it for a lot more than your father paid. I could look for something that better suited you."

"Thank you. Maybe in a year or so. The condo is really very nice, besides my father would be terribly hurt if I even considered selling. No need looking at the garage. I don't own a car."

Mr. Ryan said goodbye, and handed me his card. "I'll be happy to show you other properties when you're ready."

With the set of keys in my hand, I took the elevator back to the tenth floor, opened the door to what was to be my new home and sat on the floor the middle of the empty living room and cried my heart out.

When I was through with tears, I looked around and began to visualize where my furniture would go. Like it or not this was my new home. Better make the best of it. After checking out every room, I locked the door, took the elevator to the lobby, and had the doorman hail me a taxi.

By three in the afternoon, I was back home. Time to begin sorting through the things I wanted to take with me, and things for the goodwill. It hadn't turned out quite as I'd been led to believe, but it meant moving back to the city and for the moment that's all that mattered.

    I started to unpack. I hadn't touched my suitcases since I returned from Montana. At the bottom of one of the cases was the jewelry box Cole had given me. Opening the lid I took out the earrings and held them up to the light. They were truly beautiful. I placed one on each lobe and looked in the mirror and then I started to cry again.

Chapter 18

On moving day, Sam and I drove into the city, with the trunk of Dad's car piled high with boxes and suitcases, the overflow on the back seat. The moving van was due to arrive at the condo at noon. God love Sam. He offered to stay to give me a hand until it was time to drive my father home.

I felt a certain excitement to see all my things again. The furniture fit well and indeed the rooms did look larger. It didn't take the three men long to move everything and put the furniture in place. Boxes marked bedroom were piled on the floor in the corner of my room. They stacked the kitchen boxes on the floor in the dining area. The rest of the boxes sat in the middle of the living room floor. I had my work cut out for me.

By the time Sam left a few minutes before five, I'd already started to unpack the boxes. I'd made the bed and hung towels in the bathroom while Sam hooked up the television to the cable the building provided. No need to hurry with the kitchen. There must be a million restaurants in the city that did food delivery.

Dad called my cell phone to be sure I was all right before he had Sam drive him home. I assured him I was fine. I promised to call if I needed anything.

I'd given myself a week to get organized and began in earnest to get settled. By mid-afternoon I decided to take a break. It seemed like a good time to go for a walk and explore the neighborhood. In just a few short blocks, I found a couple of interesting bistros, a charming coffee shop, Starbucks, a wine shop, a small, but very expensive gourmet grocery, boutiques, and hotels. Everything one could want within walking distance, one of the joys of living in the city. I did find the city noises and the rush of people hard to get used to after the quiet of Montana.

I'd worked non-stop, emptying boxes and hanging pictures. When the condo was in some semblance of order it was time to start the search for a job. I wanted to stay in advertising. I'd spoken with a headhunter who specialized in advertising and forwarded him my resume.

Picking up the phone I punched in Amy's number, the last item to be checked off my to-do list, anxious to let my best friend know I was back in town. Amy and I grew up together, best friends since kindergarten. I'd ignored her texts and calls most of last year, just as I had ignored everyone's overtures.

Her cell rang several times before Amy picked up.

"My Caller ID says its Julia. Is it really you?"

"It's really me."

"Oh my God, I can't believe it. It's been ages since I've heard from you. How are you? Where are you? What are you doing with yourself?"

"I'm here, back in New York and settled into my new condo and ready and eager to pick up where I left off. Anxious to see you. I know I should have returned your calls, Amy, but I was in such a funk I didn't want to talk to anyone.

"I can't wait to see you, kiddo. How are you feeling? All the operations over with, I hope."

"I feel great. No more surgeries. Everything has been put back together, but enough about me. What's with you?"

"Not much has changed. Bill and I are still together although hard as it was to believe Nancy and Steve split about a month ago. Hey, now that I think about it, several of us are meeting for dinner tomorrow night at Dino's in the village. Why don't you come along? I know everyone would be glad to see you."

"That sounds great. What time?"

"Seven. Bill and I can pick you up."

"Not necessary. I'll meet you there."

"I'm so excited, Julia. It will be wonderful having you back. I've missed you. See you tomorrow."

I put the cell phone back on the kitchen counter, wondering what it will feel like being alone, without Roger.

After dropping copies of my resume in the mailbox addressed to several of the large advertising companies, I bought bagels at the coffee shop for breakfast and stopped at the grocery store a block away to begin to stock the kitchen with food. I'd been living on takeout all week.

Unlike my prior time in the city, I was really enjoying doing things on my own without Roger or my dad to oversee my every move. It felt good having only myself to answer to.

I heard the phone ringing as I unlocked the door to the condo. I rushed to answer, dropping the packages on the floor. A male voice asked to speak to Julia Johnston.

"Speaking."

"Hi, Julia. It's Fred Wilcox from Great Job's Inc. A new inquiry just came across my desk, an opening in a small advertising company you might want to explore. I'll e-mail you the details. If it sounds like something you might be interested in give me a call and I'll try to set up an appointment. Good jobs don't stay open very long, so let me know one way or the other ASAP."

"Thanks, I'll let you know."

Sitting down at my desk, I booted up the computer and waited for Fred's e-mail. The information indicated the agency was a small, private company, not part of a large corporation or a franchise. The duties were varied. The salary was okay though not great, but they offered advancement and bonuses.

I jumped at the chance. Being employed was the most important thing in my life right now. For my own sanity I needed a job. I replied to Fred's e-mail and asked him to try and set a time for an interview.

I took my time putting put the groceries away knowing I had plenty of time to get ready for dinner with Amy. Life was looking up, dinner with friends tonight and maybe a job interview next week.

So much had happened since the last time I had dinner with old friends. While I was excited to see everyone, I wasn't sure how comfortable I'd be on my own. Roger had been by my side since I first moved to the city. I checked the clothes in my closet and put on the same yellow sheath I'd worn to family night at the club. I took a silver necklace I'd bought in Mexico years ago and a pair of silver hoop earrings out of my jewelry box. On a whim, I reached for Cole's present as well. The earrings were perfect with the necklace. I'd wear them tonight instead of the hoops.

Grabbing a paisley shawl, my purse and cell phone, I headed for the elevator. The doorman hailed a cab for me and gave the driver the address in the village. I hoped for the best. Being on my own was all new and different.

The place was mobbed for a Tuesday night, but they did serve the best Italian food in the village. I saw Amy and Bill at the bar.

When Amy spied me, she rushed over and gave me a big hug. "I'm so happy you decided to come. Let me have a good look at you. You look wonderful, Julia. Where did you get that great tan?"

"I just got back from a month on a ranch in Montana. Bill, it's good to see you."

"You, too, kiddo. We've all missed you. Here, take my seat, the rest of the gang should be here soon. Let me buy you a drink."

That felt a little awkward. Shouldn't I buy my own drink? Before I could give it too much thought, everyone showed up. After another round of drinks, we were shown to our table, five couples and me. Nancy couldn't be too broken up over her spit with Steve as she had a date she introduced as Jim. She seemed quite attracted to him.

Everyone seemed glad to see me. Thankfully no one mentioned Roger. I wouldn't have known what to say. As it was, most of the conversation went right by me. I felt like an outsider. I'd been away so long I'd lost track of who was in and who was out. By ten, we'd all finished coffee. The tab was placed on the table in one of those black leather covers. Bill checked it out and split it five ways over my objection. I insisted I be allowed to pay my share or I couldn't do this again. After much back and forth it was agreed this would be my welcome home party. I could pick up my share next time.

After the usual round of goodbyes, I said goodnight and took a taxi home. The evening had been disappointing. After the "good to see you, Julia," it was almost as if I wasn't there. The men talked about their golf game, politics, and the stock market. All I heard from the women was ugly gossip and back stabbing. I wondered what would be said about me behind my back. Feeling like a fifth wheel wasn't what I'd expected.

Chapter 19

Today was the big day. I'd put aside all thoughts of Tuesday's dinner with my old friends. Maybe I'd been hypersensitive. On edge about the interview, I thought I'd left plenty of time for the nine o'clock appointment. I hadn't considered the taxi might be stuck in traffic. Horns were honking, heads leaning out car windows trying to see what was holding up traffic.

"Is this going to take long?"

"Who knows? According to the cab driver this was just the normal New York rush hour screw up. I tried to get him to do something, anything, raising my voice at him over and over again. Telling him I was going to be late. He turned and looked at me with disgust.

"Look, lady, stop screaming at me. Whad'a you want me to do? If you gotta be someplace on time, take the subway. Now shut up and get off my case or get out of my cab. I'm doing the best I can."

I was getting antsy as I watched the meter ticking away adding money to the fare. The last thing I wanted was to be late. After what seemed an eternity, the police arrived and the traffic began to move if only at a snail's pace.

The cab stopped in front of an old brownstone that had been converted into office space. The sign in front of the building read Charles Crawford Advertising Company, LTD, Jorge Ramos, Attorney at Law, and Howard Hammond, CPA. I climbed the steep flight of stairs and entered the building. The door on the right was the attorney's office, the one on the left the CPA's. The ad agency was up another flight. I'd count the staircase as my morning's exercise.

The double glass doors that greeted me at the top of the stairs had the name of the agency printed in large gold letters. I took a deep breath and opened the door, telling myself I could do this. A very pretty, youngish blond sat behind a reception desk. Trying to smile, though my stomach was in knots, I said, "I'm Julia Johnston. I have a nine o'clock appointment with Mr. Crawford."

"Please have a seat. I'll let Mister Crawford know you're here."

I watched her pick up the phone, heard her say, "Miss Johnston is here." After a long pause, I heard her say, "Yes, sir. I'll see that she fills out forms before I send her in."

She reached into a file cabinet and retrieved a few pages of paper. Attaching the pages onto a clipboard she motioned to me.

"Please fill out the forms. Mister Crawford will see you as soon as you finish."

I glanced at the first page. It was personal information some of which was part of my resume. The last two pages were inquiries regarding my former employment and why I wanted the position and what I could bring to the business.

Having answered all the questions, I returned the data to the receptionist. She thanked me and picked up the phone.

"Yes sir, I'll send her right in." She smiled and motioned to the right.

"Mr. Crawford will see you now. It's the last door on the left."

I started down the hall hoping I'd chosen the right outfit. The weather was too warm for a wool skirt and sweater. I wanted to look attractive, but business like. After a dozen tries, with clothes still strew all over my bed, I choose an old Diana Von Furstenberg wrap dress I bought years ago. I stopped in front of the door, took another deep breath, put a smile on my face, and knocked.

"Come in."

Mr. Crawford was sitting behind a huge modern glass and steel desk in front of a bank of windows. In his late forties, I guessed, wearing a bold, very ugly blue-striped shirt, a horrible blue flowered tie, and matching flowered suspenders. With his slicked back black hair, he looked like something out of a fifty's movie or

Mad Max, different than the business-look of the men in my old agency.

"Have a seat, Julia. I've read your resume so let's skip that part. Tell me about yourself."

His Brooklyn Italian accent was more than evident as he spoke. I glanced around the room. Every inch of the walls space was covered in framed ads and awards. I settled into a chair in front of his desk as directed.

"Not much to tell. As you can see, I graduated from Dartmouth. I worked for Saint Andrews Advertising for several years. I find the industry exciting and challenging, and I'm looking for an opportunity to prove my worth."

"Yeah, Yeah. I get all that. What I don't get is why you haven't worked for Saint Andrews or anybody else for well over a year. What have you been doing with yourself? Your resume isn't clear whether you left of your own accord, or you were let go."

I hadn't expected those questions. How much should I tell him? I took a moment thinking better be truthful.

"I was in a major automobile accident well over a year ago. It required several surgeries that kept me out of action until now."

"Any problems, health wise, that is, our damn employee health insurance is high enough without complicating it with any more issues."

"I have no issues. I received a clean bill of health."

"Glad to hear it. So, Julia, we're a small company. Everybody does double duty. Our clients are mostly small to medium-sized businesses. We don't do large corporations. We let the big boys deal with those headaches. We keep our clients happy not only with what we produce for them, but also with our hands on approach. We all work hard and we work as a team. I don't need any prima donnas."

"I've never had a problem getting along with my co-workers."

"Good. I'll have the receptionist show you around. If a call to Saint Andrews backs you up, the job is yours if you can start immediately. We're really shorthanded. For the record, we have a three-month trial period. Until then, the job's temporary. No benefits. Make the cut and you become a permanent member of our staff and the benefits kick in."

"Thank you, Mister Crawford. I'm anxious to get back to work."

The receptionist, whose name was Jean, showed me around. The office took up the whole upper floor. She introduced me to the sales and art staff, mostly men in their thirties and forties. I counted about twenty people in all. Saint Andrews must have employed at least a hundred most were a lot older. This group seemed a lot friendly as well. I liked what I saw.

After filling out more forms with the woman in charge of human recourses, I was on my way home by noon. Either I had a job or I didn't. I'd know by the end of the day.

I spent the time waiting for the phone to ring. Close to five, Jean called to tell me I was to start work the following Monday at nine. I breathed a big sigh of relief. Everything was falling into place.

The more I thought about my interview and the paperwork, the more I realized my father must have paved the way for my job at Saint Andrews. I never had an interview. The only person I met with was from Human resources who gave me a few papers to fill out. Between my father and Roger, I'd never really been allowed to achieved anything on my own. Everything had been handed to me on a silver platter. I had a lot to prove.

I'd just hung up after a long conversation with Amy turning down an invitation for dinner with the gang when my cell phone pinged.

"Hi, Julia, it's Nancy. It was so good to see you last week. What's up?"

"Not much although I might have a new job with an ad agency if I get by the trial period."

"That's great. It seemed almost like old times the other night, didn't it? Anyway, the reason I called is Jim and I are invited to a cocktail party Saturday evening. He suggested you come along and meet a friend of his. Jim thought we could all go out to dinner afterwards."

"Gee, Nancy, I don't know."

"Come on, Julia, you have to get back into the dating game sooner or later."

I hesitated, hating the idea of a blind date.

"Jim says he's a nice guy, good looking, a VP of something or other at Jim's company."

"If he's so great, why does Jim have to fix him up?"

"He's just getting back into dating too after his divorce, but no more questions, Julia, I'm not taking no for an answer. Jim and I will pick you up at six on Saturday. If you don't like the guy, you never have to see him again. Besides, I'll be there to make sure all goes well. It's so good to have you back. We've all missed you."

Strange, I didn't think the crowd acted as if they missed me at all, but maybe Nancy was right. I didn't have to fall in love, just find a likeable escort. I'd feel better going out if I wasn't solo. Anyhow, I'd probably meet a lot of new people once I started working.

I waited downstairs for Jim and Nancy when a black Mercedes sedan stopped in front of the no parking zone in front of the building. Jim got out and opened the rear door. "You look very nice, Julia."

I didn't like the sensual way he stared at me. Wasn't he supposed to be Nancy's boyfriend? He never took his eyes off me as he said, "My friend Jamie is in for a big surprise. I'm sure he's not expecting anyone as glamorous as you."

We stopped outside a newer, high-rise building on Fifty Ninth Street off Fifth Avenue in what was known as millionaires row. He left the car with the doorman and we walked toward the elevator. Reaching the forty-fifth floor, Jim led the way. There were only two units on the floor with the door to one ajar. Jim held the door open explaining the apartment belonged to one of the senior vice presidents of his company.

The place was unbelievable. Huge windows dominated one side of the room with an unbelievable view of Central Park. Some decorator had done a fabulous job that must have cost a small fortune -- everything done in black and white. The walls were covered with expensive works of modern art. The living room full of what appeared to be well-heeled New Yorker's. The women wearing fashionable and expensive designer clothes, dripping in costly jewelry.

I felt out of place as Jim and Nancy began to circulate leaving me to fend for myself. I noticed a bar setup in one corner of the dining room. An elaborate assortment of trays of finger food, and numerous covered chafing dishes was set up on the long dining room table. A server was slicing roast beef, turkey, or ham for each guest as they circled the table. The host had spared no expense.

I had a feeling this was going to be a long evening and I had better play it safe. I wandered over to the bar asking the bartender for a tall glass of tonic with a slice of lime. No one would guess it was without either vodka or gin.

As I started to move away from the bar, a tall, good-looking, well-dressed man in his forties came along side me. "Don't you drink, or are you just being smart."

"I beg your pardon?"

"I watched the bartender pour straight tonic in your glass. Just curious? I'm always attracted to pretty women. I haven't seen you around this crowd before. New in town?"

"Let's say I've just returned to New York after sometime away."

"Names David Harrington. What's yours, pretty lady?"

"Julia."

He smiled, "Julia what? Are you here with somebody?"

"Just Julia. Yes, I'm here with friends. Nice to have met you, Mr. Harrington."

I walked back to the living room looking for Jim and Nancy; Jim seemed antsy wondering out loud where the hell Jamie was. He was anxious to leave. He asked if we wanted another drink as he left for the bar, returning several minutes later.

"So, Julia, I think you've caught somebody's eye."

"What are you talking about?"

"David Harrington. I just ran into him. He asked who you were. Wanted to know how to get in touch with you. He's the VP of sales in our company. Quite the ladies man."

Before I could say anything, Jim smiled. "At last, there's Jamie now."

I turned to see a slim man of medium height, dark hair, in a well-tailored business suit, late thirties or early forties. As Jim had indicated Jamie wasn't unattractive.

"Jesus man, what kept you? I thought you'd never get here. Want to grab a drink or can you wait 'til we get to the restaurant. I've mingled long enough with all the right people now I'd really like to get the hell out of here."

Nancy looked disappointed as she asked, "What's your hurry, Jim, it's a lovely party. Let's give Julia and Jamie a little time to get to know each other."

"They can get to know each other at dinner, Nancy. I don't like mixing business with pleasure. It's too damn easy to say the wrong thing after you've had a few drinks."

We left, walking the few blocks to *Café Francais*, a new upscale eatery that had been open for only a few months. We found seats in the large bar, with its dark wood paneling and subdued lighting. The dining room was small and intimate, every table and booth taken.

After a long and very uncomfortable wait in the bar, we were seated in a booth, Jamie alongside me across from Jim and Nancy. So far, Jamie had said next to nothing as he downed two double bourbons and water. Jim and Nancy were trying hard to keep the conversation flowing.

I tried to start a conversation with Jamie, asking what he did at Jim's company. In a matter-of-fact manner he answered, "I'm one of many vice presidents in international finance." The conversation stopped there.

"Julia works for an ad agency. She's just returned to New York after being away for over a year," Nancy said. But that fell on deaf ears as well.

I sipped my wine and played with the salad. The evening, so far, was proving to be uncomfortable and embarrassing. At some point, the conversation turned to family, and Jamie began to loosen up. He went on and on about his two boys, who much to his concern, lived with their mother. Lamenting that he only gets to see them every other weekend. Information spilled forth about the bitter divorce. Details I had no interested in. He kept talking as he pulled out his wallet and passed around pictures of his sons.

"What handsome boys, you must be very proud of them." I didn't know what else to say. The rest of the conversation, which was turning everybody off, was devoted to describing more of the nasty details of his recent divorce. I couldn't wait for the evening to end, vowing never to date divorced men with children.

Somehow, I got through the meal. When the evening came to an end, I thanked Jamie for dinner, telling him how much I enjoyed meeting him and declined his offer of a ride home.

"Thanks, but you all live in the opposite direction. I'll take a cab."

Settling in the back seat, I gave the cabbie my address and breathed a sigh of relief. Never again would I go on a blind date. Never, never, never.

By the time I reached home, I had a text message from Nancy apologizing, hoping I'd forgive her and promising the next time Jim arranged a blind date she'd check him out first.

I spent Sunday shopping for groceries and getting organized, ready to start work on Monday. Dad called and we had a long conversation about my new job and how the condo was working out. He was upset I'd accepted the job without consulting him first. He said he intended to check the financials of the company, warning me not to sign any agreements without his approval.

I bit my tongue. He meant well, but I could see the problem that had eluded me my entire life. Time to grow up. I was even more bound and determined to make my own way, my own decisions, sink or swim. If I could learn to deal with chickens, I could learn to handle anything I put my mind to.

After Thursday's traffic problem, I opted to take the subway. Taxis were a luxury I could no longer afford. The subway station was an easy two-block walk. Thank God, I left myself lots of time. I'd never taken the subway before. Surviving the shoving and pushing of people rushing down the stairs to the platform, I stood in line to purchase a Metro Card. It cost me one hundred and twelve dollars for a monthly card.

The whole experience was scary. An older woman took pity on me as I tried to figure out which train, I needed to take from the various destinations on a big board. I told her where I wanted to go and she told me which train to take, walking with me to the platform and pointing out where to stand. She advised me not to be too polite or I'd never get on or off the car. Just push ahead like everybody else.

The fact that I was twenty-nine years old, and so ill equipped to deal with things other people faced on a daily basis was a shock. I thought I was so sophisticated, so worldly. I had a lot to learn if I was going to make it on my own.

The subway car was crowded, standing room only, body-to-body contact. I held on to a pole as the car lurched every time the train came to a stop or started up again. When the train reached my station, I pushed my way off and climbed the stairs to the street. Welcome to my new world, a real working-class New Yorker. I returned home having survived the evening subway rush, exhausted, but happy.

I'd been assigned responsibility for several accounts to begin with, more to be added once I learned the ropes.

The week was over before I knew it. I was too tired to think of anything outside of work and home. Saturday was the only time I had to shop and run errands. The fact that I didn't have a Saturday night date never occurred to me. The Longhorn bar was only a fleeting memory

Chapter 20

Today marked a whole month since I started working for the agency and my first paycheck. I'd grown accustomed to the subway and enjoyed the people I worked with. The boss made a not too subtle pass at me a time or two, but when I showed no interest, he backed off. The appointment to meet with one of our clients on Tuesday would be the first real test. Time to see if I was up to the job.

I arrived at Casa Bella in Soho at noon on Tuesday, and was greeted by the owner, Mario Ricci. Casa Bella was the original of his four-restaurant chain. He'd been a client of the agency for several years.

"So, you're taking over from Gina, the new mama. How is she?"

Mister Ricci must have been at least sixty. From the look of him, he was his restaurant's best customer, the suspenders holding up his pants a testament to a job a belt could never accomplish.

"I've never met Gina, but from what I hear, she and her baby boy are doing just fine."

"Good, Good. So, what can I do for you? What's your name, *Bella Donna*?"

"Julia. I'm here to get to know you and make sure you're happy with our services." I was stumbling to find the right words. Maybe I should have worked something out before our meeting.

"Come, follow me. We'll talk over lunch."

I followed him into the kitchen. Several workers hustled about as the restaurant was beginning to fill with the lunch crowd. Mario pointed to a small table in one corner of the large kitchen. "Sit, I'll be right back."

He returned with two glasses of red wine.

"Thank you, Mister Ricci, but I don't think I should drink on company time."

"So just say this isn't drinking. It's aiding your digestion and making a client happy."

He sat across from me, smiling. "So, now that that's not a problem, we eat. I like eating in my kitchen. I can keep an eye on everything. Luigi," he caught the attention of the cook, "lasagna for me and the lady."

"I couldn't"

"I prefer doing business over wine and good food. So, relax and enjoy."

One of the cooks set two plates of food and a carafe of red wine in front of us. "*Buon Appetito.*"

The food was delicious. Mister Ricci asked a lot of questions about me, claiming he needed to know the people he did business with. We'd finished the last of the meal before I had a chance to ask how his restaurants were doing. There appeared to be a lot of competition in the area.

"So, so, Julia. Lunch has slacked off a little bit, but dinner is good every night but Wednesday. Wednesday, I don't know why, is way too slow. I don't begin to break even."

I saw a chance to prove myself.

"Let me give some thought as to how we can do a better job of advertising. See if we can't improve Wednesday's dinner business."

"You figure out a way to improve Wednesday and you've got my business forever. How's your lasagna? You like it?"

"Like it? It's the best I've ever tasted."

Mario poured another glass of wine for us. "You like to cook?"

"When I have time. I spent a summer in France years ago, learning how to cook."

"The French, they make cooking too complicated. *Cara mamma mio* taught me to cook watching her in our family's kitchen. She never had a recipe. Mama would open the icebox and what ever was there she turned into a meal, pasta, frittata, chicken, veal. She always had a pot of minestrone soup on the back of the wood burning stove. In our house you never threw away leftovers, Mama just tossed them into the pot...vegetables, tomatoes, pasta, wine, the pot was never emptied, always simmering. You like Italian food?"

"Oh, yes."

"I make you a deal. You come on Wednesday night. It's slow in the kitchen and I'll teach you to cook Italian in one easy lesson. You can forget the French. You'll make your husband very happy. The best way to keep a man happy is to fill his stomach with good food and wine."

"I'd love to take a lesson in your kitchen, but I'm not married."

"Boyfriend then."

"No."

"Well then, you come alone and we'll eat whatever you cook together. I think some guy is missing a bet. If I was twenty years younger, I'd make a pass at you."

I looked at my watch. Two o'clock. I needed to get back to the office.

"Thank you for the wonderful lunch, Mister Ricci. I like this kind of a business meeting."

"It's Mario. I told you business over food and wine is better than behind a desk. See you next Wednesday. Be here by five."

I took a cab back to the office. After two glasses of wine, I wasn't ready to tackle the subway. Besides the meeting was on my expense account.

By the following Wednesday, I had a plan ready to present to Mister Ricci. When I arrived, the hostess pointed me toward the double doors that led to the kitchen. The chef in a white coat and chef's tall toque greeted me with *"Ciao, Signorina, come stai?"* He paused, "I say, hello, how are you?" He spoke with a heavy Italian accent. "I'm Luigi."

"I'm Julia, and I'm fine, thank you."

"So come. Mario say's I am to teach you how to make the pasta for your dinner tonight."

Luigi tied an apron around my waist and pointed toward a small metal bowl and a hand-cranked machine. He placed a dish of loose salt, a slightly beaten egg and a container of flour on the counter in front of me. I was directed to make a well in the flour for the egg, add a pinch of salt and mix them together until they formed a ball. When I didn't see a mixing spoon I asked Luigi for something to mix the items with.

"You have the mixing tools right here," he held up his hands. "You need to feel the dough to know when its ready. It will speak to your hands."

With Luigi's help, the whole thing congealed into a workable ball of dough. He wrapped the ball in saran wrap and placed it in the big double-door refrigerator, removing a similar looking package. After many tries with little success getting the dough to feed through the machine, I finally mastered the art. Feeding the dough through the slot in the top of the machine, and using the crank handle long strings of fresh pasta came out the other end.

I was very proud of myself. Once I got the hang of it, it wasn't hard at all. Luigi said he'd toss the pasta into a boiling pot of water after we finished eating our salad. Fresh pasta cooked *a dente* in less than two minutes.

"Remember in order to be a good cook you must feel the dough for bread or for pasta. You don't need a recipe you need only a spoon and your taste buds they will tell you if you need a little more seasoning, a little more salt or pepper, maybe a dash of wine. Taste and smell make a good dish, not words printed on a page, Capischi."

I watched as a different individual put salad greens in a bowl tossing them with red vinegar and olive oil from a bottle containing an amazing assortment of herbs.

The table in the corner was set for two, a carafe of red wine waiting. At six, Mario arrived. He gave me a warm greeting pointing to the chair he was pulling out.

"Good to see you again, *Bella Donna*." He poured the wine as the salad was placed in front of us. "So did you make fresh pasta for us?"

"Yes, thanks to Luigi."

"I'm afraid the sauces are already made and there are no recipes, but you will learn to improvise."

Finishing the last of my dish of pasta, with a certain sense of achievement, I said, "I have a Wednesday plan."

I went into great detail about a buy-one-get-one free Wednesday night all you can eat pasta feast.

"All you serve is pasta, so there's no waste."

I think I had him really interested in the idea when I convinced him people love to get something for nothing, so when they get a free dinner, they're more likely to spend money on drinks and wine, and even desert.

"So, you see, Mario, it generates a greater profit as well as filling the restaurant."

It didn't take long for Mario to see the benefit in the plan, giving me the go ahead to print coupons redeemable for the two for one offer, and permission to increase his advertising budget. If it went well in Soho, he'd think about doing the same thing one night a week in his other restaurants.

I went home feeling great. My first success and I'd done it all on my own. Not only had I made a client happy, I'd learned to make pasta.

Chapter 21

Summer and Fall had come and gone before I realized it. With the exception of a horrible weekend in the Hampton's, my life was falling into a pattern. I worked long hours leaving no time for a social life.

The Hampton scene was the final straw in my relationship with what had been my best friend, and the rest of our crowd, as well. Had something changed in my life? I didn't feel comfortable in their company any longer. We had nothing in common. Had I been blind to how superficial they seemed. There must be something more to life than cocktail parties and what I gleaned from some of their comments, meaningless sex.

I couldn't believe Amy and Bill had split. They'd lived together for years. I thought they were the perfect couple, always assuming they'd get married when they thought it was time to have children. I was devastated their relationship couldn't stand the test of time. Nancy and Jim were no longer seeing one another. She'd latched on to some other guy. Just more examples of why I never wanted to be involved again.

Amy was having a hard time coming to grips with the fact that Bill was out of her life and already involved with another woman. Feeling sorry for her I promised I'd go along to the annual end-of-the-season party in the Hamptons since she didn't want to go alone. We were staying at Amy's grandparent's house. They were vacationing someplace in Europe. Spain, I thought. The weekend began on Friday night with a BYOB party at somebody's rental and soon developed into a debacle. I didn't know most of the couples. The single men were either older or gay.

Watching Amy, I had a hard time understanding her behavior. I tried to get her to slow down. She was trying to hard to be the life of the party. After downing way to many drinks, she went off to bed with the first guy who looked at her twice, leaving me alone to fend off a bunch of single-purposed males. Sex being all they had on their minds. I didn't see Amy until the following morning, having no idea how or when she got home.

Amy slept late complaining of a hangover as she wandered into the kitchen for coffee. She looked like hell.

Thank God she agreed to spend Saturday afternoon at the beach, skipping the afternoon cocktail hour. We didn't have much to talk about. I asked what she'd been thinking after she apologized for taking off and leaving me alone.

"What got into you, Amy? I can't believe you'd sleep with some guy you didn't even know. Do you even remember his name?"

I didn't buy her answer, nor was I interested in the details of what went on between Bill and her. She was crushed by the breakup. Worried she'd lost her appeal. That much I could understand and even sympathize with, but was the solution to hop into bed with the first guy who came along. Was sex just some sort of sport with everyone a player, just fun and games with no real meaning?

Saturday night was a replay of Friday, just different people with too much to drink and no other purpose than to have fun, meaning sex. By the time I got home on Sunday, I knew the time had come to cut all my ties with the old crowd. Were none of them capable of commitment? If it was all about having fun and sleeping around I couldn't play that game. Better to stay unattached.

The phone was ringing as I opened the apartment door. Picking up the receiver, a voice said, "Julia, its Dave."

"Dave. I'm sorry, Dave who?"

"David Harrington. We met at a cocktail party several weeks ago. I got your number from Jim Clausen."

"Yes, of course. I remember you now. You wanted to know why I was drinking straight tonic."

"I'm the one. I found you an intriguing woman and if you're not spoken for, I'd like to get to know you better. Will you have dinner with me Friday night?"

I thought for a minute. He'd seemed nice enough, maybe a little too confident, but Jim did say he was in sales. At least he had no relationship to any of the old crowd. Maybe I needed to be more open to meeting men. That didn't mean I had to play by anyone's rules but mine. Sleeping around held no interest.

"I think I'd like that. Yes, I'd be happy to have dinner with you."

"That's great. Give me your address and I'll pick you up at seven on Friday."

I gave him the information, and hung up. Well, at least it wasn't a blind date. An evening out would be nice.

I left work a little early, wanting to have plenty of time to change. I had no idea where we were going. Basic black seemed safe. My black wool dress with its multi colored silk jacket would take me anywhere. I started looking for just the right piece of jewelry when I saw Cole's earrings. I picked one up and held it in my hand. It brought back all kinds of memories, things I didn't want to remember. I placed it back in the box. It didn't seem right to wear Cole's earrings on a date with another man.

David was standing beside a very expensive Porsche Coupe talking to the doorman. When he spied me, he opened the passenger door.

"Good evening, Julia. You look lovely. You're even more attractive than I remembered. Let's be on our way."

"Fabulous car, Dave. My brother drives a Porsche."

"She's my mistress. Buckle up and hold on. We were off with a roar. Hope you enjoy the place I've chosen."

David handed the car keys to the valet and helped me out of the car.

The maître'd greeted him by name, saying his table was ready. "Your usual, Mr. Harrington?"

"Please. What will you have to drink, Julia? I'm having a martini."

"Chardonnay, please."

The drinks arrived. David seemed easy to be with, I was surprised how comfortable I felt in his company. He was doing most of the talking, which pleased me. The place was crowded, the bar overflowing with typical New Yorkers on a Friday night. The perfect place for getting acquainted, all very casual, not too intimate.

We'd exchanged the usual questions and answers -- where did you grow up, where did you go to school, who do you work for, when David changed the subject.

"I've been trying to figure you out all evening and for the life of me I can't understand where you've been. Why I haven't run across you before, and why you're unattached? You're damned attractive, bright, easy to be with. I asked Jim about you, but he said he didn't know anything, only that you were a friend of his significant other. What gives?"

"I'm no mystery woman. My fiancé and I were in an automobile accident almost two years ago. He was killed and I spent over a year in and out of hospitals and Rehab. I just returned to New York when we met. No hidden secrets. No mysterious past."

"Well, that explains a lot. Sorry about the accident. Must have been hard to take."

"It was. Time has a way of helping you deal with tragedy, but what about you? Still single, no girl friends?"

"No one special at the moment. I've had my share of great girlfriends, but I'm not the marrying type. I try to make my life as happy and as uncomplicated as possible."

"Don't we all. Tell me, what makes you the happiest?"

"Maybe this isn't the right time to answer that question if you want a truthful answer."

The waiter approached, poured the last of the wine and placed the check in front of David. "No rush, sir.

Whenever you're ready."

David paid the bill, saying, "Come on, let's get out of here. I know the perfect place for an after-dinner drink where we can get to know each other even better."

We stopped in front of an apartment building on west 29th street. The doorman approached and started to open the car door. "Hold off a minute, Charles." He'd noticed my reaction.

"Where are we?"

"My place. I have a full bar and its quiet. We can continue our conversation there. I'd really like to know you even better."

Before I could say a word, David said. "As a gentleman, I suppose now's the time to answer your question. I like to keep everything open and above board, Julia. The thing that makes me the happiest is laying naked next to a beautiful woman like you."

I was dumbfounded. Well, at least he was honest. "Sorry, David, sex is something I take seriously. I don't consider it just another way to say thank you at the end a very nice evening. I can take a cab home."

David started the engine. "No. I'll take you home. Somehow, I'm not surprised. Disappointed, but not really surprised."

We drove the rest of the way without a word exchanged between us. Stopping in front of my apartment house, I opened the car door before the doorman was visible.

"Thank you, David. I enjoyed the evening."

"I enjoyed being with you, Julia, and you know what, I'm glad you turned me down. I'll call you later in the week. Maybe we can have dinner again."

I hurried to the elevator not knowing what to think. Had I reached the age where all eligible men had only one thing on their minds regarding women?

I closed the door to the apartment. I'd try to sort it all out another day.

Chapter 22

December had arrived. Dad asked all of us to come home to celebrate Christmas. Not a problem for me, but my brothers and sister had kids and family obligations of their own. Years had gone by since we'd all been together at the holidays. Our family celebrations had come to an end when our mother died.

My office would be closed between Christmas and New Years. Going home gave me an excuse for turning down invitations from the old crowd. My social life at this point was nonexistent, though I did spend an occasional Wednesday evening in Mario's kitchen. Luigi was an excellent teacher and I was having fun. My friends would never have understood.

By Friday, I was ready for a quiet weekend. I'd spent the last week working out the details of an ad campaign with a prospective client. I hoped to sign him to a contract. I was exhausted. He was difficult to deal with. Just as I was about to sit down to Chinese take-out in front of the television, the phone rang.

"Hi, Julia."

I recognized the voice. I hadn't heard from David since our evening ended with my turning down his not-too subtle-invitation to his bed.

"It took a lot of soul searching for me to make this call, Julia. I'm not used to women turning me down and I admit I don't handle rejection very well. Anyhow, I'm swallowing my pride and with my tail between my legs, I apologize for misjudging you."

"Nothing to apologize for. You were honest about what a nightcap in your apartment meant."

"I'd like to explain one thing I didn't make clear. I'm not keen on one-night-stands. I wanted to be honest when I told you I'm not the marrying kind, not into permanent commitments. My idea of a perfect relationship is more akin to good friends with benefits. I like women. I treat women well."

"I'm sure you do, David." I wondered where all this was leading.

"The reason I mention all this is I'd like you to give me another chance. Go out with me again. I find you intriguing, seductive, and oh so desirable"

I could feel my cheeks redden. He was hard to read. "Let me think about it."

"I'll call you next week. I promise I'll let you set the limits. You decide when the time is right. I have reservations in Aruba for a week the end of January. I'd like to take you with me. Think about it."

I put the phone down. My mind swirled with a million different thoughts. David was charming, glib, and dangerous. He was the kind of man it would be easy to give in to. I'd already ruled out getting involved in a permanent relationship, but was a friend with benefits the answer? Was it any less scary? I wasn't sure I was experienced enough to hold my own with a man like David.

True to his word, David called the following week. I agreed to have dinner with him and test the waters. I'd see if his word was to be believed. I'd be leaving for Connecticut the following week with plenty of time to decide if I wanted to continue to see him.

We went to a small French bistro tucked off on a side street in the village. The owner greeted David like an old friend.

"We haven't seen you in a while, Mister Harrington. Your table is ready."

"I only bring special people here, Julia, and it's been a while since I've had anyone special in my life."

Was he to be believed or was he just too smooth?

"I have the bottle of champagne you requested on ice, Mr. Harrington. This way, please."

We were seated in a far corner of the small restaurant. One of those special places you kept secret hoping it never grew too big to lose its charm.

"I've taken a chance and ordered Pierre's specialties in advance for us. I hope you don't mind."

"No, I think that's very thoughtful. I can't wait."

After the waiter had uncorked and poured the champagne David raised his glass. "Here's to what I hope is the start of a wonderful friendship."

At least he didn't add with benefits. The dinner went well, the food was delicious, but hard as I tried, I couldn't learn anything more about David that wasn't superficial. Different from our first meeting, he turned the conversation back to me at every chance making me uncomfortable. I needed to know more about him. We lingered over coffee and desert, being the last to leave.

David stopped in front of my building. "I offer no nightcap this evening, my dear. I'll call you soon," He leaned over and gave me a very sensual kiss. "Goodnight."

I stepped out of the Porsche as the doorman greeted me, more confused than before.

The early train was packed, every seat taken with people anxious to get home for the start of the Christmas holidays. I settled into my seat looking forward to some time off and excited at the prospect of the whole family being together.

The clickety, clack of the wheels as they traveled over the rails was almost hypnotic. I watched the scenery change as I looked out the window, thinking about my date with David last night. I couldn't figure out whether his attraction for me was the chase or was he really interested in a long-term friendship as he called it. He could have his pick of beautiful, charming, intelligent women. Why me? I was afraid I was no match for him. I closed my eyes and nodded off to sleep.

I awoke when I felt the train coming to a stop and reached for my suitcase. Steeping off the platform I was happy to see Sam waiting for me.

"Here, Miss Julia, let me take your bag. Your sister and all her kids are already here, and more family is arriving later. I'm so happy I'm goina' see y'all together again. It's been a long time, ever since the Misses passed. The house seems so quiet these days."

A Ford explorer was parked in the driveway. I thanked Sam as he carried my suitcase into the house saying he'd put it in in my room. I followed the sound of children's voices, and opened the side gate to the backyard.

A kickball game was taking place on the lawn. My father and my sister Jennifer were cheering on her four sons.

"Hi, Sis, Dad."

Jennifer put her arms out and gave me a big hug. "How's the new job? Bet you're glad to be back in New York with all your friends. A month in Montana would have been the death of me. Feeling well?"

"I've no complaints. When did you get here?"

"About an hour ago. Dad and I are watching the boys run off a little nervous energy."

"I can't believe how much they've grown. Is Bob here?"

"He and Peter are playing nine holes of golf at the club. Adam and his brood should be here soon."

I felt a sight chill. "It's cool. Think we'll get some snow? Wouldn't a white Christmas be the perfect touch? What about Annie and the kids?"

"Peter took the train from the city. Annie's driving with the kids. They should be here soon"

I smiled at my dad, "Well, you got your wish, Dad. All four of your kids and nine grandchildren will be here for Christmas. I'm going inside. I'll see you all later. It's too cold out here for me."

I ducked my head in the kitchen to say hello to Mattie. She was busy with dinner preparations, happy to have her brood home again. The smell of familiar food cooking filled my nostrils and my stomach began to growl. I'd had a quick breakfast of toast and coffee before I caught the train. I was starved.

I left Mattie to her cooking. As I passed the living room, I caught a glimpse of a large Christmas tree, every branch decorated with the old ornaments I remembered helping place on Christmas tree limbs growing up. Hanging from the mantel were four stockings with our names embroidered in gold thread -- ones we'd hung as kids on Christmas Eve. Where had Dad found them? I hadn't seen them in years. I began to choke up, a lump in my throat. Mother would have been so happy to see us all here together.

After unpacking my things, I laid down on the bed and stretched out thinking about the incredible year that was coming to an end. From Connecticut to Montana to New York and now back home, so many emotions packed into twelve short months.

Dinner was wonderful, noisy and somewhat out of hand with so many children at the table. I was paying particular attention to the interplay between husbands and wives, holding them up as examples of wedded bliss. Did they seem happy, content with their lives? How did they treat each other? Did they still seem in love or were they comfortable, or distant, or worse, snapping at each other?

My siblings had all been married for some time. If relationships couldn't seem to last could marriage really work in our day and age? So far, my siblings seemed to be good symbols of its merits. Somehow, they'd beat the seven-year-odds when so many marriages end in divorce.

My week at home was coming to an end, the rest of the family left soon after Dad told us the reason, he wanted us all home for Christmas. He was planning on selling the house. This would probably be the last of family Christmases, and probably our last visit to the house we all grew up in. Everyone seemed ready to pack and go home early after the announcement, taking with them their own feelings about the house being sold.

I stayed on to sort through things I'd left behind when I moved to the city and chose a few pieces of furniture and some artwork to send to New York. We were all given the opportunity to take what furnishings we wanted.

I found it hard to believe Dad would sell the house. Of course, I never considered the upkeep or the commute, but as he explained his reasons, it made sense. He was looking for an apartment in the city, and had rented a housekeeping cottage at his club in the meantime. He planned on spending weekends golfing with his cronies, spending time with the friends he and mother had enjoyed for years.

The deciding factor was when Sam and Mattie decided to retire. They'd bought a house on a small piece of land in Mississippi, years ago. Now they wanted to spend the rest of their years there. Who could blame them?

For me, it felt as if the umbilical cord had finally been cut. Once the family home was sold, I'd no longer have a safe haven to return to.

Chapter 23

Being back at work after the holidays were over had proved to be a nightmare, my in-box was full to overflowing. Trying to catch up I stayed late every evening. Getting things done was a lot easier when the office was quiet and the phone didn't ring. The reward for leaving the office late was the ease in finding a seat on the subway. I didn't have to guess whether the body, too close for comfort, was a simple case of overcrowding or just some pervert getting his jollies.

Home at last. All I wanted was a long soak in the tub and early to bed. I'd not heard from David during the week. Just as well. I wasn't ready to go off on a week's vacation to Aruba or any place else with him. I was sure he'd be good company and practiced in the art of making a woman feel special, in and out of bed, but how long would it take for him to be attracted to someone else he found even more irresistible. No. The best thing to do was to put an end to our friendship now, before it got out of hand. The benefits would all be one sided, I'm sure.

I rolled over, pulling the covers up close, and glanced at the clock on the bedside table. Seven-thirty. No need to get out of bed that early on a Saturday. I was about to go back to sleep when the phone rang.

"Miss Johnston, it's Charles, the doorman. There's a gentleman here to see you, says he's an old friend."

I thought it must be David. He was the last person I wanted to see. "Please tell Mister Harrington I'm unavailable."

"The gentleman say's his name is Cole Clayton."

Cole? I was a loss for words. Good God what was he doing here.

"Do you want me to send him up, Miss Johnston or should I send him away?"

"It's okay, Charles. He is an old friend. Please send him up."

I ran to the bathroom in a panic, brushed my teeth in a hurry, ran a comb through my hair, and applied a bit of lip gloss. I searched through the closet pushing hangers aside looking for the beautiful Asian silk robe Roger's mother gave me as a gift years ago. My stomach was in a knot. My hands shook as I tied the sash. I heard the doorbell.

"If you'd allow a weary cowboy carrying bagels and smears to enter, maybe even being as hospitable as to provide a much-needed cup of coffee, I'd be most grateful."

I opened the door.

"Come in. I'm speechless. This is a total surprise. What brings you to New York?"

"Delta Airlines red eye special."

I laughed. How could I not? He could be charming if he wanted to. Quite irresistible. "God, you can be difficult. You know what I mean. Why didn't you tell me you were coming?"

Cole handed me the paper bag, "I'll tell you over coffee. The bagels are still warm, fresh out of the oven."

I made coffee while Cole looked around the condo.

"Great view, really nice digs. Not a bad payoff for spending a month with me."

"Don't put it that way, Cole."

"How else should I put it? Wasn't that the deal?"

"You know the offer was made before I ever met you. You make it sound heartless. Sit down. Coffee's ready."

I put the bagels on plates, my hands shaking, nervous with his being there.

"Now, will you tell me what you're doing here?"

"Long story, but at the moment I'm finding it hard to concentrate. You look very sexy in that robe."

I felt uncomfortable considering the way Cole was eyeing me, as if he had x-ray vision. His eyes undressing me.

"I missed you, you know. By the way, Julia, what happened to all the letters you were going to write?"

I felt my cheeks redden. "I'm sorry. I should have written, but I guess I was trying my best to put Montana behind me and move on."

"Was it that easy for you to move on? I thought we had something special happening between us. Something more meaningful that just a roll in the hay."

I took a long drink of coffee. There was no good answer to Cole's question. I needed to change the subject. "You still haven't told me what you're doing in New York."

"I guess you're going to avoid answering any personal questions. Am I right?" He took a moment before he continued, pouring the last of the coffee into his cup. "I'm here about a plan I've been working on. It could become a reality if I can get financing. New York is where the investors are. I'm hoping to talk some of the big money boys into lending me the funds to begin building."

"Cole, that sounds great. Is this is what you were alluding to before I left? Now, will you tell me what its all about? I'm really excited for you."

"I'd much rather talk about you. Tell me what you're doing? Are you happy being back in the big city? Most of all, I'm almost afraid to ask, are you involved with anyone?"

We talked for a long time before Cole asked if I would do him a favor.

"Of course, anything."

"I plan to be in town for a week. Hotels in the city are damned expensive and I'm too old for the YMCA. Right now I'm on a really tight budget so, can I crash on your sofa? We could sort of reverse the circumstances. I'll clean and cook in exchange for room and board."

"You can be so sarcastic. Of course, you can stay, but why is it necessary for you to go out of your way to make me feel guilty."

"I'm sorry, Julia. It's just my frustrations talking. I'll go retrieve the suitcase I left with the doorman. Just a suggestion, but while I'm gone you might want to get dressed. That robe is much too inviting, especially since I know what's hidden underneath all that silk."

It didn't take much to make me feel self-conscious. I could feel a warm flush come over me as I tightened the sash.

"If you haven't any plans for the day, Julia, how about we spend it together."

"I'd like that, Cole."

"Try to think of something fun to do." He walked toward the door. "Be back in a few minutes."

I took his suggestion and hurried to throw on some clothes. The gentle knock on the door told me Cole had returned.

Putting his suitcase on the floor in the hall Cole said, "I have an idea. I just thought of it coming up in the elevator. What say we play tourists for the day and explore the Big Apple?"

"That sounds like fun. I'm game."

Having snowed the day before slush was everywhere, dirty gray banks of snow left behind by the snow plows piled high. Thank God I'd been smart enough to put on a heavy sweater under my winter jacket, and tights under my jeans. I could still feel the cool air as we stood in front of the apartment building.

"Where should we start, Julia? You pick someplace to explore. Someplace you've always wanted to visit, but never got around to it."

"How about the Guggenheim? At least it will be warm inside."

"Come on, you don't consider this cold, do you? It was twelve degrees when I left home last night. No, museums are out, too boring. I think we need to do something we'd thought of doing as long as we lived here, but never got around to it."

I could see Cole trying to come up with an idea, and then as if a light went on, he smiled, putting his arm around me. "Come on. We're going to visit the Statue of Liberty."

"In the dead of winter?"

"What better time? We might even have her all to ourselves." Cole took out his cell phone to check for information. He grabbed my hand. "Let's get going. The ferry leaves from Battery Park."

We had a ten-minute wait for the next ferry along with a handful of out-of-towners.

"Check this out, Julia. We get two for the price of one Ellis Island is included as well."

Cole was like a kid, so enthusiastic about the tour. "From the first day I first arrived in New York, this was the one of the things I wanted to do, but I never seemed to have the time."

Once we boarded, rather than sit inside the warm cabin, Cole wanted to stay on deck in order to see New York's skyline from the harbor.

I'd never viewed the city from that vantage point. I could see as far as the George Washington Bridge. The skyline was a forest of tall buildings. What a fabulous sight. The weather began to warm a bit as the sun peeked through the clouds.

We'd missed the tour guide's stories he was relating to the tourists in the cabin, but I had a vague knowledge of France's gift to the United States. The good thing was we had the space to ourselves. A strange sense of ease was beginning to take over. The nerves had subsided. I really felt happy to see Cole again. When he wasn't being hurtful, he made time together fun and he did have the ability to make me laugh.

The trip didn't take long, no more than fifteen minutes to reach Liberty Island. Miss Liberty was a magnificent sight seen from the harbor. I don't think I'd ever really paid much attention to her before, or realized just how enormous the statue was.

The entrance to the pedestal was located directly behind the statue in a white tent where the park rangers wanted to see our reservations before allowing us to enter as they checked our belongings. We stopped to read Emma Lazarus's poem on a tablet, "Give me your tired your poor, your huddled masses yearning to breathe free." After looking around the museum studying all the exhibits, we visited the gift shop. Cole found a small metal replica of Lady Liberty and insisted on buying it for me as a remembrance of the day. We even contemplated climbing the stairway to the crown. The view was supposed to be unbelievable. Three hundred and fifty-two steps didn't sound to bad, until I heard it was the equivalent of twenty stories and backed out. We wandered around until the time came to get back on the ferry for the tour of Ellis Island.

Going through the old deserted building was amazing, trying to imagine the millions of people who entered the United States for the first time through Ellis Island. According to the plaque in front of the building, it opened in 1892, and closed in 1954. Cole had his arm around me as we listened to the tour guide's history lesson before we toured the facility.

As we were leaving, Cole stopped and starred out on the harbor. "Just for a moment, Julia, just try and imagine the emotions my great grandfather must have felt, taking his first steps onto the soil of the United States after leaving Norway. What he must have thought as the first thing he saw was the Statue of Liberty. He was nineteen years old, spoke no English, had only a few dollars in his pocket, and didn't know a single soul in America. It must have been overwhelming."

I turned to look at him.

"You're quite the story teller."

"No, just a lonesome cowboy a long way from home."

Four and a half hours later, I plopped down on the sofa, glad to be home. Exhausted.

"Did you enjoy being a tourist for a short time?"

"My compliments, Cole. What a wonderful way to spend the day. I can't remember the last time I had as much fun."

Sassy's words came to mind as I spoke. "Somehow we get so busy we don't have time to enjoy the wonders around us. I loved every minute, Cole. I haven't spent that much time out of doors since I left the ranch."

Cole walked toward the kitchen. "Don't suppose you have a beer in your frig?" He opened the refrigerator. "Looks like you don't have much of anything in here. I'm starved. What say we clean up and go have dinner somewhere?"

"Great idea. I'm starved as well. I have wine if that will do."

"It'll have to. Any idea where we can go that isn't New York expensive?"

I thought for a minute. "I know just the place, and its casual. I'll call for reservations. They might be busy. Its Saturday night."

The taxi let us out in front of Casa Bella. The hostess seated us saying, "Mario is helping in the kitchen tonight. He wants to say hello. I'll tell him you're here."

"So you're on a first name basis here. I guess you must come here often on dates if the owner wants to say hello."

"No, Mario's a client, but I have spent a few Wednesday evenings in the kitchen learning to cook *ala Italianio*."

"You're kidding."

"No, for real. It's been fun and Mario has become a good friend."

"Julia, you amaze me. You're so full of contradictions. Will I ever know the real you?"

Mario approached our table, wiping his hands on his white apron. He had a big smile on his face when he saw Cole.

"Hello, *Donna Bella*. I see you brought your boyfriend."

"Mario this is Cole Clayton. He's visiting from Montana, he's just a friend."

"His eyes tell me something else, I think he's more than just a friend. It's how I would look at you if I were younger or single."

Mario shouted at one of the waiters. "Hey, Julio, bring my friends a bottle of *Chianti Classico*."

"The wine is on the house. Luigi is not here tonight so I'm the chief." With a wide grin he winked at me. "I'll make everything special for you and your maybe yes, maybe no, boyfriend."

Mario shook Cole's hand and started to walk away. "I'd like to spend more time visiting with you kids, but I have to get back to the kitchen or nobody eats. Ciao."

"He's a kick. So, you told him you didn't have a boyfriend."

"He keeps asking and I keep saying no. He can't seem to understand why I'm single."

"Neither can I. I'd change that in a minute if you'd let me."

I let the remark go by unanswered. We finished dinner and the bottle of wine both agreeing we'd had a busy day, time to call it a night.

Chapter 24

I suggested Cole have the first turn in the bathroom while I made the sofa into a bed.

"Okay if I take a shower? You could join me if you want."

"No, thanks. I prefer to shower alone."

"Just a suggestion. You know it's a great a way to save water. We westerners are big on conservation. That's why in the old days cowboys only showered once a month when they came to town on payday. You can save a lot of water that way."

"I'm impressed. Go shower."

I tucked sheets, a blanket and a pillow under my arm and did my best to make the sofa a comfortable place to sleep. By the time I arranged everything, Cole appeared, hair wet, barefoot, in grey sweat pants and a white tee shirt, handsome as ever.

"Thanks again for letting me stay over, and for a great day. You don't have to lock your door. It's your house, I'll play by your rules."

"Goodnight, Cole, see you in the morning."

"Goodnight, Your Highness."

I laughed as I closed the door to my bedroom. It had been a great day.

I awoke to the smell of coffee, put on my robe and opened the bedroom door. The sheets and blanket were folded on the floor alongside the sofa. The sofa pillows had been fluffed and back in their place.

"Coffee smells good."

"I'll pour you a cup. I checked your frig again, as well as your cupboards. They're almost bare. No wonder you stay so skinny. You never eat. I found enough to make eggs and toast. Breakfast when you're ready."

Cole handed me a mug of hot coffee. Just what I needed.

"Thanks. It won't take me long to shower and get dressed."

We'd finished the last of breakfast when Cole asked if I had plans for the day.

"No. We can spend it together if you like. What would you like to do?"

"Well, I've been thinking and I believe I have a great plan. Julia, have you ever had a picnic in Central Park?"

"Of course not, but you're not really thinking of a picnic in the middle of winter?"

"Why not? The park's there and we have to eat. Besides this feels warm compared to Montana. What say we stop at that coffee shop nearby, the place where I bought the bagels, and have them make us lunch to go."

"You're not kidding. You really want a picnic in January."

"Come on, be a sport. Every tourist wants to see Central Park."

With our lunch in Styrofoam boxes stowed in a large plastic bag we started walking along a wide tree-lined path. The air felt fresh. Yesterday's windy cold evening was replaced by mild weather for January. "The park must be spectacular in the spring, Cole, when all the deciduous trees are in full bloom."

For some reason, my eyes were drawn to the expanse of lawn, green shoots peeking through the dusting of snow. It brought back memories of the ranch, memories of the endless green meadows and trees.

We gave way to the joggers as they ran by, amazed at the number of dog walkers and people just out for a Sunday morning stroll in the middle of winter. I swore I heard the songs of birds. I didn't think any birds except for the damn pigeons lived in New York.

We'd walked some distance without speaking, admiring the scenery. Cole held my hand as he said, "Checking out the park was also something I promised myself I would do. Somehow the magic of the city's bright lights got the best of me and I forgot there was anything but work, parties, booze, lots of booze, and more work. What about you, Julia? Ever been to Central Park?"

"I'm embarrassed to say no, it's been just another part of the skyline. I can't begin to imagine what a dramatic change New York was for you after growing up on a ranch in Montana."

"It was overwhelming. I was about as naive as anyone could be. I'd never been outside Montana before coming here for grad school, but New York was my dream. Having watched how hard my dad worked and how little he had to show for it, I decided early on, the ranch was not for me. I wanted the big city and all the glamour thinking that was all that was important. Needless to say, I learned my lessons the hard way."

"But you've never regretted leaving?"

"Hell, no. I came to understand, though Dad worked hard, he had all he ever wanted out of life, all that mattered to him was right there on the ranch. It took a long time for me to realize he never yearned for anything else."

"I know I've asked you before, but I find it hard to believe you've never once considered moving back to New York."

"Never."

"None of this makes any difference?"

"Great place to visit, Julia, but no I'll never move back."

We walked along, hand-in-hand without the need for words. I never realized all this beauty had been here, within easy reach and I'd never bothered to take advantage of it.

Finding a bench in a quiet secluded spot off the main path we settled down. My growling stomach telling me it was time for Lunch.

Cole handed me the Styrofoam container with my name on it. Inside was a brie, avocado, and beansprout sandwich, a small container of red potato salad, and a can a herbal tea. Curious, I glanced over to see what was in Cole's box. The three-decker BLT, large container of potato salad, chips and a coke, the differences between us were evident. I smiled as I thought about Sassy teaching Cole's father to eat sushi.

When we were finished, I gathered the containers, put everything back in the plastic bag and dropped it in the nearby trash can.

Cole put an arm around me as I settled back on the bench. "Look around you, Julia. Look what the park has to offer. What's amazing is this is all here to enjoy and it's free. I'm always surprised how much fun you can have without spending a nickel."

I missed what else Cole was saying as I thought about the way he viewed things. He was so different from the other men I'd met, even Roger.

"Somehow you make the simplest things feel magical." While the words just slipped off my tongue, it was true. Cole made me see things in ways I'd never seen them before. I remembered the day at the rodeo where Cole showed me a different life style and for the first time let me get close enough to see his sense of humor. Most of all the day we rode to the grove where his grandfather was buried, without holding back he spoke of the things he held dear. All he wanted out of life was to hold on to the ranch and one day hand it down to a son.

I brushed my thoughts aside when I realized Cole was asking me a question.

"So tell me Julia, what do you do with your spare time?"

"What spare time? I don't seem to have any. I've been putting in long hours at the office. I guess work takes up most of my time."

"What happened to all the friends you seemed so anxious to get back together with."

"I don't know. Either they'd changed during the time I was away, or I've changed, but one-by-one I've given up on them and gone my own way."

"I'm not surprised. The Julia that arrived at the ranch was sure different from the Julia who left a month later. You're not dating anyone?"

"No. The dating game hasn't gone well. I had a disastrous blind date and a recent offer of a friendship with benefits I turned down. I guess I'm out of sync with the dating game. What about you, Cole?"

"No, no one. A guy can only chance having his heart broken so many times. Besides, I doubt anyone could live up to the girl I want."

Time to change the subject. "You still haven't told me about this secret plan of yours and the meetings this week."

"It's not complicated, just a big undertaking. Do you remember the lake where we went swimming?"

I nodded, yes, as I tried to block out all that had happened by the lake.

"The plan revolves around building a conference center on a piece of the land facing the lake, sort of a retreat, a place where groups could hold meetings away from distractions."

"Please tell me you're not building log cabins, not after all you said about dude ranches."

"No way. There's nothing rustic about the plan. Everything is designed to be a modern, up-to-date facility. I've got the plans in my suitcase. I'll show them to you when we get back to your place."

The expression on Cole's face had changed. He seemed really animated.

"It's a pretty major project, maybe too big for anyone to chance providing financing, but it's worth a try."

"I'm impressed. You're certainly not thinking small. I can hardly wait to see the drawings. I'm really excited for you."

"If I can make it happen, I can keep the ranch afloat, maybe even replace the old cow and calf operation and get rid of the guy I lease the land to. The county already gave me a thumbs up. They promised a building permit if I can get the funding."

"It does seem to solve all your problems."

"Yeah, but it will all have been a pipe dream if I can't come up with the money. I've a date tomorrow with an old buddy from my New York days. He's a big wheel in one of the private investment banks. I'll see what he thinks."

"Come on." I stood and grabbed Cole's hand. "Let's hurry home. I can't wait to see the plans."

Chapter 25

Cole laid out the set of prints on the dining room table. I felt a sense of eagerness as I looked at the rendition of the exterior elevation.

"Wow, this is fabulous. Did you draw these?"

"No, I did some rough sketches and sent them to an architectural draftsman."

"Is the exterior of the building really made out of logs? With the large amount of glass, the plans are an imaginative, very modern concept of an old west design. From an art standpoint, it's spectacular."

"Look here, Julia." Cole began to flip through pages of blue prints showing me the interior elevations. His fingers tracing the flow. "See, you enter the building from the wide front porch, and the first thing you see as you walk through the double doors is three stories of glass, the entire back wall of the lounge. The lake and trees become the central point of interest."

"Dramatic." I took a closer look at the plans. "Where do the staircases on either side of the entrance hall go?"

"They go to the conference rooms on the second floor and the bedrooms on the third floor. There's an elevator for anyone who doesn't want to climb the stairs. The rest of the first floor is the dining room, bar, kitchen, gym, and employee's quarters. That's it, all the makings of a small hotel. What do you think?"

"Oh, Cole, it looks wonderful. I'm so proud of you. I had no idea you were so talented."

"I have talents in other areas as well if you remember."

My cheeks began to redden. I couldn't help smiling though I wasn't about go there.

"How long do you think it will it take to construct?"

"Once I get the financing, it should be done in a year." Cole started to roll up the prints and replace them in their cardboard tube. "That is if the weather doesn't become a problem. The key to the whole thing is the money."

"Your meeting is tomorrow?"

"Yes. Ten o'clock tomorrow morning. It's sink or swim."

"I've got my fingers crossed. Have you got a name for the facility, yet?"

Cole seemed taken aback. "I never gave a thought to a name. You know what. I'll make that your department. You're the one in advertising. I'll leave the name up to you.

"I'd like that. Give me a little time. I'll try to come up with something that befits your fabulous plan. How about I open a bottle of wine and we celebrate."

"I'll go for the wine, but there won't be anything to celebrate until the cash is in hand."

Cole turned on the television and asked if it was okay if he watched the football game.

"Of course. Why don't I make dinner? We can eat in front of the TV while you watch the game."

"Good plan, Your Highness."

I busied myself in the kitchen, putting a pot of water on to boil for pasta. I thought of Mario and all he said about how his mother cooked and opened the refrigerator. What could I add to make the pasta interesting? I pulled out butter, Parmesan cheese, a half empty box of mushrooms, tomatoes, and a bottle of green olives with pimentos in the center. Opening the cupboard, I retrieved a bottle of olive oil and placed it on the counter. I tossed together a green salad, realizing I hadn't cooked a real dinner since I left the ranch.

I drained the pasta and added the olive oil tossing it together with all the ingredients I'd assembled and carried everything to the living room. Setting the tray on the coffee table just as the second quarter was coming to an end. Cole was so engrossed in the game he seemed surprised when I said, "Ready for dinner?"

"It's almost the end of the first half, only seconds to go. Looks like the Cowboys have the game in the bag. Your timing couldn't be better. Let's eat." Cole glanced at the large bowl filled with steaming pasta. "This looks great. I'm starved. I almost forgotten you knew how to cook."

Maybe it was the fresh air because I was hungry too, or maybe it was the enjoyment of not eating alone.

"This is terrific, Julia. Mario's recipe?"

"No, Mario's concept."

When I finished in the kitchen, I sat down next to Cole to watch the end of the game. He moved closer to me and put his arm around my shoulder. "I bet this is what old married folks do on Sunday during football season."

How cleaver. Not the first time he alluded to how married people spend their time. I let it pass. I wasn't interested in being married people.

When the game ended. I said goodnight, leaving Cole to make up the sofa. "I'll be up early. I'll try not to wake you. Tomorrow's a workday."

I slept well and awoke to the sound of the alarm. I showered and dressed trying to be quiet. I opened the bedroom door hoping I wouldn't wake Cole. Much to my surprise, he was awake sitting on the sofa. I noticed him giving me a careful examination.

"You look very nice this morning, Your Highness. I've never seen you in your city clothes before. I'd say you're the picture of a successful New York business woman."

"Stop kidding. I've got to run or I'll be late. Give me a call after your meeting. I'll be anxious to hear how it went." I grabbed my purse off the hall table. "Good luck, today. I hope everything goes your way."

"Thanks. I'll call to you later."

I left, thinking how much the big tough cowboy sitting on my sofa looked like a scared little boy.

I kept checking my cell phone all afternoon. Not even a text from Cole. I hoped it wasn't bad news. Around four-thirty he called.

"How did it go? Did you get the loan?"

"Well, it wasn't a yes or no, just a maybe with strings attached. Long story. Tell me where your office is and I'll meet you in a half hour or so."

I gave him directions and hurried to finish the few things I needed to get out of the way before I called it a day.

Shortly before five, I started down the stairs to wait for Cole. I almost didn't recognize him as he walked toward me dressed in a dark blue, expensive looking well-tailored suit, light blue shirt, and maroon tie, carrying a brief case. He looked like he belonged on Wall Street.

"Tell me what happened, Cole."

He took my hand. "Come on. There's a cocktail lounge I spotted around the corner. I could use a drink. I'll tell you all about my day."

We entered the darkened lounge and walked toward a booth. The place was almost empty. A few hangers-on sat at the end of the bar, a tad too early for the after-work crowd. The cocktail waitress, in the skimpiest of outfits that seemed to be the required lounge attire, showing far too much cleavage, came to take our order.

"Don't keep me in suspense. What happened?"

"It wasn't all bad, just a bunch of if's. Hank, my banker friend, liked the concept and loved the plans. We talked for hours about what it would take for the bank to finance the deal. The long and short of it, they offered a construction loan for a year, which would convert to a business loan if the building was completed within that time frame."

"That's wonderful, Cole. I'm so happy for you."

"Yeah, that's the good part. The catch is I have to put the ranch up as collateral until the project is finished. The other kicker is I have to have at least two confirmed conferences booked for the first year of operation."

"Wow, that's going to be tough. How do you get anyone to commit to hold a conference in a place that doesn't exist?"

"Yeah, that's the kicker."

The drinks arrived. I'd never seen Cole drink hard liquor before. "What's the plan?"

"For starters, Hank gave me a list of businesses and foundations I could call using his name. I spent the day at the bank making calls and setting up appointments. Any ideas?"

The bar was getting crowded by the time we'd had a second drink. The noise level was growing to the point that any serious conversation was out of the question.

"Let's catch a cab for home, Cole. We can order in and put out heads together to come up with some selling points."

We'd pushed the empty cartons of Chinese take out to one side of the dining room table. A yellow legal pad sat in front of Cole. He'd loosened his tie, undone his collar, and rolled up his shirt sleeves. After several hours of tossing around ideas we came up with a list of talking points and a selling plan not much different from an advertising campaign.

"You're very good at this stuff, Julia. I never could have put this together by myself. I'm a numbers guy. How do I thank you?"

"You don't have to thank me, it's been fun. Let's just say it's the least I can do after you put up with me for a whole month. Besides, I'm enjoying the challenge. Sort of the way I feel about my job. I'm proving I don't need anything handed to me. I can stand on my own two feet."

Cole started to clear away the mess, picking up the empty cartons, the beer bottle, and wine glass. "Question, Julia, but don't get me wrong. This is a really nice condo, but it's sort of a surprise. Not exactly what I expected your place would look like. I don't know I imagined you living in something not quite this sterile."

I followed Cole into the kitchen and began to put the glasses and silverware in the dishwasher. "Guess you know me better than I thought. I had nothing to say about the condo. My father had already purchased it. He brought me here and handed me the keys. I can't complain. After all, it was a gift, but I'd have preferred one of the great old converted brownstones. Speaking of surprises, you looked very handsome today all dressed up in a business suit, carrying a brief case."

"Better than boots and a Stetson, you mean. More like the way you like the men in your life to dress."

"Really, Cole? I only meant I saw a different side of you."

"There's where you're dead wrong. There's only one side to me, no matter what I'm wearing. Don't let the jeans and boots confuse you. Clothes don't make the man."

"Don't get your back up. I was paying you a compliment."

"Let's just say I'm a little sensitive about how New Yorkers look at anyone different, seeing them as yokels."

"Please believe me. I never looked at you that way."

I stood and stretched, rubbing the back of my neck, stiff from bending over the table. "It's late, I should be going to bed."

"Come sit with me for a bit. I'm to wired to sleep."

Against my better judgment, I sat beside him as he put his arm around me. The conversation was light until Cole turned and gazed straight at me, a serious look about him.

"Have you any idea what you want out of life? Any thought about what things might look like ten or twenty years from now?"

"Where did that come from? It's a really weighty question for so late at night."

"I know, but believe me, it's important. What do you see yourself doing?"

I tried to form a picture in my mind, but it was blank. Why would Cole ask such a question? Why would I even think about my life in those terms? My days all ran into one and another. In my life only today existed. I had no time to think about tomorrow, certainly not in terms of years. Nor did I want to. "To be truthful, Cole, I haven't given it any thought."

"You've never thought about getting married, having kids?"

"I did once in an abstract sort of way. Remember I was about to be married until fate intervened."

"That happened a lot of yesterday's ago, Julia. What about now? Is that something you see in your future?"

"I don't know, Cole. It's complicated. Relationships seem so different today from my parent's generation. Sure, people got divorced then, but it wasn't the norm. I read somewhere the average length of a marriage these days is seven years. Maybe our generation isn't capable of long-term commitments, always searching for the shiny object in the distance."

"That may be everybody else, but how about you?"

I stood and walked toward the windows, looking out on a full moon and a sky full of stars, the tall buildings in the distance. "How did we get into this conversation, anyhow?"

"Just one more question, Julia, and I'll call it a night."

"Okay, what's your question?"

I felt Cole standing behind me, "Are you capable of an until death do you part kind of commitment, or have you built a huge wall around your feelings?"

Cole's presence, the warmth of his body as he stood without an inch of space between us was sending chills down my spine.

"It's complicated. In a way, maybe what I've seen happen to relationships among my friends is holding me back."

"Maybe it's because you've never really been in love before, and still too afraid to let your guard down. Afraid to take a chance on love, afraid you might get hurt. You're so afraid of failure, that you can't see that love is worth taking a chance?"

The gentle kiss on the back of my neck caused me to turn around. He looked at me with such longing in his eyes. Before I could say anything, I was in Cole's arms. He held me close for a moment before he whispered in my ear.

"Go to bed, Julia. I'm not sure how long I can keep my hands off you."

Chapter 26

Cole and I were to meet at the same cocktail lounge after work. I hurried knowing I was late. Pushing open the door to the lounge I tried to adjust to the darkened interior, It took a second or two before I spotted Cole in the same booth we'd sat in the night before.

"Sorry I'm late." I tried to catch my breath. "I couldn't get off the phone with a client. Did you order already?"

"No, I waited for you."

The same waitress, much too be old to be wearing her revealing outfit, stopped at our booth.

"Well, you two lovebirds back again?"

I don't know why I bothered to answer, but I did. "We're just friends."

"Sure you are." Her Brooklyn accent and her flippant attitude were typical of New York. "I've been around long enough sister to know friends don't look at each other the way you two do. What'll you have?"

"I'll have any beer on tap. What about you, Julia?"

"Vodka tonic, please." Turning toward Cole I said, "Quick, tell me what happened today?"

"Well, where should I begin? The day started off with a meeting with one company VP in charge of meetings and got a quick and firm no, followed by meetings with two foundations. One had plans in place for the next two years. The other said maybe. They'd run it by the director and let me know."

"I hope you're not too disappointed."

"Not really. Each time I pitched the center I sounded more confident. Sort of like my old Wall Street days of pitching stocks and bonds to investors. I've got one company and three foundations lined up for tomorrow. At least Hank's name gets me in the door. The rest is up to me."

"Do we need to tweak any part of your presentation?"

"No. Like I said, it's up to me, but it's a hard sell when the place only exists on paper."

"Maybe if you offered a discount for signing early."

The drinks arrived along with a bowl of chips. We must count as regulars by now.

"That's a great suggestion. It might overcome some concerns, but I'd have to run the numbers to find the break-even point. The most important thing is to get a commitment. The following year should be easier if I have a track record."

"You're right. Once the center is a reality, we can advertise all over the country, even Canada. Maybe even the rest of the world." I paused. Cole looked like the cat that swallowed the canary. "What's so funny?"

"Not funny, damn right encouraging. Do you realize you just said we could advertise instead of I could. Sit still, I'm going to see what's on the juke box."

Cole slid in beside me. "This is the best I could do. They don't play songs like, Achy Breaky Heart, in this part of the country."

As the musical introduction to the song finished, I recognized Elvis Presley's voice.

Wise men say, only fools rush in
but I can't help falling in love
with you.

Shall I stay
Would it be a sin
I can't help falling in love with
You.

Like a river flows surely to the sea

Darling so it goes
Some things are meant to be

Take my hand take my whole life
for I can't help falling in love
with you.

"I hope you listened carefully to the words old Elvis sang. The song says it a whole lot better than I ever could." Cole took a long swallow of his drink. "I can't help falling in love with you, Julia."

I was speechless. I knew how he felt. I just choose not to think about it or us. Besides, he'd never put his feelings into words before. I finished my drink placing the glass on the table. What seemed like minutes passed before the silence was broken. When Cole realized, I was going to let his confession pass he changed the subject.

"Want another drink, Julia?"

"No, thanks. One's enough for me."

"Then let's grab a bite to eat and head for your condo. I've got numbers to run before tomorrow's meetings. Elvis or no Elvis."

Cole used my computer to log onto his. He worked at least two hours, while I curled up on the sofa and tried to read a book. I couldn't concentrate. Elvis words keep replaying over and over again in my head. Remembering Cole's words. None of it something I was prepared to deal with.

When I heard the sound of the printer, I got up and walked over to the desk.

"You finished?"

"Yes. I've broken it down as best I could to so much per head. The more heads the less per person. It's a really good deal compared with some of the other conference centers. I just hope I haven't made this too generous." Gathering the copies from the printer and placing them in his brief case, Cole ran his hand across his brow.

"Tired?"

"In a way, but still optimistic. I've got three more days to get the deal done, but even if things don't pan out, I've spent time with you and that's been worth it. Come here."

He reached out his arms and held me close. "You have no idea how much it's meant to have your help. You know, we make a great team. I meant every word of the song, Julia. A day never went by that I didn't think of you, that I didn't miss you."

There was that silly grin again. "I missed you almost as much as old Charger did."

He kissed me and I was lost. The wall I'd erected between us came crumbling down. Tonight, I wanted him. I wasn't thinking about tomorrow. If truth be told, I wanted him from the moment I saw him at my door.

As Cole began to make love to me, I realized how much I'd missed his touch, the feel of his body close to mine. His rough calloused hands caressing my body. Was this love? No, not now, I don't want to go there.

Half awake, half asleep, content with Cole's arm was wrapped around my waist, holding me close. This was heaven until I realized what time it was. No matter how much I hurried, I was going to be late for work. I put one foot on the floor as Cole opened his eyes.

"Good morning, Your Highness, where are you going?"

"I'm late. I have to go to work."

He reached out and pulled me back to bed. "If you're late you might as well be good and late. This is more important to our future and a lot more fun." He began to run his hand over my body and I no longer cared what time it was.

As a nod, once again, to Cole's heartfelt conservation speech, we saved water by showering together. A really sexy sensation I'd never experience before. We downed a quick cup of coffee and hurried off, each to our own day's calling. Any passerby looking at the two of us, noticing our silly grins, the kiss before we went off in different directions, the joy in our steps wouldn't have to guess the reason. Cole promised to call if anything happened.

I entered the office trying to reach my desk before running into anyone. No such luck. George was standing in the hall outside my office talking to one of the sales staff.

"You certainly look happy this morning, Julia. Not your usual business-like manner."

Good God, I felt sure he could see the look of embarrassment on my face as I tried to concentrate on what my boss was saying.

"I was about to leave you a note. Doug Jones of Sterling Inc. has been trying to get in touch with you for the last two hours. He finally called me, but he won't talk to anyone but you. I suggest you put whatever happened last night that put that smile on your face behind you and call him. Oh, yes, somebody called David Harrington, has been trying to get in touch with you too. Lady, I don't have time to take your phone calls."

After the awkward scene with George, I picked up the phone, my cheeks still hot. I settled the problem with Doug Jones. No big deal. I knew I should call David, but I put it off and spent the rest of the day waiting to hear from Cole.

By five, when he hadn't called, I started for home, stopping at the grocery to pick up a few things for dinner. It was after six before I received a text from Cole saying he was running late. He probably wouldn't be home for a while.

Had he run into old friends? Maybe he even called his ex-wife? All kinds of suspicions were running through my head. The pitfalls, I thought, of caring for someone. The knock on the door didn't come until well past ten.

As I stood beside the open door, Cole reached over and gave me a big kiss on the forehead. I could smell the alcohol on his breath.

"You've been drinking."

"Absolutely. I'm three sheets to the wind and happy as can be. You're my lucky charm."

"What are you talking about?"

"Hank and I had an extra-long happy hour celebrating the two foundations I signed up today for conventions to be held at the yet unnamed-conference center, and I love you," his words were slurred. "Have I told you today I love you, well, if I haven't' let me tell you now how much I love you? I told Hank I loved you a thousand times and he says he loves you, too."

"Take off your coat silly and sit down before you fall down and tell me what happened."

"What happened is I'm getting the loan, so if the dam don't break and the river don't flood, we've got ourselves plan A. Oh, and I love you."

Before I could say another word, Cole put his head back against the sofa pillows and fell asleep. I took off his shoes, undid his tie and tried to make him comfortable. When I finally got his legs up on the sofa, he moved around until he was lying flat on his back, sound asleep. I put a blanket over him and decided there was nothing else to be learned tonight. Cole could tell me all about it in the morning.

Sometime in the early morning hours, I felt him near me. I fell back asleep, happy.

Cole was still fast asleep when I crawled out of bed. It wasn't until I was about to leave that I heard him stir.

"God, I feel awful. My head's pounding. Do you have any aspirin?"

"I think there's a bottle in the medicine cabinet. I'm not surprised your head hurts." I laughed. He looked terrible as he pulled himself out of bed and with an unsteady gait walked toward the doorway. I felt sorry for him as he stood holding on to the door frame in his jockey shorts and tee shirt, his hair tousled, still half asleep.

"You were dead drunk."

"Forgive me. I hope I didn't make an ass of myself. I don't even remember how I got here. Hank and I started out celebrating and it's all sort of hazy from there."

"Nothing to forgive. Congratulations on the loan. Take a couple of aspirins. A cold shower should help. I made coffee. I've got to go or I'll be late again. Hope you feel better."

"I couldn't feel any worse. I'll take your suggestions, but first I think I'll crawl back into bed. I'll call you later."

I was glad my day was busy leaving me little time to think about the week coming to an end. Cole would be leaving, only this time it wouldn't be so easy to put him out of my mind.

He phoned in the late afternoon saying he had just finishing signing a raft of papers at the bank. He'd meet me at home. We were going out to celebrate.

The conversation ended with Cole asking me to take tomorrow off, his last day. He'd be leaving on the red eye. He insisted we had a lot to get straight between us.

Cole waited in the living room while I changed. He glanced up as I entered the room. "Wow. You look elegant, Your Highness. You really are beautiful, Pretty Lady, beautiful whether its jeans and no makeup or the way you look tonight."

"Thank you. That's very nice. For a lonesome cowboy, you do have a way with words, but you haven't told me where we're going."

"*Le Bernardin*. Hank recommended it as the best French food in town." With a broad grin he looked straight at me, "and I know you're an expert in French cooking."

I let him get away with the reminder of my comments about learning to cook in France. "I've heard it's great food, but I'm sure it's really pricy."

"Everything in this city is, but I want us to celebrate and you deserve the best. Besides, think of all the money I saved on hotel rooms. Come on. We don't want to be late."

Chapter 27

I was in no rush to get up. I found myself trying to forget Cole was leaving. Breakfast conversation was a little strained, both of us reluctant to admit we'd be saying goodbye by day's end.

"Want to take a walk, Julia? I've something I want to suggest, but I need to put my thoughts in order. A little fresh air should help."

We walked along, not saying a word. Cole seemed deep in thought. His head tilted slightly downward paying no attention to where we were walking without a destination in mind. When Rockefeller center came into view, I realized how far we'd walked. I suggested we stop for hot chocolate at the café overlooking the rink. It would feel good to sit down for a bit. I was tired and something hot in my stomach would feel good. The morning was really cold.

"You ever ice skate as a kid, Julia?"

"No, I did ballet."

"In one of those cute little tutu's? I bet you looked adorable."

"Don't laugh. My mother told me I looked like an angel in my pink tutu. She even proclaimed me the star of one Christmas performance of the Nutcracker. How about you? Did you ever try ice skating?"

"Nope. Too busy learning to rope steers."

"It does look like fun. What do you think, I'm game if you are? I'm sure they rent skates."

"No way, Julia. I'm not about to go out there and make an ass of myself."

We watched the skaters for a while. I realized I'd never been to the center before, not even to see the world-famous Christmas tree.

"Want another chocolate or are you ready to go home?"

"I'm ready, but I'm not walking another step. It's either the bus or a cab."

I hung up my jacket asking, "Ready for lunch?"

"Lunch can wait. It's time we have the conversation you keep putting off. We need to talk about whether or not we have a future together."

I started to walk away. That was one conversation I wasn't ready for.

"Don't leave. You can't keep walking away forever. We've got to settle this once and for all. I've been giving a lot of thought to trying to come up with a solution you'd be comfortable with. It's something we have to decide now, not something we can discuss over the phone. You have to look me in the eye and say yes or no., Okay?"

I began to feel very uncomfortable as he continued. My fingers curling and uncurling as I tried to listen without letting my emotions be involved.

"First Julia, you know I'd marry you in a minute if you'd have me. I understand you're scared about commitments, and to tell the truth, I don't want to go through being hurt either.

Cole motioned me to sit beside him. "Here's what I've been thinking. Let's move in together, give it a year. If we still feel the same way about each other after a year's time, we'll get married. If it doesn't work out, we can both walk away as friends. No hurt feelings. Look, I know you've never once said you loved me, but I know we wouldn't be sharing a bed if you didn't have some feelings for me."

I looked at Cole in disbelief. "You're serious."

"Yes. I'm dead serious."

"That's impossible. You live in Montana and I live in New York. What are you talking about?"

"I'm asking you to come to Montana. We're so good together, Julia. Not only that, we make a great business team. There'd be so much you could do marketing the new project. Things you're so much better at than I could ever be."

I couldn't believe what I was hearing. "Let me get this straight, you're seriously asking me to move to Montana?"

"What I'm asking is for you to take a chance on love. Take the leap of faith that we could build a great life together, raise a family, have what everyone hopes to find...a lifetime partner to love."

I got up and walked to the window, my safe zone. I hadn't expected this.

"You're asking me to give up everything, move to Montana and help you make your project a success. I was surprised, dumbfounded. I admit the tone of my response sounded caustic as I said, "What do I get out of the deal?"

"I know you don't mean that, Julia. You're just putting your guard up. What you get is a chance at happiness. Look, keep your condo, lease it out, ask your boss for a leave of absence. Anytime you're not happy, you're free to go, free to come back to your condo, your job, but for God's sake, isn't it worth taking a chance."

Cole came and stood behind me, his arm around my waist.

"I knew you had no idea what real love was all about when we made love for the first time. Knew you'd never felt the way you felt with me before, Roger or no Roger.

How will you feel if twenty years from now you're alone with only a job to occupy your time and energy? Think you'll regret not having the courage to take a chance? That you threw away the possibility of real happiness for a condo and a job? Think New York will be enough on the cold winter nights you spend alone in your bed?"

I could feel the tears begin to run down my cheeks I wanted to say yes, but somehow, I just couldn't bring myself to say the word.

Cole held me in his arms.

"I want to say yes, but I'm so scared."

"What are you scared of? Your feelings for me, or what?"

"In a way, yes, but what will my family think about us living together? My father will be horrified. What about your friends?"

"Dry your eyes and think about Sassy. She didn't give a damn what people thought. Her love for my dad was all that mattered. They had ten wonderful years together. Do you think she would have traded that for what some busybody or her family had to say? I don't think so."

Cole brushed the hair from my face as he lifted my chin, our eyes met. "I have to leave tonight, that's a given. When I get home, I'll be up to my ears in work. This whole project is on a very tight schedule. I have to be ready to break ground as soon as it starts to thaw. I'll compromise. I won't press you for an answer today."

Thank God I thought. I needed time to think. So many thoughts swirled around in my head.

"Julia, I understand you well enough to know you don't act impulsively. You're more comfortable thinking with your head rather than your heart and it's not like I'm asking you for a date to the prom. I'm asking for a lifetime commitment. One I'm more than ready to make. That said, let's make a deal. I'll wait until mid-February, let's say Valentine's Day, for your answer, but I can't keep waiting, hoping forever. If you're going to break my heart, please do it by February."

I didn't know what to say. I felt helpless. He was putting me in the one place I didn't want to be. I'd have to make a decision, as Cole put it, a plain and simple yes or no.

"I'll relent, Julia, and make it even easier for you. Just leave a message. You don't have to talk to me. If the answer is no, then that will end it for me. I won't bother you again. If it's yes, then all you have to say is when and I'll be there as fast as the old truck will go. But please, please, Julia, don't throw our chance away."

Cole walked away. I could tell the conversation was over. "How about you fix us something to eat while I pack."

Chapter 28

When the door closed behind Cole, I stood in the hall feeling a sense of anguish. I didn't know what to say in those last few awkward moments, and just like that he was gone. I let him go without so much as a goodbye.

I spent a sleepless night, pulling the covers over my head hoping to block out the morning sun. Cole's words, as he left yesterday, still rang in my ears. The scent of his aftershave remained on his pillow. I wasn't ready to get up and face the day. Around noon, I put on a robe, made a pot of coffee and wandered around the apartment, lost. I missed our mornings together. Damn it, I missed him.

Why did he have to come back into my life? I'd managed to put Montana behind me. Damn it, everything was fine until he showed up. Maybe I wasn't what one would call happy, but I was busy, more or less content.

Cole's probing questions were forcing me to take stock of my life, my future, go places I didn't want to go. He was making me face what my future might hold, and he'd given me only a few short weeks to make the most important decision of my life. Damn him,

I stretched out on the sofa. I didn't want to think about Cole today. I'd think about everything tomorrow and turned on the television. I flipped from channel to channel, only to find one football game after another, I tried scrolling through the channels again, but everything seemed so insipid. At last I came across an old film on Turner Classic Movies. I'd forgotten movies used to be in black and white. Life seemed so much simpler then, love conquered all. The hero came home from the war and everybody lived happily ever after.

Tears ran down my cheeks at the end of the film. Why was I crying over a dumb movie? Or did my tears have little to do with the picture?

I never bothered to get dressed, just wandered around the apartment lost for the rest of the day and went to bed early. At least sleep would end my jumble of thoughts.

Dad called on Sunday to say the house had sold. The closing was in thirty days. He asked about my job and we chatted for a bit. I never mentioned Cole. He seemed happy his moving to the city would mean we could spend more time together. He had someone he wanted me to meet.

Monday. Thank God for the office. It meant an escape. I had no time to think about anything except work, only the desk calendar reminded me of my Valentine Day deadline.

The lunch meeting I had with a new client didn't go well, I couldn't concentrate on the task at hand, and barely touched my food.

Friday came and went and I faced another weekend alone. Saturday morning, David called.

"Hey, Julia, you haven't returned any of my calls. I was hoping we could get together."

I really didn't want to talk with him, but I would have to sooner or later. "I'm really sorry, David. I meant to call you, but it's been hectic. I've had a house guest this week."

"You're excused. I haven't given up on you as yet, not ready to accept our budding relationship as a lost cause even though you missed out on a great trip to Aruba. The weather was fantastic. I've called because I've been invited to spend a week, over the President's holiday, aboard a friend's yacht in Florida. I'd like to take you along. They're great people and it should be fun. We'd be chaperoned more or less. There'd be no way I could take you out to sea and have my way with you. Just kidding, I'm not that kind of guy. So what do you think? Would you like to come along?"

"That sounds very nice, David. I just don't know if I can take the time away from the office. "I'll let you know in a few days, I need to check my work calendar."

"Great. It sounds as if there's hope for me after all. Maybe we can do dinner before then. Call me."

"I promise. I'll be in touch in a few days."

I hung up the phone wondering why I didn't just say no. David wasn't what I wanted. I needed to be honest with him. I wasn't interested in seeing him again. I told myself it had nothing to do with Cole.

February arrived. The deadline was creeping up. Sunday had turned out to be one of those rare warm sunny days in the middle of winter. I had a strange desire to go for a walk in Central Park. So far, I'd put off any decision regarding Cole's proposal, but time was getting short and if nothing else, I owed him a yes or no answer. I kept telling myself it was ridiculous to even consider rushing off to Montana. I was happy her. This is where I belonged, but something kept bubbling up just beneath the surface.

The park was crowded with joggers and walkers, couples strolling along the paths, people sitting on blankets spread out on the rare grassy areas, everyone enjoying a welcome break from the cold of winter. A few trees had started to sprout leaves. Here was a beautiful world I'd never experienced before Cole.

I had no idea how far I'd walked, my mind running wild in all directions. I spied an unoccupied bench and decided to sit for a while and watch the people pass by, remembering the fun Cole and I had picnicking on a cold January day. Somehow, here alone, without Cole, a large part of the magic was gone.

Flashbacks kept returning of my time at the ranch, how I hated every minute of it until I stopped fighting the surroundings and let my guard down and began to enjoy the beauty and solitude. I could see Bear, his tail wagging at the sight of me. I remembered how much I enjoyed riding Charger, his long easy stride taking us for miles of rolling pasture, the snowcapped mountains in the distance, listening to birds singing, watching cows and calves grazing, swimming in the lake. It wasn't the middle of nowhere, the ranch as I recalled Cole describing it was in the middle of God's country. Maybe he saw it that way, but there was no kidding myself, the ranch was miles from anything or anybody. Absolutely the middle of nowhere.

With nowhere to go I'd learned to slow down, to enjoy my surroundings, and as Cole put it, "to smell the roses." I remember laughing, feeling happy and at peace, laughing. Something's I hadn't felt since I've been back, except for the week Cole was here. And God help me, I remembered the sensual nights in his bed and mine.

I sat for the longest time, finally willing myself not to remember anything else. Everything was all too confusing. The temperature began to drop as the sun hid behind the clouds. Time to head for home.

I poured myself a glass of wine and picked up the Sunday newspaper, my eyes drawn to the date on the masthead, February ninth. I had five days left to give Cole my answer.

For some reason the subway seemed more crowded than usual on Monday morning, positive the guy behind me was rubbing against me on purpose. I moved further down the crowded car trying to find a spot to squeeze into, but no one was interested in giving me any space. We were all in a hurry to get to work on time. The paycheck never enough to cover the city's high cost of living. Pushing, shoving, and rushing from place to place were all part of living in New York. No wonder everyone was so short tempered.

I pushed my way off the car at my station and headed up the long flight of stairs. When I reached the sidewalk, rain had begun to fall. Without my umbrella, I hurried as fast as I could, hoping to get to the office before I was drenched.

I spent the whole day at my desk trying to avoid looking at the calendar. The constant reminder my day of reckoning was fast approaching. True to his word, I hadn't heard from Cole. It might have been easier if I had, but he was going to leave the answer to me. I had to make the decision all on my own.

I called David making it clear, no matter how much I enjoyed the time we spent together, what he was suggesting was not an arrangement I was comfortable with. Telling him, his interest in me was very flattering and he was good company, but it wouldn't be fair to lead him on."

"I'm really disappointed, Julia. I'd imagined we'd share a long and enjoyable relationship. You seemed different. Maybe that difference was the big attraction, but I'll never know, will I."

We chatted for a few more minutes before ending the conversation. I felt relieved. David's friends with benefits wasn't what I wanted out of life. Good lord, what did I want?

Thursday rather than head for the subway, I walked around the corner to the cocktail lounge Cole and I had stopped at. I found an empty booth and slid into the seat just as the barmaid approached. "You want to order now, honey or wait for lover boy?"

"I'll have a glass of Chardonnay, and I'm not waiting for anyone."

"Hope it's not splitsville with you two. He looked like a keeper to me, but then I've been wrong before. Twice divorced"

Why I returned to the lounge or why I put money in the jukebox to hear Elvis sing again was hard to explain. Was I looking for ways to make up my mind or trying to convince myself Cole and I lived in two different worlds?

I finished my drink and hailed a cab. It had begun to drizzle. Besides, I wasn't in any mood to cope with the subway.

Pushing the plate of half-eaten scrambled eggs aside, I sat at the table for the longest time, my thoughts running in all directions. Food held no interest. All I could think of was my telephone call to Cole tomorrow night. I'd spent hours the last few nights in bed half asleep rehearsing what I was going to say when I called. Trying to find the best way to say no without hurting him, maybe leaving the door ajar a tad if I changed my mind. I'd awake in the morning exhausted without a final conclusion.

The more I tried to frame an answer the more words failed me. The more I knew it had to be a yes or no, that there wasn't room for maybe, the more I began to panic. I had to call. I couldn't just blow him off.

I grabbed a muffler and my winter coat and decided to go for a walk. I needed to get out of the apartment. There was a refreshing chill in the night air, the city aglow in bright lights, tall skyscrapers, as far as the eye could see. The moonlight reflected off glass walls of the tall buildings. A steady stream of traffic filled the streets. The constant sound of horns honking as impatient New Yorkers vented their frustrations.

I was enjoying the excitement off nighttime in the city, enjoying walking past crowded restaurants, hearing music coming from the gay bar on the corner. Montana had none of this to offer. The peanut shell laden floor of the Longbarn couldn't begin to compete with what was within walking distance of my condo.

Then there was Cole. I wouldn't allow myself to think about him in terms of love. What did that over-used word mean anyhow? Yes, I felt alive in his company and I realized I only laughed when I was with him. Yes, I admired his strength, his straight arrow approach to life, and loved the little boy he could be sometimes. I loved his sense of humor, and couldn't deny the way my body reacted when he kissed me, when he made love to me. No one I'd met, not even Roger, could hold a candle to him. Was that enough to compensate for being isolated from everything I'd known and loved?

I remembered the morning we left the building together, Cole in his suit and tie with a brief case in hand. We'd kissed before we went our separate ways for the day. If only he'd move back to New York, everything would be so simple. I'd say yes in a minute. We'd have everything -- well-paying jobs, my condo, enough money to take advantage of all that New York had to offer.

I'd walked for what felt like hours. Realizing the time was getting late, I turned and walked back toward my building. As I passed the tall buildings they suddenly seemed to loom like giant trees in a forest. Sassy's words came rushing back to me. Was I missing the forest for the trees?"

Remembering the trip to Yellowstone brought back the sweet smell of pine needles. I remembered the varied aromas of the ranch. The pasture grass and wild flowers, the smell of the cattle, horse sweat, all triggering a nerve and bringing a sense of contentment. I took a deep breath as my nostrils filled with the pungent smell of diesel fumes and auto exhaust. No wonder no one opened their windows. In the City you didn't snuggle under the covers as the cool fresh night air billowed in though open windows.

The doorman greeted me as I returned. Exiting the elevator I walked down the hall to my unit slipping the key in the lock. Closing the door behind me I stood in the hall and looked around. Everything was new, the upscale kitchen, down the hall the bathroom's huge shower, the soaking tub, and sinks in the middle of the long wide marble counter top. Cable television, cell phone service. Everything anyone could ask for.

The ranch house was old, nothing had changed since 1950s, the only exception being the fabulous patio with its modern outdoor kitchen and barbeque. I'd bet anything, the patio was Sassy's addition to the house. The kitchen was dated, with old tired appliances, a bathroom without a stall shower. I'd be crazy to give up everything I had here for Cole and the Longbarn Bar and Grill on a Saturday night.

Who was I kidding? Sure, I'd miss all the luxuries of my condo and all that New York had to offer, but how could I give up the one thing I'd fought so hard achieve--my independence. God knows Cole was set in his ways. Who would give in? Was love and even passion that might fade worth it?

Chapter 29

Dreaded Friday, February 14th arrived. One way or the other I would always remember Valentine's Day. I hung my coat in the closet, put my purse on top of the dresser, and changed out of my work clothes. My hands were shaking as I reached into the refrigerator, taking out what was left of a bottle of Merlot. Carrying a wine glass in one hand and the bottle in the other, I sat down at my desk and opened the top drawer. There, sitting on top of a stack of papers was the note pad I'd been scribbling on for days, the checklist of the things I needed to say to Cole before I gave him my answer.

I'd picked up the phone twice to dial Cole's number only to put it down both times. I almost finished a second glass of wine hoping it would give me courage before I finally called Cole. The phone rang several times before the answering machine picked up.

"This is Cole. Leave a message and I'll get back to you."

The sound of his voice brought tears to my eyes, but I breathed a sigh of relief knowing I didn't have to talk to him.

I heard, "At the tone please record your message. When you are finished, you may hang up to end the call."

"Hi, Cole, it's me." I hesitated. "I've been giving a lot of thought to your proposal, I've had a lot of reservations about how it could work. I love my job, I have my condo, my family would be unhappy, and lots of things could go wrong."

By now the tears had turned to sobs. It seemed like forever before I could get the next words out. I took a deep breath, scared to death of what I was about to say next.

"Cole, all the words,..." That's as far as I got as the answering machine cut off. In a panic I dialed the number again needing to finish the rest of what I wanted to say. I waited as the phone rang, again his familiar voice saying, "This is Cole, leave a message and I'll get back to you."

What I heard next was, "Sorry your message cannot be recorded. The message box is full. Try again later."

No. No. This can't be happening. Cole wouldn't hear my answer. He'd think I was going to say no. When in spite of all my concerns I was about to say yes. God, what do I do now?

I dialed his number again, hoping he'd pick up the phone, but I got the same recording. No, no I said over and over again. This can't be happening. I banged my fist on the desk so hard it sent the wine glass flying, leaving droplets of red wine on the white carpet.

Stupid, stupid, stupid. Why didn't you just say yes and leave all the rest of the dribble for another day. No, in your own childish way you had to remind him of all you were giving up. Believing he had to understand all you would be sacrificing for him. Now for sure he wasn't going to answer the phone. Why couldn't I stop crying? What should I do? What could I do?

I started to pace up and down the living room. I kept dialing his number every few minutes, before I realized with two hours difference in time, he was probably out checking on the horses or feeding Bear. I'd wait a few hours and try again.

I called again before I got ready for bed and got the same damn message. No point in going to bed. I knew I'd never fall sleep. I was a nervous wreck. At midnight I called again. Cole didn't answer. He'd turned off the answering machine. I hug up and waited a few minutes and dialed again. He still didn't pick up. There was no use sending him an email. If he wasn't going to answer my phone calls, he sure as hell wasn't going to open an email.

Panic set in. I told myself just keep calling until he was so annoyed, he had to answer. It took three tries letting the phone ring forever before Cole finally answered.

"Julia, stop calling.'

"Don't hang up, please. I didn't get to finish what I wanted to say. Your answering machine cut me off. Please, Cole hear me out.

"I got your message. There's nothing to say. You said it all. Goodnight."

"No. No, please don't hang up. That was my head talking, I don't know why I needed to tell you all my reasons for concern. Just stupid and childish, I guess. Cole, my heart says yes, a million times yes. I love you, I've been miserable ever since you left, and yes I'm coming. My guard is down. Don't say anything. I'll call you tomorrow when I calm down and have things sorted out. All you need to know is I love you and I'm coming as soon as I can."

My hands were shaking by the time I hung up the phone. I knew I had to give it a try. For weeks I'd been kidding myself, when the truth was, I knew I loved him, I missed him and I couldn't imagine what life would be like without him. I remembered Sassy telling me, it's not where you live, but who you live with.

I lay down on the bed, mentally exhausted. I don't know whether it was the wine on an empty stomach or the sheer relief of having made the decision, but I slept sounder than I had in months. I knew there'd be some rough spots, but I could hardly wait now that I'd made up my mind to see Cole again.

On Monday I asked for an appointment with my boss. His secretary said she'd squeeze me in after lunch. My next call was to George Ryan, the real estate agent my father used to buy the condo. I told him I wanted to lease the condo for a year, furnished or unfurnished, it didn't matter. I'd be gone in two weeks. He assured me it wouldn't be a problem. Once we agreed on the price he said, "I guarantee you'll have a signed lease on your condo by the end of the day. I have several clients looking for a place like yours."

The last call was to my dad. I asked him to have lunch with me one day this week figuring it would be easier telling him my plans in a crowded restaurant.

Next, I checked flights to Billings and purchased a one-way ticket for fourteen days from today. March 3rd would be the start of my noble experiment, lovers with benefits.

The next two weeks would be busy, too busy to think about changing my mind. Funny, I no longer felt nervous or concerned. A huge weight had been lifted, the decision made. The time couldn't pass fast enough. I called Sassy, impatient for her to answer.

"Julia, how nice to hear from you. Are you well?"

"I've never been better, but I have a favor to ask. Could you pick me up at the airport on the third of March? My flight gets in at three o'clock."

"Of course, my dear. I'd be delighted. Just one question, what took so long?"

I couldn't help laughing. "I'll tell you all about it when I get there. Thanks again."

The meeting with my boss went as well as could be expected under the circumstances. I gave him my two-week notice. He was surprised, of course, and disappointed. After all, I hadn't been with the firm a full year. He thought some other agency had snapped me up. When I explained it was a personal matter and I might want my job back in a year he offered no promises, but told me to check with him first.

I rushed home to call Cole. He picked up on the first ring.

"Julia, I've been walking on air since your call. You're really coming? You're not going to change your mind?"

I related all the things I'd already accomplished.

"You mean you really quit your job?"

"Yes, and I've made my plane reservations. One way. No return ticket."

"Maybe you really do love me."

"I spoke with Sassy. She'll meet me at the airport at three on the third of March. I'll wait for you at her house."

"I need you Julia, this is going to be the longest two weeks of my life."

We talked forever, neither one of us wanting to hang up, until Cole said, "Gotta' run, Babe. I still have horses and Bear to feed and a million things to get done before you arrive. I'll call you tomorrow evening. By the way, Your Highness, I love you."

Chapter 30

Arriving a few minutes early I was seated at the table I'd reserved at the Four Seasons nervously waiting for my father to arrive. The popular luncheon place was jam packed. Every table taken. I ordered a glass of Chardonnay trying to formulate the proper words to tell dad what I was planning. I knew he wouldn't be happy no matter how carefully I crafted my intentions. .

I didn't have to wait long. My father, as usual, was prompt. He leaned over and kissed me on the cheek, before settling into the chair across from me.

"This is a wonderful idea, Julia. We should do this more often. How are you, dear?"

"I'm fine, Dad, thank you."

"And your job? Are you still enjoying working at, what's was the name of the agency again?"

The waiter arrived with the menu. Father ordered a dry martini, careful to request his favorite brand of gin and the exact amount of vermouth.

"So my dear, we haven't spoken in some time. Fill me in on what's happening in your life. Still enjoying your condo?"

I swallowed hard. There was no way to sugar coat my plans. I blurted out, "I'm moving to Montana, Dad."

"I'm sorry, dear, did you just say you're moving to Montana?"

"Yes."

The look on my father's face was one of bewilderment. "I don't understand."

"It's a very long story, Dad, but I've met a wonderful man, and I've fallen in love. I'm leaving in March to be with him."

"Whoa, back up." His steely eyes looked right through me. "Where did you meet this individual? Montana you say? I bet your Aunt Sarah had something to do with this?" Taking a long drink of his martini, almost emptying the glass, he said. "I should have known better."

My stomach began to feel queasy. I knew the rest of my announcement wouldn't be an easier, nor did I have any reason to believe my father would understand. I'd never confronted him before. "In a way, yes, she's involved."

I watched Dad try to regain his composure. It wouldn't be like him to make a scene in a public place. This obviously came as a shock to him.

"You do seem to be rushing into this. Not at all behaving like the sensible girl I know you to be. Why haven't you mentioned this individual before? Where and when is this wedding taking place? You could at least have given the family a chance to meet him. "

Dad was confused, hurt, not used to my making decisions without consulting him.

"Julia, this is all too sudden. At the very least you should have spoken to me first. I'm your father."

He finished the last of his drink as he looked at me with the same expression, he used to correct me when I was a child.

"Usually, though it may seem a bit old fashioned, its customary to ask the father for his daughter's hand."

"I know this comes as a surprise, Dad. It surprised me too, but sometimes you have to follow your heart."

"Poppycock."

I drank the last of my wine and almost considered a second glass, but I knew the worst was yet to come.

"You still haven't told me anything. Does this mean you'd be moving to Montana for good?"

I took a deep breath and hoped I didn't start to cry. From the look on my father's face, he seemed devastated that he'd been kept in the dark.

"I'm sure you're not going to appreciate or even understand what I'm about to tell you, Dad, but I'll try and do my best to explain. Please don't interrupt before I'm finished."

I inhaled. Wondering if the words I was about to speak would test the bonds between us.

"His name is Cole Clayton. He owns a large cattle ranch a couple of hours outside of Billings. Right now, he's in the process of building a conference center on his property and, yes, if everything works out, it would mean living in Montana forever."

I could see my father processing what I'd just told him.

"The lawyer in me is listening carefully to your every word, Julia, but something is missing here."

Hoping for the best, but expecting the worst I dropped the bombshell. "You're right, something is missing, it's the part about a wedding you're not hearing. We've agreed to live together for a year. If things work out, we'll be married then."

The look on my father's face was not a surprise. Thank God we were out in public or he would have exploded. I could see the veins at his temple throbbing.

"I'm beyond disappointed in you, Julia."

The tone of his voice was biting, his look like a knife to my heart.

"I can't believe you'd agree to anything so stupid. Have you lost your mind, child?" He motioned to the waiter to bring him another drink, not bothering to ask if I cared for a re-fill.

"If he won't marry you now, what makes you think he'll be any more likely to marry you in a year? There's an old saying, though I admit its rather crude, why buy the cow if she's already giving you the milk for free."

"He offered to marry me, Dad. It's what he wanted all along, I'm the one who's hesitant."

"Well, if you don't love him enough to marry him now, do you think it's going to be better a year from now?"

Dad was beginning to lose control. His voice was getting louder, his cheeks were flush, you'd have thought I was telling him I'd robbed a bank.

"Really, Julia, for a smart young woman I don't understand how you could even consider such an arrangement."

"You don't understand. I'm not sure about marrying anyone. I need to know this is for real before I commit. I knew this would upset you, but I'm a big girl. I need to make my own decisions."

"But, my daughter, living with a man she's not married to. Thank God your mother's not alive to hear this. Have you even spoken to your sister or your brothers?"

People were beginning to stare as his voice could be heard above the noise. The menus still unopened, Dad shooed the waiter away. I tried to smile. Tried to bring the volume of the conversation back a notch without much success. He was fuming.

"No, I haven't spoken to them as yet, but I know you'll like him when you meet him and so will they."

"At the moment, Julia, I don't see myself agreeing to such a meeting. I don't have much respect for the man. How much do you know about him anyway?

He pushed back his chair and reached for his wallet throwing two twenty-dollar bills on the table. "I promise I'll be checking into the man's background," he shouted as he turned and walked away from the table. "I don't want to hear anymore."

I felt every eye in the room was on me as the tears began to run down my cheeks. The waiter approached and asked if I was ready to order. I pointed to the money and walked out unable to say a word for the lump in my throat. The meeting with Dad was even more unpleasant than I'd expected. This was something I couldn't share with Cole. I needed to keep it to myself.

Trying to balance work and the long list of things I had to accomplish in the few remaining days was taking it's toll. As many items as I'd check off the list, dozens more remained.

The condo was leased. The new occupants were to take possession on March 15th. The moving company was slated to begin packing and storing everything I left behind. The telephone needed to be disconnected, insurance policies changed, friends and clients called.

By some miracle, when the third arrived, everything was done, and I was on my way to the airport, two suitcases jammed full in the trunk of the cab. The few things I couldn't carry on the plane had been boxed and were on their way via the postal service. No turning back now.

Exhausted, I fell asleep as soon as the plane's wheels left the ground. I awoke to hear the pilot announce we were twenty minutes from landing. The stewardess, busy collecting articles to be discarded, making sure all tray tables were up, and seat belts in place, meant my journey was over. This was the beginning of an adventure. The tearing down of all the walls I'd erected these past few years to keep emotions and commitment out. I was ready to build a future with the man I loved. I watched as the city came into view.

With a feeling of excitement, and only a few butterflies in my stomach, I walked toward the baggage claim, easily spotting Sassy.

"Good to see you, Julia. Believe it or not, it's been almost a year since I met you here for the first time. I'm surprised it took you this long to come to your senses. Follow along. I'm parked close by."

I placed my cases in the car and climbed in alongside my aunt.

"How are you, Sassy? You look fabulous as usual."

"I'm fine, my dear. Cole called to say he'd be here around five. I was hoping we'd have more time to spend together, but I understand how anxious he is to see you. Tell me how my brother reacted to your decision."

"Exactly as you would expect...furious, hurt, questioning my morals as well as my judgment."

"Don't be too concerned. He'll come around sooner or later. You're the apple of his eye. He'll feel different once he meets Cole. I'm sure he considers this my fault and I'll gladly accept the blame."

Sassy stopped the car in front of the familiar surroundings of her home suggesting I leave my cases in the trunk for Cole to remove. She unlocked the front door. "Would you like a snack?" As you know it's a long drive to the ranch. I understand they don't even serve peanuts on planes any more. I remember when flying was a dress up affair, and people were treated like royalty rather than cattle."

"A snack sounds great."

We sat at the breakfast room table, a teapot between us.

"I fully approve of you two taking time to make sure the relationship works. Divorce can be such a messy affair, especially if children are involved."

"I'm glad somebody understands."

"You understand it's going to be a big change from city life, and all that you've been used to. A month's visit is a lot different than a lifetime. As for Cole, his divorce knocked the pins out from underneath him. It's a leap of faith for him, too.

"He's only spoken of her once."

"Oh, he's well over her. My concern was he'd never trust another woman again. I knew after spending a few days with you that you two were meant for each other. You have as many trust issues as he does. I'm positive you'll make a go of it. You're the kind of woman he is looking for.

"I hope I can meet him half way."

"No, Julia, never half way. Relationships only work when you're willing to give at least sixty percent. If each of you is prepared to put the other first, meeting them more than halfway, the relationship can't fail."

"I worry about hurting him."

"How could you hurt him? You love him."

"For one thing, I'm a worried I'll miss New York, having a job, places to go. I'm not sure I can be happy being dependent."

"Rubbish. Besides from what I hear about the conference center, you'll have a full-time job."

I looked at my watch -- a little after five. Cole would be here, soon. As I helped Sassy clear the table, my mind was working overtime. No matter how many times I swore I'd changed, was I really capable of throwing caution to the wind and leading with my heart instead of my head.

Sassy asked about the center and I was telling her all I knew. I stopped speaking in mid-sentence when I heard the old truck belching as Cole stopped in the driveway. Without giving it a second thought, I did what my heart wanted and flung open the front door running down the steps into Cole's outstretched arms. "Hold me tight. Tell me I'm home. Promise you'll never let me go."

"Your home in my arms where you belong, and I promise I'll never let you go."

"Let's head for the ranch. Let's not waste a minute."

"You're sure Sassy won't mind if we just take off?"

"I assure you she'll understand."

In less than five minutes, Cole had thrown my suitcases in the tailgate, we'd said goodbye to Sassy, and were on our way home. Her last words brought a smile to Cole's face as she wagged her finger at him. "I'm warning you both, Hank and I are watching you. Don't disappoint us. Were counting on you two to enjoy all the years of happiness we wished we'd had."

I wondered if she saw me as a younger version of herself and Cole as his father. Was she reliving her past through us?

I sat close to Cole feeling the warmth of his body, my hand resting on his leg.

"I can't believe you're really here. The whole time I was driving to town I kept thinking I'd pull up to Sassy's house and she'd tell me you'd changed your mind at the last minute. You can be sure, woman, I'm never letting you out of my sight. I've been seriously thinking of taking away your shoes so you can't run off."

"Really, Cole, where would I go. I've burned all my bridges behind me. Tell me all about the project. What's happening? Anything new at the ranch?"

"Well, the grading's done and they've begun laying the foundation in between snow storms. The weather has slowed the progress a bit, but John promised to put on a few extra men as soon as the weather clears to make up for lost time." We'll drive out there tomorrow so you can have a look."

Cole had one arm around me and the other on the steering wheel. He turned and smiled as he drove off the road and stopped the truck.

"Is something wrong?"

"Nothing this can't fix." He reached over and kissed me, holding me in his arms. "Sorry, I couldn't wait. God, for once I wish the old truck had a back seat. You look so damned sexy sitting there. He kissed me again and pulled back onto the highway. "Hold on. I might break a speed limit or two, getting us back home."

We sped along for miles before Cole spoke again.

"Juanita's gone home for the evening. I've told her all about you. She's looking forward to meeting you, but beware, she's a little over protective of me. She's worked for us on and off since I was a kid. If you reach in the back there's a basket full of sandwiches Juanita made.

I placed the basket on my lap and peeled back the napkin covering the contents -- neatly wrapped sandwiches, chips, cookies, and a thermos.

"Grab a sandwich and hand me one. I'm starved. I didn't have time for lunch."

I unwrapped a sliced beef sandwich handing it to Cole.

"The food looks inviting, but I'm not hungry. I had a bite a Sassy's."

For some reason the drive seemed longer than usual, maybe because I was in a hurry to get home, surprised at what I was thinking as I glanced at Cole. Finally, we drove over the cattle guard, and the house came into view. The porch lights were on, snow covering everything, but a freshly cleared path to the front door. I saw Bear leap off the porch.

Cole grabbed my luggage as Bear came running toward me, his tail wagging. He brushed against me so hard he almost knocked me over. He whined a hello as I bent down to pet him.

"Somebody's glad to see you. Wait until Charger finds out you're here."

Cole put the cases down and closed the front door.

"Leave them. There's nothing I need." I couldn't hold back a grin as I faced him. "What I need is you. Follow me, and you better hurry."

At that moment all my inhibitions were gone. I started to undress as I ran up the stairs toward the bedroom, dropping my blouse on the top step. I could hear Cole laughing as he ran up the stairs behind me. "What happened to the Julia who thought beds were for sleeping?"

My bra dropped on the landing as Cole reached the top step and grabbed me. "Time to rope this heifer and bestow the Clayton Brand upon her."

Cole was kissing me while he was trying to undo his belt buckle. In no time there was a pile of clothing on the floor as we ran for the bed. Seconds later I knew I'd made the right decision.

Chapter 31

"Are you awake?"

I opened my eyes to see Cole standing in the doorway, my bra in one hand, my blouse in the other. "Found these in the hall," he said, trying to suppress a laugh. "You sure were in a hurry to get to bed."

I pulled the covers over my head. "Please don't tease me. I'm just glad you found my clothes before Juanita did. What would she think?"

"If I promise not to tease you, will you come out from under the covers? Time to get up. We've got a busy day ahead, but you're safe, I gave Juanita the day off. I thought we needed to settle in without anyone around. She won't be back until Monday."

"That's a relief. Be a sport and bring my cases upstairs while I hop in the shower."

I pulled on a pair of jeans, a nylon turtleneck and a warm sweater, and headed downstairs. I needed coffee. Everything looked just the same as it did last spring. I felt right at home.

"Good morning, Your Highness. Coffee?"

"Yes, please." I noticed juice and a plate of muffins on the table.

"Hungry?"

"Starved."

"This is day one of our noble experiment and off to a good start. I like having breakfast across the table from you, but don't expect me to cook your breakfast every morning, Your Highness."

"Of course not. If I remember, your breakfast must be on the table no later than six-thirty. Somehow it feels as if I never left. What's on tap for today?"

"I thought you'd like some time to unpack and get settled in, then we can take a ride to the building site and then we're expected at the Longbarn tonight. Everyone is looking forward to welcoming you back."

"I can't believe you have everything so well organized."

"I've had two weeks to think of nothing else but your being here. I wanted everything to be perfect."

After breakfast, Cole said he needed a few minutes on the computer, and then he'd be ready to help with whatever I wanted.

I finished the dishes and went upstairs to unpack. Three of the four drawers in the highboy were opened a bit showing me they were empty. He really had thought of everything. The small closet was half-empty as well, extra hangers in place. I looked around wondering where I'd find space for all the boxes I'd sent.

I made the bed and tidied up the bathroom, feeling lucky Cole was as neat as he was. I'd lived with a college roommate my freshman year and shared an apartment with three friends my first year in New York, hating every minute of it. But this was going to be a different kind of adjustment. I'd no longer be a guest in this house and I'd be living with a man for the first time.

When I finished unpacking, I called out to Cole and heard him answer, "I'm down the hall."

Cole had moved his desk, computer, and some of his clothes to a bedroom I didn't even know existed.

"You have enough room for your stuff?"

"For now. How sweet you made room for me."

"Clayton hospitality at its best. If you're finished unpacking, we can take a ride to the building site."

Cole stopped the truck in front of a large graded area, some distance from the lake. He said the area was for parking, and large enough to double as a helicopter pad. There was a chill in the air. Cole took my hand as we walked onto a huge rectangle outlined with concrete footings every few feet. Columns of re-bar rose up from the footings.

"What do you think?"

"I hadn't realized it would be this large. Truthfully, I'm awe struck."

"Well, you better hope I guessed right. Our future is right here on this plot of ground. They start pouring concrete next week, if we don't get any more snow. Pray for an early spring."

"I know you'll make this work. I'm so proud of you."

"Well, keep cheering me on. To be honest, Julia, I'm scared shitless. As the old saying goes, I bet the ranch on this one.

We walked past the temporary electrical pole stepping over the footings until we were standing in the middle of what was to be the building.

"Imagine you're standing in the entrance and you look straight ahead. What do you see?"

"The lake."

"Now imagine your viewing the lake through three stories of glass. Looking out on the view in the spring with all the trees leafed out and the sun shining on the lake."

"Spectacular. With subtle outdoor lighting, you could capture its beauty at night as well."

"Great idea. I told you we make a great team. I'll pass the suggestion on to John."

We walked around the area, hand-in-hand, both of us lost in are own thoughts until I began to shiver, pulling up the collar of my jacket.

"Let's go. Nothing more to see here for now. We can stop at the barn on the way back to the house. I'm sure old Charger will be glad to see you. If the weather's better tomorrow we can go for a ride."

I walked into the barn, surprised to see Charger standing in deeply bedded shavings, wearing a heavy winter blanket. His mane had been pulled, his tail combed, the clippers taken to his bridle path and ears. He looked up and nickered when he saw me. I started to cry.

"You groomed him. He looks like he's ready to go to a horse show. Thank you."

"Then why the tears?"

"I don't know. It's all the little things you thought of. It's hard to put into words, but their happy tears." All I could think of was Sassy saying relationships are sixty-forty. "I know it's your way of saying I love you."

Cole and I spent the rest of the day by the fire in the living room talking about the project, holding hands, making plans, glad there was no one around, happier than I'd ever been. Sitting on the old leather couch, Cole's arm around me, my head resting on his shoulder, I felt sorry we had to leave this behind for the crowd at the Longbarn.

We arrived a little late. All of Cole's friends were at the bar. The men in one group, as usual, the women in another. The greetings included hugs, and kisses, and words of welcome back.

After a bit, Charlene took me aside, saying we needed to talk. I followed her to a quiet corner of the room.

"It's none of my business," she started to say, "But I have to ask, only because I think the world of Cole and I don't want to see him hurt. So, Julia, what are your plans?"

"My plans?"

"Yes, are you planning on staying around or are you leaving again after a week or two? Cole moped around after you left he couldn't seem to get you off his mind. The guy's so head over heels in love with you he can't see straight. If you're not planning on staying go now. Don't string him along. He's too nice a guy to get thrown under the bus."

"I'm not going anywhere. I'm here to stay. I love him. We're going to make it work between us. So don't worry. The last thing I want is to hurt him."

"Well now, that's good news. Glad to hear it. It takes a big load off my mind. I thought from the beginning, you two seemed right for each other. Honestly, girl, I'm glad you're staying. I know we'll be great friends. Let's go find the boys before they wonder what's happened to us."

We ate, drank, laughed, and danced. None of this was New York, but somehow it felt right. Cole's friends were genuine. No phony airs. They cared about one another and I felt comfortable in their company thinking they cared about me too.

Chapter 32

Juanita had prepared breakfast for Cole by the time I walked into the kitchen Monday morning. Short, stocky, according to Cole part Indian, part Mexican. Juanita was a woman of about forty with jet-black hair in a long thick braid down her back, her light brown skin a reflection of her heritage.

She'd started working for Cole's family over twenty years ago, about the time his mother was first taken ill. Her husband, Hector, had worked for Cole's father for many years and continued to work for Cole as the ranch foreman. Their son Hector, Junior had been hired to pick up some of the slack caused by Cole's spending most of his time on the project.

Juanita gave me a warm greeting, asking how long I was going to stay. I glanced in Cole's direction. He hadn't gone into much detail about our relationship, it seemed.

"I'm here for good, Juanita, and so happy to meet you at last. I hope you'll share your wonderful recipes. You were a lifesaver when I stayed here last spring. I'd open the freezer and find Juanita's specials. The wonderful dishes you left behind."

Juanita had assumed I was a short-term guest, not someone who would be invading her territory, or her kitchen. She'll be shocked when she goes into Cole's bedroom and discovers where I spent the night.

Sitting down next to Cole, I reached over and gave him a kiss. "Good morning. I didn't hear you get up."

"Didn't want to wake you. I need to get out to the building site before the work starts, but I didn't want to leave before seeing you. I've a couple of details to go over with John. What are your plans?"

"I'd like to get started on an advertising layout as soon as possible. If I can download the interior plans, I can start working on a decorating scheme as well. The earlier we get a handle on most of the details the faster things will go. I'm hoping my things arrive today. I need my computer to get started."

The days began to fall into a routine. Cole was gone by the time I got up. I spent mornings doing research on successful conference centers, advertising layouts and gathering decorating ideas. When it warmed up a bit and most of the snow had melted, I'd spend time in the afternoons riding Charger. Juanita did all the cooking and the chickens were her responsibility. Thank God. Her kitchen was off limits. She let me know in no uncertain terms I wasn't welcome in her domain. She left every afternoon at four having prepared our dinner. All that was left for me to do was re-heat everything in the microwave. By the time Cole came home I'd changed and was ready for our evenings together.

As hard as I tried, I couldn't get to first base with Juanita. She was convinced I was evil, up to no good, otherwise Cole would have married me. In her mind if I were a respectable Christian woman, I'd be sleeping in the guest room.

Our days grew busier, each of us with a different aspect of the project. I had no spare time. When Cole asked if I missed New York, which he did quite often, I could say, in all honesty, not yet.

The building was moving along slower than we'd hoped for. Finding workers was proving to be difficult. John moved two trailers onto the property hoping to attract men willing to stay on the job during the week and go home for the weekends. Cole was beginning to worry. We both knew it would be a disaster if he had to cancel the first conference booked for next May.

By July, the building was framed, with the exterior facing of logs in place, all three floors accessible by ladder, and the roof completed. Cole had started doing a large share of the construction himself, hoping to move the project along faster.

I borrowed Hector's truck and started taking lunch to the building site giving us the opportunity to spend more time together as Cole had begun to stay long after the other workers had quit for the day. Most evenings he wouldn't come home until dark. We'd have dinner and he'd fall into bed, exhausted. I could have been upset that we had so little time together now, but I knew how much he had riding on the project. We still had our weekends.

I had the advertising campaign ready, and the target markets identified. All I needed was sufficient funds to start buying space in the trade papers and printing up brochures. I was disappointed when Cole didn't feel he could spare the funds. I wanted to use my own money, but Cole would hear none of it. Knowing how important the early advertising would be I went ahead anyway. If I paid the bills myself, he'd never know, at least for a while, anyway.

Each day brought us closer to our one-year goal. For me, each day was happier than the last. I couldn't imagine going back to my old life. Cole was my life now. If we could just get the center off the ground everything would be perfect.

Cole had left at his usual time for the construction site so I was surprised when I saw his truck come barreling down the driveway an hour or so later and come to a screeching stop in front of the house, leaving a cloud of dust behind. Cole stormed inside slamming the back door behind him. The expression on his face spelled trouble. I'd never seen him so angry.

"What happened?"

"A bombshell just dropped. This morning John handed me his copy a cease-and-desist order from a judge in Billings. Some idiot filed a lawsuit against the construction and John said for the moment everything had to stop.

"Cole, calm down, what are you talking about?"

He pushed past me toward the kitchen. "I need a drink. What the hell am I going to do? It could take forever to get a court order lifted. I don't even know an attorney."

"Juanita," he shouted, "Pour me a double scotch on the rocks and hurry."

I'd never heard Cole shout at Juanita before. "Slow down, I'll get your drink. We need to sit down and try to figure out what this is all about."

I took Cole's drink to the patio, Bear sensing something was wrong, rubbed against him as Juanita asked if he wanted anything else.

I watched Cole down his drink in one long gulp.

"Yeah, Juanita, pour me another scotch."

Just then, the mail truck stopped and the postman got out and walked to the front door.

"I'll get it Cole. It's probably for me."

Toby, the mailman handed me a large envelope marked Certified. I took the receipt to Cole to sign noticing the return address had the name and post office box number of an attorney in Billings.

Cole tore open the envelope and pulled out multiple pages stapled together. It was the lawsuit.

When he'd finished scanning the contents, he handed it to me.

"Some son of a bitch is claiming the noise generated by the project is disturbing the spirit that dwells in the God damn lake. For Christ sake, what kind of crazy shit is that? The suit claims the debris from the construction is contaminating the lake, claiming the lake will continue to be polluted after the construction is completed and the breeding grounds for the various species of fish will be destroyed by the run off from the septic system."

"That's nonsense."

"Well, some idiot judge doesn't think so. Read it yourself. The lawsuit claims the construction is destroying ancient Indian artifacts, and is being built on sacred land belonging to his tribe."

"Who filed the suit?"

"Some guy named Hawkins." Cole started to pace up and down, hands on his hips. "This morning was the first I heard of it, but Goddamn it, the crew is already packing up to leave."

"Cole, please stop pacing. You're making me nervous."

"I'm making myself nervous. Shit we're already cutting it close. This whole thing is some sick joke, but I can't stand to lose another day. Who knows how long this will take to be settled. There's been a lot of crazy uproar lately about destroying ancient Indian relics."

Cole looked at me with despair written all over him.

"Jesus, Julia, where am I going to find a good lawyer? If this thing drags on, I'm done. The project, the ranch everything down the tubes."

"Leave it to me. I just happen to know one of the best lawyers in the country."

I left Cole nursing his second drink and more carefully reading the legal papers and went back into the house and dialed my father's office. I told his secretary this was an emergency, not sure dad would even take my call. Our last meeting hadn't ended well and I hadn't spoken with him since. I could only hope he'd tempered his feelings about my decision by now.

I waited, nerves on edge, thinking please, please answer the phone. When Dad came on the line, he wanted to know what kind of trouble I was in. Was I ready to come home? I tried to speak, but he kept talking over me. "Had the damn cowboy abused me?"

"Please Dad, stop. Give me a chance to explain."

I relayed the facts begging him to fly out at once. "It's my whole future Dad, my happiness at stake."

He grumbled, as I knew he would, lecturing me with a long list of I told you so before he promised to be on the next plane. Warning me in no uncertain terms that the Cowboy had better not have laid a hand on me. He'd let me know the arrival time.

I rushed back to the patio, excited to tell Cole my father was flying out tomorrow. I hardly thought he'd enjoy a ride in our truck, so I planned to call Sassy and have her meet him. They could drive out to the ranch together. I was babbling on a mile a minute knowing that as soon as my father arrived everything would be under control.

Cole didn't seem pleased. "You shouldn't have called him without asking me first."

"Hey, my love, we've access to one of the country's best lawyers. Why not let him play on our side. Besides it's about time you two met."

Chapter 33

I watched from the living room window as Sassy and my dad got out of her car and started up the walkway to the house. From the looks on their faces, neither smiling, I guessed they'd been arguing non-stop during the long drive. Each of them was strong willed, but I bet my dad was no match for Sassy.

As I opened the door, trying to stay calm, my dad greeted me with a great deal of reserve. Not even a kiss on the cheek. "How are you, Julia?" His question delivered in the same way he'd address a casual acquaintance not his daughter.

"I'm fine. I can't thank you enough for coming, Dad."

His attitude came as no surprise. I'd expected a rather cool reception and he didn't disappoint me. I'd been worried about Dad and Cole meeting ever since I hung up the phone yesterday hoping it would go well.

I led the way to the living room trying to remain in control of my feelings as I listened to my father. "From the sound of your telephone call, Julia, your problem is a matter of life or death, or at the very least financial ruin. What's this all about?"

"Cole will fill you in when he gets home. He should be here any minute now."

I wasn't surprised by the look on my father's face as viewed the living room with dismay. I'm sure this wasn't how he expected his daughter to be living, but I had all I could do to suppress a laugh when he saw the moose head, antlers and all, over the fireplace. He seemed both fascinate and repelled.

"So this is your new home, Julia. It's modest to say the least. You can't possibly be happy here. This place is a million miles from anything and anyone, in the middle of a God forsaken nowhere. I hope you've come to your senses and are planning to return home with me."

"Let's not talk about anything but the lawsuit for now, Dad. It may be hard for you to understand, but I am happy here."

Thank God Sassy intervened. "You look wonderful, Julia. I do hope Cole won't be long. I should be leaving soon. I hate driving these back roads at night."

I pointed toward the couch motioning for them to sit. Hearing the sound of voices, Juanita appeared from the kitchen. Once she saw Sassy, her face lit up.

"Oh, Miss Sassy. I'm so glad to see you. It's been such a long time since you've been to the ranch."

The two women embraced. "It has been a long time. It's wonderful to see you too, Juanita. How is Hector? I hope you're taking good care of my niece."

"Your niece?"

"Yes, Juanita. You mean you didn't know Julia and I were related?"

"No. I only know she is Mister Cole's girlfriend."

My father was fidgeting, I could tell the conversation was making him uncomfortable.

Juanita turned toward me smiling. "Unless you need something, I'm leaving now, Miss Julia. Everything is ready in the kitchen."

Juanita had a different tone to her voice and the smile was the first I'd received from her. I thanked her and said no, everything was fine.

Sassy kept glancing at her watch. "If Cole doesn't show up soon, I'll have to leave you to battle it out without me."

I heard the truck come down the driveway giving one last belch. Cole was home.

"Good God, what was that?"

"Nothing, Dad. Just Cole's truck."

I breathed a sigh of relief as he walked into the living room holding out his hand as he walked toward my father.

Dad rose and accepted the handshake. "So you're the cowboy."

"Cole Clayton, sir, but I prefer cattleman or even rancher." He turned toward Sassy giving her a hug and a peck on the check. Thanks for being the chauffer. How about a drink?"

Sassy declined, saying she had to leave. Without prompting, dad said good idea and asked for scotch and soda. I followed Cole to the kitchen to help with the drinks.

"Thank God your home." I hugged him as he kissed me. "Don't get upset, his bark's worse than his bite. The fact that he's here means he's gotten over being mad at me."

"Well let's pour a little scotch into the ole boy and see if we can mellow him out."

I carried the salsa and chips as Cole brought the drinks. I smiled as I saw Cole had poured his beer into a glass, guessing my dad wouldn't understand drinking beer straight out of the bottle.

Sassy said goodbye, promising to be on tap for whatever she could do to help. I walked her to the door, assuring her I'd be fine. "Dad will eventually come off his high horse. Cole can be very subdued, very charming when he wants to be, as you well know."

"I'm delighted to see you so happy, my dear. Your father's not going to let you down and I'm sure Cole will win him over. I gave Sassy a hug and thanked her again for making the long drive"

Closing the front door behind me I walked back into the living room hearing my dad speaking in his best lawyerly manner.

"Well, young man, if I understand the gist of your problem, a lawsuit has been filed and a judge has stopped construction on your little center project. Correct?"

"More or less. Every day construction is stopped I'm less likely to finish before the construction loan expires. I'm not only losing borrowed money, but every lost day brings me closer to canceling the conference scheduled for May and then the whole house of cards collapses."

"Tell me, young man, just how much business experience do you have, except ranching of course, which I'm sure is an entirely different world than what I'm used to dealing with. I hope you didn't venture into this project blindly?"

I could see Cole's back stiffen. God I hope his holds his temper. He so resents being judged by wearing levis and boots.

"Not blindly sir, as far as business experience is concerned, I have a bachelor's degree from the University of Montana and a

MBA from Columbia, so despite what you might think I'm not some uneducated backwoods cowboy."

The tone of Cole's voice worried me. Please Cole, please, I thought, don't get your back up.

"Actually, sir, I did quite well working on Wall Street until my father's death brought me back home."

Dad's expression changed. He seemed to back off a bit. "So, I assume you obtained all the necessary permits before you started construction, right? Was there an environmental impact study? No questions or restrictions on your permit regarding whatever is claimed about the issue of Indian relics?"

"I did it by the book. As far as artifacts or so-called relics are concerned, the whole State of Montana is one large collection of artifacts. The Indians were here long before we were. Remember this was buffalo country." He smiled before he asked if he could get my dad another drink?"

"Fine, yes that would be fine."

"Follow me. We can talk on the Patio while I get the fire started. I'm barbequing steaks from steers raised on the ranch."

Cole poured the drinks while I started making a salad and warming Juanita's special Mexican chili bean dish.

When we were seated at the table, my dad commented on the fine choice of wine as he sliced into his steak. Dinner was going well.

"Do you know the individual who filed the suit?"

"I know who he is. Says he's an Indian. Calls himself Billy Longhair, but his name's Chester Hawkins. He could be a half-breed, but as far as I know he's nothing but a small-time con artist. He preys on tourists selling them junk he claims are Indian relics. He owns a small sliver of land on the far side of the lake."

"Do you think he's sincere in what he states in the suit?"

"Hell, no."

"What do you think he's after?"

"Money. I think he's betting he can shake me down."

"Good, that makes our job a hell of a lot easier."

"Surely you're not suggesting I pay the guy off."

Dad smiled, picking up the wine bottle and refilling his glass. "Of course not. We'll just make him think you're willing to reach some financial agreement. We'll attempt to bet him at his own game. Do you think he's in this alone? What about the lawyer who filed the lawsuit, do you know him?"

"Never heard of the guy, but I can't imagine any respectable lawyer would take Hawkins seriously."

I interrupted the conversation to suggest that Cole clear the table while I saw to the dessert and coffee.

"Yes, your Highness, Will do." Cole said as he picked up the dinner plates. "You'll notice, sir, your daughter has taken a step upward from Princess."

I hoped the last remark had gone over my dad's head. I couldn't wait to get Cole alone as I started to slice the fresh baked pie Juanita had made earlier. "It seems to be going well don't you think? He seems to be softening his approach."

"Time will tell. I hope you're right, but I'm not sure it isn't the booze talking. I poured him two stiff drinks and he's been hitting the wine pretty hard. We'll see how he feels when he sobers up."

By the time we'd finished coffee, Cole had pushed the place mats aside and had the plans spread out on the dining room table. I could tell by the look on my dad's face he hadn't imagined the center as anything that large. He seemed impressed as he went over sheet after sheet of the blueprints.

"I must admit this comes as a surprise. I had no idea you were planning anything of this magnitude. I guess I underestimated you, young man"

"Maybe you shouldn't have underestimated your daughter as well, sir."

The look on my father's face changed. I hadn't expected Cole to go there.

"Let's just let that subject matter wait for another time, Cole."

"Right. Tomorrow morning I'll drive you to the building site."

"Fine. It has been a long day. Let me sleep on the facts and come up with a plan of action."

"Good. I can't afford to lose too many days."

"As for me, young man, I can't be in this Godforsaken place for too long. I have clients who need to get in touch with me and I can't seem to get cell phone service in this wilderness."

"Yeah, it's spotty at best."

"Then if you'll excuse me, by my time clock it's late. I'm still on New York time. I'm ready to turn in."

I took my dad upstairs to the guestroom while Cole stacked the dishes in the sink for Juanita to do in the morning.

"What do you think of him, Dad?"

"Well, he's not exactly what I'd expected. Seems like a well-educated, clean-cut sort of fellow. That still doesn't mean I approve of you two living together and he's not who I would have chosen for you. This place, alone, is far from what I would have expected of you, but I can't understand why you don't get married if you're so sure you can survive out here in the wilderness."

"I suggested we get married a month ago. After all I have substantial funds of my own that could help ease the bind Cole is in, but he won't hear of it. He wants to do this all on his own. He's afraid of involving me, of putting my money in jeopardy. We'll marry when the project is signed, sealed and delivered. Until then, I'm helping out in whatever way I can with the advertising and decorating and loving every minute of it."

We said goodnight. I looked for Cole hoping he'd started to close up for the night.

"What did he have to say?"

"Only that you weren't what he'd expected."

Cole split the last of the wine between us. "Did he approve?"

"Not in so many words. He's finding it hard to believe I'm happy here."

"I can't blame him. Sometimes I find that hard to believe myself."

"I'm happy where ever you are my love. I've developed a something for lonesome cowboys. What's the song girls who love cowboys sing? I remember now. "Stand by your man.""

Cole laughed as he handed me my glass, "You better remember. I expect you to stand by your man. Drink up. Let's call it a night. I have a feeling tomorrow is going to be a long busy day."

I climbed into bed alongside Cole as he reached over and turned off the bedside lamp, drawing me close.

"Maybe tonight's not such a good idea. If my dad hears moaning, groaning, and creaking bedsprings it will blow his mind.

Chapter 34

The first thing Juanita said to me in the morning was "Why didn't you tell me Miss Sassy was your aunt?"

"It never occurred to me. Why?"

"She's a very fine lady, your aunt. She took good care of Mister Hank, Mister Cole's Papa, when he got sick. I think she loved him very much."

"Just as I love Mister Cole."

"Good. He's much happier now that you're here. Not so happy when you left."

I knew from here on in, Juanita would no longer be a concern.

I found my father and Cole having coffee in the dining room. "Sleep well Dad," I asked.

"To damn quiet for me. Not a sound except for some damn hoot owl. Cole is going to show me around his project. You coming along, Julia?"

Thinking it would be a good idea in case things got out of hand, I nodded Yes. "Have you come up with a plan of action, Dad?"

"I have. Cole and I have just been discussing the plan, but Cole will have to carry the ball. He's going to set up a meeting with Mister White Beard, Long Beard, or whatever the hell his name is. As Cole's attorney, I can't meet with him without his lawyer being present, and of course I can't practice law in this state without passing the bar or getting special permission from the court. I'll have to check Montana's laws regarding what type of consent is required to record conversations before their meeting. It would help if Cole could get the meeting on record."

Cole called Hawkins after breakfast and set up a time and place to meet. Cole suggested the ranch would be a good place, but Hawkins wanted the meeting in a public place. He suggested a bar and grill about ten miles away. The meeting was set for three in the afternoon. Having a time and place settled, we were ready to take dad to the building site.

If only I'd had a camera, the look on my father's face as he climbed into Cole's tired old truck was priceless. Watching as he placed his shined shoes on the floor mats covered in dead grass and dried cow manure, all I could think of was my dad's Lincoln sedan, which Sam kept polished and vacuumed for the trip to and from the train station five days a week. I sat in the middle trying not to laugh as we bounced along the dirt road to the lake.

Once dad saw the lake, and the size of the building, he seemed impressed. "This is quite an undertaking, young man. What a fabulous site. I could see myself coming here as a meeting place, removed from all the glitter of Vegas, or Pebble Beach's golf courses. You could really accomplish something here."

We walked around the structure then down to the lake.

"How's the fishing, Cole?"

"Great. Lake Trout, Rainbow Trout, White Fish, Bass."

"Well, next time I'll bring my fishing gear."

I knew the battle was won if my dad was talking about coming back. Cole had passed the test.

We drove back to the house for lunch as Dad coached Cole on what he needed to get Hawkins to admit. "You need him to set a price and confirm the only thing he's interested in is the money. Tell him you'll have your attorney draw the papers. The number one priority is to have him agree to let you record the conversation. Say you need to be sure your lawyer gets the information right."

They decided I should go along, but not enter into the conversation. My job was to be a witness and to record the events as well, just in case something was unintelligible on Cole's recording.

Dad was going to stay behind and get in touch with Sassy, convinced she would know everybody of importance in Billings. He was sure she'd know the judge and could get us an appointment for tomorrow.

The bar was a dark, dirty dump a mile off the main road. A few old men were sitting at the end of the bar. A couple of guys in cowboy boots and jeans were drinking beer and shooting darts, as the jukebox blared. The pool table was unoccupied.

A man in his late sixties or early seventies was seated in the last booth. He'd pulled his snow-white hair into a ponytail, a white beard covered part of his sun-leathered face.

I followed Cole as he walked over to the booth. "Are you Chester Hawkins?"

He nodded.

"I'm Cole Clayton. Can I sit down?"

"Who's the woman?"

"She's my girlfriend, just along for the ride. You want a drink, Hawkins?"

"Yeah, a Bud on tap."

"I'll be right back. You want something, honey?"

I shook my head no, feeling uncomfortable, surprised Cole could seem so cool.

Cole returned with a pitcher of beer and two glasses. "Well, Hawkins, should we get down to business?"

"Yep, that's what we're here for."

"Okay, but before we get started, can I record our talk? I want to be sure if we come to some sort of an agreement my lawyer gets the facts straight so he can draw up the necessary papers."

"Don't make no difference to me."

Cole placed his cell phone in the middle of the table as I reached inside my purse and put my cell on my lap hidden from sight.

"So Hawkins, I've got a question. What do you hope to gain by stopping my construction?"

"What do you mean?"

"What makes you think there'd be a lot of noise when it's finished and what do you care anyway, you don't spend much time here."

"I got my rights, Cowboy, and gul darn it, peace and quiet is one of them."

Cole placed his Stetson on the seat beside him, unbuttoned his jacket and picked up his glass, the amber foam still fresh on the beer.

"And what's this nonsense about the spirit God who lives in the lake. I've never heard that tall tale before."

"My grandfather, Chief Big Bear, told me all about the spirit and what would happen if he was disturbed."

"Come on, don't shit me, Hawkins. You're no more Indian than I am. Who the hell is Chief Big Bear? What do you really want?"

Cole refilled Hawkins glass and watched as he took a big swig.

"You know, Clayton, I could tie this up in the courts for a long time, dragging a lawsuit out for years, costing you a lot of time and money. At least that's what my lawyer tells me."

"Yeah, I know all about that, so what do you want to go away?"

Hawkins was twisting strands of his beard between his fingers as he took his time to answer.

"You know, Clayton," he said in a hushed tone. "I've kinda' fallen on hard times. A little nest egg to tide me over in my declining years would help,"

"Let me get this straight. If I pay you, you'll withdraw your suit. So how much to settle?"

I could see Hawkins eyes brighten, his attitude begins to change.

"Well, I could overlook the noise, and all the relics you'd be destroying. All those things that belonged to my ancestors, for say two hundred and fifty thousand dollars."

"You're shitting me. I don't have that kind of money. I could maybe come up with twenty-five thousand if you agree to withdraw the suit now and promise to go away, but you gotta agree not to file another suit."

"No deal. I can't get by for long on that small amount. I know you got lots of dough, let's say you double it, say fifty thousand, then we got a deal."

Cole took a big breath, seeming to be deep in thought before he answered. I was amazed Cole seemed so comfortable, so much in control of the situation because my heart was beating fast and my palms were sweaty. I could hardly wait for this to end. This whole thing was way out of my comfort zone.

"I can raise fifty, but not a cent more, that is if you agree in writing to drop the law suit."

Hawkins had a grin on his face from ear to ear, "You got a deal, partner."

"Okay, I'll have my lawyer draw up the papers and cut you a check for fifty grand."

"It's got to be a cashier's check."

"No problem, I can do that." Cole reached across the table for the pitcher of beer, refilling Hawkins glass again.

"One question, just between you and me. This was all bull crap from start to finish, wasn't it? What made you think I'd pay off?"

Hawkins took a long drink, wiping the foam from his lips on his shirt sleeve. "Well, it's like this. One of the guys that worked for your contractor used to come in here every night for a few beers. He kept complaining about how hard he was workin'. The contractor saying if they didn't finish on time, you'd go broke. But you was promisin' them a big bonus if they finished ahead of time. I got to talkin' with the guy and figured out it was you he was working for. I knew your old man. Knew he was loaded, what with that big ranch of his and all them cattle. Figured if you'd pay a big bonus, you'd pay a few bucks to get rid of me."

"How'd you get a lawyer to go along with this scam, Hawkins?"

"Hell, the old guy ain't doin' much lawyering anymore. He's got a drinkin' problem, dead drunk most of the time. Don't think he's seen the inside of a courthouse in years. But the old coots smart as a whip, if you can sober him up long enough to get somethin' done. He put the papers together and he was going to do the negotiatin' with you. I promised him twenty-five percent of whatever I got, but seein' as how I did all the negotiatin' myself, don't see why I got to give him a dime."

"I sure got to hand it to you, Hawkins. You managed to pull off this scam and come out ahead. I'll call my lawyer as soon as I get home and we'll be in touch in a day or two at the most. I just need time to transfer some funds."

Cole turned toward me, "Come along, honey. Let's get out of here. I've got to make a couple of phone calls before the bank closes."

I shoved my cell phone into my purse and waited for Cole to stand up.

"Nice doin' business with you, Cowboy. You got one good lookin' woman there. Where'd you find one as pretty as that who's smart enough to keep her trap shut?"

"It's easy. You just gotta' school em' early in the relationship."

As the door to the bar closed behind us, I felt a sense of relief for the first time. "Cole you were wonderful. The guy just hung himself. Call my father and tell him the good news."

"The news can wait until we get home. No way am I going to turn on my cell phone and chance losing any part of the conversation."

My dad finished listening to the recording, a broad smile covering his face. I have to hand it to you, Cole, you'd make a damn fine trial lawyer. You nailed every point. The judge is going to throw this suit out as soon as he hears this recording. You've got a good case against Hawkins for extortion. Do you have a local attorney?"

"Not interested. I've already lost a few days. I can't afford to lose any more time and I'm sure not interested in spending any money on lawyers. Besides, what good would it do to send the old coot to jail? He sure as hell doesn't have any money I could sue for? Maybe this'll teach him a lesson.

"Have it your way. I spoke with Sarah, and I'm not the least surprised she knows the judge very well. We have an appointment in his chambers tomorrow at two o'clock. Assuming all goes according to plan, I'll be out of here on the six o'clock flight back to New York."

My dad and Cole were getting along famously, no more talk of weddings. They spent the evening discussing plans for the center, Dad offering to draw the basic contract protecting the center, and binding any meeting holder to specific terms and conditions. He said he'd spread the word. He knew a lot of the right people in New York.

With dad's suitcase in the tailgate, the three of us sat crammed into in the front seat of Cole's truck. He'd vacuumed the interior for our trip to Billings. Cole looked very business-like, wearing a suit and tie for our appointment with the judge. Even dad commented on his appearance, telling Cole he looked more like he belonged on Wall Street than any main street in Montana.

We drove along without any conversation for quite a while before dad, the lawyer in him, started to question Cole.

"Julia said you returned to the ranch after the death of your father."

Cole proceeded to tell my dad the same story he'd shared with me. When he finished, Dad asked, "Don't you have any desire to leave the ranch and get back to the world of big business? Your talents seem wasted here. I'm sure you'd receive a pretty penny if you sold the ranch. Just think you and Julia could build your lives together in a city filled with things to do. I'm sure you both miss the wonderful restaurants, the theatre, all the things a metropolitan area abounds with."

Another long stretch of silence followed before Cole spoke. "Once I couldn't conceive of living anywhere else. My dad was a tough taskmaster, but a great role model. It just took me years to appreciate what he taught me. Growing up here the isolation and the hard work tended to get in the way of the example he was setting. None of it made sense until I returned to the ranch following his death."

My Dad seemed to be taking in the story without interrupting. Not his usual behavior.

"My dad was a man of honor, a man of his word. He did business on a handshake. We kids were taught respect for others and a belief in honesty. Most of those rules didn't apply on Wall Street. I found myself doing things that weren't necessarily dishonest, but they tilted the game in my direction. What happened to the other guy as long as I came out ahead wasn't important. It was all about money, and power. That's how the game's played in that world, but you know that better than me."

There was another long pause before Cole continued. He seemed to be giving careful thought to what he said next. I knew that wasn't easy for him, but he seemed intent on letting my father see who he was.

"My New York friends were only friends on the surface. They were great people to party with, but not in a crisis. Relationships in the power set I ran with were based on how much money you had and who you knew. Business was a daily dog-eat-dog challenge. When it all came crashing down, the folks who were there for me were the people I grew up with. Good down to earth friends. The further I got away from New York, the more I began to realize how phony my life had become. No, I have no desire to return to that rat race.

"All very interesting, young man, but what about Julia? Look at all the things she's been used to, things she'll be giving up. Is that fair?"

"That's not for me to say. You'll have to ask her how she feels about our life. But I made it clear from the beginning I'm here to stay."

Dad turned toward me, expecting an answer just as we hit a bump. The road was badly in need of repair. It gave me a minute to calm down.

"Please, Dad, give me some credit for understanding what I'm supposed to be giving up and recognize what I'm getting in return. Besides when the Centers operating, all sorts of interesting people will be here for me to interact with, the best of both worlds."

Conversation came to an end as we neared Billings. Like most business districts, parking was a problem. The parking lot adjacent to the courthouse was full. We drove around for a few minutes before Cole found a space several blocks away. It was a relief to plant my feet on the ground after the long drive. Every bone in my body ached after being crammed into the front seat. Dad looked unsteady as he stepped out of the truck.

"Without a doubt," young man, "that's the most uncomfortable ride I've ever had, including a jeep on safari in Africa. Julia, do you drive this piece of junk as well?"

"Sometimes, why?"

"Why, my dear? Isn't it obvious? If Cole wishes to place his life in danger that's his prerogative, but in my opinion, you should be driving a safer vehicle. Consider it an engagement present or what every you want to call it, but I'm not leaving here without giving you a check for a new truck, or car, or van or whatever damn thing you want to drive."

"That's very thoughtful, Dad, but not necessary. I have no concern about driving the truck.

"You may have no concerns, but I might want to come back someday. It won't happen if I have to drive one mile in that wreck."

The look I gave Cole was meant to urge him to say something. He returned my look with a broad smile. "I'm not getting involved in this conversation, Julia. It's between you and your dad."

"Then consider it settled, Julia. I'll write you a check before I leave."

Turning the corner, Cole pointed to the large building on the corner. "The old Courthouse is long gone. I remember it being a classic structure. I came here once when I was a kid with my dad, I'm not sure why, but the courthouse left an impression. This new building looks like any other uninspired nineteen fifties structure."

The judge's clerk asked us to be seated. It wasn't long before we were ushered into the judge's chambers. Judge Peterson rose from behind his desk and greeted my father. "So, you're Sassy's brother, an attorney I understand, visiting from New York City."

I watched Dad cringe at my aunt's nickname. The judge shook his hand before settling back into his leather desk chair.

"What can I do for you?"

"Actually, I'm here purely as Mister Clayton's friend. You issued a cease and desist order several days ago against a construction project on his property." He handed the judge a copy of the lawsuit.

"Yes, I recall the order. There's been a tremendous outcry of late from preservation groups regarding the destruction of Indian artifacts and burial sites. I opted on the side of caution wanting a little more time to study the circumstances. I didn't want another protest march outside my home."

"If you have a minute judge to listen to a short recording, I think you'll see the chicanery that's taking place here. The whole lawsuit is nothing more than a shakedown. Pure and simple extortion."

Dad put Cole's cell phone on the judge's desk activating the speaker button and started the recording as we sat watching the judge's expression as he listened to the conversation between Cole and Hawkins. He handed back the cell phone when the recording came to an end, a look of dismay on is face.

"I'll lift the order immediately. What hogwash. The judge looked at Cole as he asked my dad if he was planning on suing Hawkins?"

"No, your honor. He's just a small-time con artist. I guess he saw a way to get rich quick and took a chance. All Mr. Clayton wants is to be free to continue with the construction."

Leaving the Judge's chamber, we had just enough time to drop my dad off at the airport, but not before he made out a check for thirty-five thousand dollars. Cole seemed upset, but the check was made out to me. There was nothing he could do or say.

Cole thanked my dad for flying out and saving the day. Shaking Cole's hand, Dad encouraged us to marry soon. "The last thing I want is a bastard grandchild. Take good care of my daughter or you'll have me to deal with."

"You can count on that sir. She's the only thing that really matters in my life."

"Goodbye, my dear. I can understand your interest in the young man, but why the hell did it have to be someone who lives in the middle of Montana."

My dad gave me a hug and a kiss, reminding me to keep in touch, then picked up his suitcase and walked toward the airport entrance.

As we drove out of town, I snuggled close to Cole, glad old trucks don't have center consoles. "You've overcome two big obstacles, my dad likes you, and the lawsuits behind us. The only thing left is to bring the project to completion on time.

Chapter 35

Things were moving ahead at a rapid pace. The exterior work on the building was complete, even more spectacular than it looked on the drawings, and the interior was taking shape. Though Cole and I worked long hours I loved every minute of it.

I'd set the color scheme, soft leather sofas in a sand-beige color for the reception area, Sierra teakwood coffee tables made to order by a local wood carver. Comfortable chairs covered in a flame-patterned fabric in various shades of red scattered throughout the area.

I'd managed to obtain various art pieces on loan from the Montana cowboy museum. They had more photos, paintings, and metal sculptures then they could display. Everything was in keeping with the western theme I'd adopted. Several local tribes loaned us beautiful examples of Indian baskets, rugs, and pottery.

A commercial supply house had designed the kitchen, everything in gleaming stainless steel. It looked fabulous. I'd ordered dishes, and glasses highlighting the Clayton Ranch brand.

After the only heated disagreement we'd ever had, a large framed commercial photo of Cole mounted on his roan gelding would hang over the reception desk. Agreeing on the name was easy. The building would be called 'The Clayton Ranch Conference Center'.

If we were lucky, the building would come in a little under budget, but the furnishings and extensive media systems for the meeting rooms would surely break the bank if we weren't careful. I tried to be as frugal as possible, while still making everything personal, one of a kind, nothing commercial looking.

Building the equivalent of a small hotel in the middle of nowhere was proving to be an even bigger challenge than either of us had imagined. We'd fall into bed at night exhausted, but happy. Life was good. No matter what problems arose, we had each other and a real sense of excitement as the project came nearer to completion.

The phone rang Saturday morning just as we were about to have breakfast. Cole answered. I watched the color drain from his face.

"Where are you?" There was a long pause then he replied, "What are you doing here?" Again, another long pause. I could only hear Cole's side of the conversation, but from the look on his face he was not happy with what he was hearing.

"All right," he glanced at his watch. It's eight o'clock. I'll be there by eleven."

"Who was that?"

Cole didn't answer as he rushed upstairs, returning a short time later dressed in clean jeans, a starched shirt, his dress boots and leather jacket. He grabbed his Stetson off the coat rack in the hall.

"I'll take the car. I've got to go to Billings."

"Who was that on the phone? Cole. Speak to me. What's going on?"

"We'll talk later. Gotta' go."

He left, leaving me standing at the front door without a word or even a kiss goodbye. I watched him speed down the driveway in our new Navigator wondering what in the world could have caused him to behave as he did. Something serious was going on.

I spent the day trying to think of anything except the morning's events. After roaming around the house, lost, I decided to saddle Charger and go for a long ride.

I returned just before six. The Navigator wasn't parked in front of the house. Cole hadn't returned home, yet. I wasn't sure what to do next so I fed Bear and the horses, and waited for his return. We were supposed to be going to the Longhorn for dinner.

The days were getting shorter now that fall was here. It would be dark soon. Close to seven the phone rang. It was Cole.

"Look, sweetheart, I'm hung up here. I won't be home tonight. Could you please take care of Bear and the horses? Not to worry. I'll call you in the morning."

Before I could say a word, the line went dead. Now I was really upset. I had no idea where he was or what in the hell was going on? Should I be worried?

After a sleepless night, I waited all morning for the phone to ring. By afternoon, I still hadn't heard a word from Cole. I glanced at my watch as the phone rang. Two p.m. Much to my surprise the telephone call wasn't from Cole. It was Sassy's voice the sound of which echoed a note of concern.

"Julia, is something going on between you two?"

"Why would you ask?"

"Well, my dear, a friend and I were in the dining room of the Hilton Hotel this morning and I was flabbergasted to see Cole having breakfast with Cynthia."

"Wait, you mean his ex? That Cynthia?"

"Exactly. But wait you didn't know?"

I could feel tears forming, a knot in the pit of my stomach. "No, I had no idea. He dashed out of here without saying a word yesterday morning and didn't come home last night."

"I don't understand, my dear. That doesn't sound at all like Cole. I wonder what she could possibly be doing here? Well, I'm sure there's a reasonable explanation. I'm here if you need me."

I hung up the phone feeling a sense of despair. Had Cole spent the night with Cynthia? Was he so excited to see his ex he couldn't find time to call me? My head was spinning, every concern I'd ever had about relationships was bubbling to the surface. Was he using me to complete his project and then dumping me for her? I thought of Amy and Bill, the perfect couple, if they couldn't make it work, were we any different?

From everything I'd heard, Cynthia was a beautiful woman and Cole must have had strong feelings for her. After all, he married her.

As the day dragged on, things began to look bleaker. The sun had gone down hours ago and darkness was beginning to set in when I saw headlights approaching. I'd been sitting in the darkened living room, an empty glass of wine on the coffee table, distraught, heartbroken. I'd let my guard down and look what happened. How could I have been such a fool.

Cole opened the door and called out my name. I didn't answer. He called again as he looked around the house, turning on the lights in the living room.

He seemed surprised to see me. "Why didn't you answer, Sweetheart. What are you doing sitting here in the dark?"

"Sassy called this afternoon. She saw you and Cynthia having breakfast together at the Hilton."

Cole looked surprised.

"When were you planning on telling me you'd spent the night with your ex-wife?"

"Whoa, sweetheart it's nothing like that."

"Well, what is it like? It's obvious you intended to keep Cynthia's visit a secret."

Getting madder by the minute I couldn't bring myself to look at him. All the fears I'd tried to suppress during the time he was away bubbled to the surface. I ran from the room before Cole could see me crying, I'd be damned if I'd give him that satisfaction. I raced upstairs and slammed the door to the guest bedroom. I heard Cole running up the stairs behind me, heard him knocking on the door, turning the handle on the bedroom door I'd ready locked.

"Go away. As far as I'm concerned, Cole, It's over between us. Some things can't be excused and sleeping around, especially it's with your ex-wife, is number one on my list of things that are unpardonable."

"Julia, please open the door. Let me explain."

"No. I don't want to hear any of your lame explanations. She called and you couldn't rush to her fast enough."

"It isn't what you think, Julia. Please let me in. For God's sake be reasonable. We need to talk."

"Be reasonable. That's a joke. There's nothing to talk about. I don't want an apology. What? You only spent the night with her for old times' sake?"

Cole was banging on the door with so much force I was sure it would break.

"Cole, stop. What a fool I've been. I knew relationships never lasted. I've helped you finish your damn project and now that it's almost done you don't need me any longer. To think I almost married you. Thank God I was spared that humiliation.

"You're wrong, wrong about everything. I love you and only you. Cynthia doesn't mean a damn thing to me. Please let me in."

If she didn't mean a thing to him, then why did he spend the night with her? Wasn't our sex life enough to satisfy him? I stopped answering him, hoping he'd go away.

He finally gave up. I waited for what seemed like an eternity for everything to be quiet. Thinking Cole had gone to his bedroom, I turned off the lights and opened the door a crack. The lights were off downstairs. This was my chance. I tip-toed down the staircase, reaching for my jacket on the coat rack, and opened the front door. I ran as fast as I could toward the Navigator, knowing we always left the keys in the car.

The hour was late by the time I reached Sassy's house. I parked in her driveway and walked to the front door and rang the bell. There'd been no tears on the long drive. I just got more upset with every mile. Not so much at Cole, but at myself for being so stupid in trusting him.

The hall lights were already on as Sassy opened the door in her robe and slippers.

"I've been expecting you."

"Really. How could you know I was coming?"

"Cole called. He was sure this was where you were headed. I assume this has something to do with Cynthia. Come in. I'll make a pot of tea and you can tell me what this is all about."

I followed Sassy into the kitchen where so many meaningful conversations had taken place over a cup of tea.

"So, Julia, what did Cole have to say about his meeting with his ex?"

"I have no idea what the meeting was about. Cynthia phoned and he was out the door in half an hour without one word where he was going or who he was meeting. He spent Saturday night with her."

"There must be some explanation. I know all too well how he feels about Cynthia, and how he feels about you. Cole's not the kind of man to do what you suspect. This simply doesn't add up."

I watched Sassy pour hot water into a teapot and place it along with two cups on the table.

"I suppose I should have given him a chance to explain, but I didn't want to hear the obvious followed by, I'm sorry, please forgive me. It will never happen again."

"Really, Julia, I'm surprised at you. I thought you were smarter than that. Have you so little faith in Cole or what your relationship means to him? I guarantee there's a simple explanation. Or would you rather believe you were right all along, that there is no such thing as true love, or lasting relationships.

Sassy poured the steaming tea into our cups. "I'll be the first to admit that loving a man isn't always easy, but the rewards are well worth it. Turning tail and running away isn't the answer."

I started to cry. "Why didn't he just tell me where he was going? Is she the siren's call he can't resist? Is this what our life together would be like. Cynthia appears and he runs off to be with her. I can't live like that. How many times will he break my heart?"

"Drink your tea, Julia. Don't you think you're being a bit overly dramatic? I agree he should have told you where he was going, but I think you owe him and yourself a chance to hear the whole story. The guest rooms ready. I'll call Cole and tell him you arrived safely. He was worried sick when he called earlier. Let's try and square this away tomorrow and put it right between you two lovebirds. I can guarantee you'll live to regret it if you don't hear him out."

Chapter 36

I didn't sleep well, tossing and turning most of the night. All I could think of was Cole and Cynthia making love. I didn't want to get up. I didn't want to see Cole. My world had been perfect until Cynthia arrived on the scene. Life would never be the same again. I thought Cole was different, but if even he proved to be untrustworthy, how could I ever trust another man.

Sassy called. "Time to get up and dressed, Julia. Cole will be here soon. Whether you choose to believe him or not is up to you."

Sassy was in the kitchen, "What would you like for breakfast."

"Just coffee. I couldn't eat a thing."

"Julia, you may not like what I'm going to say, but hear me out. You're not some silly schoolgirl anymore, you're a grown woman. As such you face facts, you don't run off to your room in a fit of pique, or a rush of tears and throw a temper tantrum. I'm afraid you've spent too much of your life being the baby sister, daddy's darling little girl, the delicate one, spared from all the realities of life. I would have thought your accident would have taught you a thing or two."

Sassy filled my cup with hot coffee and passed a plate of fresh fruit in my direction.

"You've chosen to believe the worst out of your own fears without giving Cole a chance to explain. Not only is that unfair to him, but damn it, don't you see how unfair it is to you? You need to grow up."

"But, Sassy...'

"Don't but me, start behaving like an adult. Think about what you're jeopardizing. Now drink your coffee and go put on some makeup and promise me you'll keep an open mind."

I felt uneasy waiting in the living room. When I heard the truck stop in the driveway, I wanted to be anywhere but here. Cole was the last person I wanted to see this morning. Sassy opened the door suggesting Cole follow her.

"Morning, Julia,"

I nodded, having nothing to say. The whole situation was awkward. Cole looked awful.

"I'll leave if you two wish to be alone."

"No, Sassy, please stay. I want you to hear what I have to say."

Cole settled into a chair across from me. It seemed to take forever before he spoke. Looking straight at me he began. "First, let me apologize for the way I handled the situation. I should have told you who was on the phone, but knowing Cynthia, her being here could only spell trouble. She insisted it was important she see me at once. She told me she was not going to leave until we had some things resolved between us.

"Before I go on, let me make one thing perfectly clear, I had no interest in Cynthia before I left on Saturday, and even less when I returned on Sunday evening. Should I continue?"

"By all means." If my answer sounded sarcastic that was what I wanted. I crossed my arms across my chest waiting for him to dig himself out of the question I was about to ask. "I'm dying to hear your explanation of how it was just fine to spend the night with her, whether you had feeling for her or not. How that makes it okay to cheat on me."

"You don't really believe that do you, Julia? I'd never think of cheating on you. When it became obvious nothing between Cynthia and me was settled and I need to stay overnight I called Bill Richardson, an old fraternity brother who lives in Billings I spent the night with him and his wife. You can call them if you don't believe me."

I was beginning to feel ashamed. Maybe Sassy was right I should have let Cole explain. I should have known better. "What was Cynthia doing here? What was so damn important you had to rush out the door to meet her?"

"I had no idea what she wanted when we met in the lobby of her hotel, Julia. I was embarrassed when she threw her arms around me and planted a kiss on my cheek. She was all sweetness and charm, so typical of Cynthia when she wanted something. It seems one of her friends had pointed out the piece you wrote about the center for the Wall Street Journal. She thought there might be something in it for her. She quoted the article, about the center attracting renowned figures."

"Go On."

"She wanted us to get back together. Swearing she'd made a horrible mistake. Telling me how she still loved me, begging me to forgive her. She rattled on about being the perfect hostess for the center, how she was used to mingling with important people. How it would be wonderful to spend part of our time in New York and part at the center.

"When I told her I was about to get married she seemed shocked. It took only seconds before she had a change of mood and a change of heart. She did a complete turnaround from how she loved and missed me to how much it was going to cost me. How she was going to make me pay."

Cole continued. "Cynthia threatened those circumstances would change if I continued with my plans to marry. How she'd be forced to sue me for the substantial amount of money due and owing her, which of course, she'd be willing to forget if we got back together."

I looked toward Sassy not knowing what to do, while I listened to more of what Cole had to say.

"She gave me one of those, if looks could kill stares, saying she needed to call her lawyer and stormed through lobby heading toward the elevators. Raising her voice loud enough to attract attention. She said we'd discuss the details at breakfast in the morning. That's when Sassy saw Cynthia and me."

Sassy looked at me as if to say, you see there is a reasonable explanation.

I uncrossed my arms, beginning to feel foolish. "What was Cynthia talking about?"

"She demanded I pay her the five years worth of alimony she claimed I owed, and for her share of the ranch, which she asserted was an undisclosed asset in our divorce settlement."

"You're kidding."

"No. I had no idea what she was taking about. Alimony? She'd already taken almost everything I owned."

"Did you agree to pay here alimony, Cole?"

"Hell, I don't know, but I can't imagine a judge granting her anything. Christ, she's loaded. She's a trust fund baby. She gets a huge check every December."

Sassy looked at Cole and asked, "What did the divorce papers say?"

"I have no idea. I never read them, just signed the damn papers and sent them back to her attorney."

"Cole, did you have your own attorney?"

"No, Sassy, of course not. Hell, all I wanted was out. I was embroiled in trying to save the ranch. I'd just buried my father, but I can see now where that was a big mistake. I should have known better. Cynthia claims I owe her a six-figure amount.

"Now, do you understand, Julia, why I couldn't tell you all this over the phone.

Cole seemed distraught as he walked across the room and sat down next to me.

God, I had no idea how I could begin to justify or even explain my reaction? If this was a trust issue, was it Cole I didn't trust, or was the issue my problem. Sassy was right. I'd acted like a spoiled child. I needed to grow up.

I reached over and took Cole's hand in mine. "I'm so sorry. I admit my reaction was childish at best, but I was just so scared. Scared I was going to lose you. Scared I couldn't compete with Cynthia."

"What in the world are you talking about? There's no competition, no comparison. I have nothing but contempt for Cynthia. The only thing she ever did that mattered was to leave me so I was free to find you."

Sassy smiled. "I'll leave you two lovebirds alone. It would seem you don't need a referee after all." She laughed as she started to walk away.

"Thanks for everything, Sassy. If Julia's ready to come home we'll be on our way.

I hugged Sassy and thanked her for her wise council and started to get behind the wheel of the behind the wheel of the Navigator, planning on following the truck on the drive home.

Cole had a length of chain in his hand attaching it to the hitch on the back of the truck.

'Get in the truck, Julia."

I stopped short. Cole had never raised his voice to me before.

Chapter 37

Cole started the truck's engine and drove off towing the car behind us. Something seemed different in Cole's attitude. He seemed distant. I couldn't quite figure it out. We drove for some time with nothing but silence between us. I was beginning to feel concerned. Something about the tight set of his jaw, the look in his eyes, his grip on the steering wheel said all was not forgiven. "Is something wrong Cole?"

"Yes. Something is very wrong. Now that we're alone there are some things, we need to get straight between us. We've lived together for over a year and I've told you things I'd never told anyone before. I've borne my soul to you. I can't believe you have so little understanding of how much I love you. That you had so little trust in me that you'd run off in the middle of the night without giving me a chance to explain. I thought you owed me more than that."

"I said I'm sorry and I meant it."

"I know you're sorry. I just thought you were more of adult then to pull such a childish stunt. Running off in the middle of the night."

That bit. I could tell Cole was hurt, but he was angry as well.

Julia, marriage isn't a game, it isn't kid stuff. It's based on trust. We've been lucky so far. Everything has been sunlight and roses, but life ain't always like that kiddo. It's peaks and valleys and without trust it's a house of cards. Much as I love you if you can't trust me, maybe we should call it quits."

His words stung. I knew he was right. I bit my lip trying to hold back the tears. We rode along for miles with neither of us saying a word. I was beginning to realize just how much damage my childish action had caused. I tried to change the subject.

"Cole, are you worried that Cynthia might really have an action against you for alimony and a piece of the ranch?"

"Why?"

"I thought when we got home, I'd call my father and we could let him deal the situation."

"Julia, haven't you understood one word I've said. You're not Daddy's little girl any longer, you were planning on being my wife. We solve our problems together. You're an adult, you don't run to Daddy or Sassy at the first sign of trouble. If you run to anybody you run to me."

As we pulled up to the house Cole said he had spoken with John at the construction site. "I've spent a lot of valuable time driving to Billings and back because of your actions. Go inside. I'll be back later. Take the time to think about what you want to do about us."

Cole started to unhitch the car, his back to me. I walked toward the house, Sassy's comment about giving sixty percent to the relationship ringing in my ears. I'd blown it. I hadn't given Cole even fifty percent. I could feel the tears running down my cheeks.

By the time Cole returned I'd had a chance to absorb all he'd said on the drive home. I'd never been forced to look at myself in that honest a fashion. I knew deep down he was right. I needed to rely on him not my father to resolve problems. God, I didn't want to lose him.

I greeted him at the door and handed him a beer. "We need to talk."

The weather was too cold to sit outside. We settled in the living room. Cole lit a match to the kindling in the fireplace and rested his hand on the mantel waiting for me to begin.

"Everything you said was true, Cole. I'd never had anyone hold a mirror up to how I behave. You made me take a good look at myself and I must admit I wasn't happy with what I saw. I know saying I'm sorry isn't enough. Can you ever forgive me? I love you and I couldn't imagine my life without you. It's time I grew up. The umbilical cord has to be cut. You're right I'm not Daddy's little girl any more I'm your partner in life."

I tried hard not cry as Cole took me in his arms.

"It's okay, Your Highness, I know you're sorry. Maybe it was a good thing we had this out between us now. We can go on from here both having learned a big lesson."

"You have my permission to kick me in the ass if I forget to act like an adult."

"No way. Your ass is much to pretty to leave my boot print, but I could run my hand across it a time or two like this. Who knew making love on a couch in front of a fire might be so much fun."

The official start of winter was a week away and we were back on schedule. The interior work would go on no matter the weather. We both felt as if a load had been lifted, the strain of the last few months had been evident on both of us. Barring a catastrophe, the construction would be finished ahead of schedule and our relationship was stronger than ever.

The advertising campaign was paying off. The Wall Street Journal piece really helped. We'd received several viable inquiries and were booked for May, June, and now September as well. If we could turn some of the other inquiries into contracts we'd be sitting pretty.

This would be our first Christmas together and I wanted it to be something special. Cole remembered there were boxes of ornaments and Christmas lights stored in the attic. We spent the better part of Sunday tramping through ankle deep snow, searching the ranch for the perfect Christmas tree, laughing over our different ideas of what constituted perfect. The thought of cutting down our own tree made the whole idea of Christmas seem so much more meaningful. Funny how the little things Cole did made things seem special. I never would have imagined hunting for a tree in the dead of winter would be fun.

"This was a family tradition we continued every year until we were adults." Cole started the chain saw. "As kids we followed after Dad and fought over which tree was the best. When Dad decided he'd had enough tramping through the snow, he got us to agree. We'd load the tree on the back of the tractor and ride home alongside him singing Christmas carols. I haven't done this in years. It feels good, Julia. Feels like I have a home again, instead of a bachelor pad.

"It's a wonderful tradition. Let's make it part of every Christmas from now on."

We decorated the tree together, not with fancy imported ornaments like the ones on our trees at home in Connecticut, but with hand-made decorations Cole's family handed down over the years. We strung lights around the house, both of us happy to be continuing rituals that spoke of home and family. When we finished, I mixed a pitcher of brandied eggnog and brought a tray filled with glasses and a plate full of Juanita's ginger cookie into the living room. The huge fireplace served more than a decorative purpose, it kept the room warm and filled it with the sweet smell of burning logs. A wonderful place to spend a cold winter evening.

I didn't remember Connecticut ever being as cold as Montana nor the snow being as deep. The chilling winds from Canada that swept down off the mountains made it seem even colder. There was always the threat of being snowed in. The herd had been moved closer to the house. They would need to be fed hay and grain stored in the feed barn at least once a day when the snow was to deep to graze. Cole explained that their thick skin and coarse hair was natural insulation to help keep them warm. I was glad Charger and Cole's roan had winter blankets and warm stalls in the barn, but I still felt sorry for the cattle no matter what Cole said. At least the rest of the horses were blanketed and had shelters that let them get out of the snow and wind.

We chose to spend Christmas alone, turning down invitations from friends. We'd been so busy, we hardly had time for one another. Christmas morning, we opened our presents. I felt like a kid again, excited to see what was under the tree. The thrill of our first Christmas together.

With the workers gone until after New Years, I thought it might be a good time to make some long overdue changes to the house. That is, if it didn't upset Cole. I gathered the last of the wrapping paper and headed toward the kitchen to make breakfast. Juanita and Hector had time off as well. Over the last of the coffee, I asked Cole if he would be okay if I took the free time to do a little re-decorating.

"Sweetheart, you do whatever you want. This is your home as well as mine, and if that makes you happy to make some changes, I'm all for it.

"You mean you wouldn't be upset if I updated most of the house."

"Hell no. Why would I care?"

"I thought you might be upset if I started changing things."

"This place has looked the same ever since I can remember. It's dark and dated, about time it got an uplift. Babe the only drawback is money, I need to be careful until the building is complete."

"What I have in mind won't cost very much. I've got furniture in storage that I could arrange to ship here. The rest is a coat of paint here and there, and we can do that ourselves if you're game. The old house has good bones and it's rock solid. We can make it something special. It deserves a facelift."

"You wouldn't want to build something new someday? Maybe something more modern."

"No way. I love this old house, there's something special about the sound of the creaky steps when you walk up the stairs, the back door that you have to slam or it won't stay closed, they're all the familiar things that make this feel like home. The old walls have seen a lot of love and the house is full of happy memories for you. Somehow, I see Sassy and your dad happy here as well. It's got good karma. If we ever needed more space, there's acres and acres of room to add on.

By the end of January, the redecorating project was finished. It was fun working together. Cole had been right all along, we did make a great team. Most of all I was overjoyed to see how great everything looked. The interior seemed so much brighter, friendlier with the new paint, and my furniture made a big difference. The worn dark leather couch and chairs were gone. Cole even agreed to remove the moose head from over the fireplace. He said the new look brought a bit of New York glamour to tried and true Montana. Even Juanita was excited by the new look and all it cost was the price of a few gallons of paint.

If only I could find a way to update the bathroom everything would be perfect. I'd give almost anything for a real stall shower. I was tired of dealing with the damn shower curtain, and double sinks would solve the chaos every morning. I couldn't imagine how two adults and three children managed to maintain their sanity with only one bathroom.

Chapter 38

The construction of the conference center was finished and it was only the first of March. Somehow Cole had managed to pull part one of his plan ahead of schedule. The kitchen gleaming with stainless steel appliances and counter tops. The soft leather sofas, still covered in plastic wrap, were already in the lobby, along with the overstuffed chairs. The tables were ready for delivery. The photos and sculptures on loan were all in boxes waiting to be put on display.

The bedrooms had been painted in muted desert tones. The feather beds and matching duvets had already been delivered. Every room had a view of either the lake or Black Angus cattle in the distance. My part finished ahead time as well. We were ready to greet the first guests due to arrive in May. The only thing left was hire and train the staff.

I held my breath as Cole and the county building inspector went through the final inspection. I watched as they shook hands. I could almost hear Cole's sigh of relief, the smile on his face couldn't be missed. The inspector closed his notebook, assuring Cole he'd passed with flying colors and he'd receive a copy of the Certificate of Occupancy within a few days. Cole walked the inspector to his truck. They exchanged a few more words before Cole turned and walked back toward me the huge smile still on his face, shoulders back, head held high. He'd had done it.

There was nothing standing in our way now. We walked hand-in-hand up the steps to the double doors and entered the lobby, even more spectacular than it looked on paper or that I'd ever imagined. Looking out at the lake through the three stories of glass was breathtaking. The dream I'd first seen as a series of blueprints on my dining room table had come true.

"Look what you've accomplished, Cole, and you did it all on your own. I'm so proud of you."

We explored every room as if we were seeing it all for the first time. We knew it would take a lot of work and a bit of luck to put the center on a paying basis, but we were both up to the task.

Finishing the tour, we walked down to the edge of the lake and glanced back at the building imagining how it would look once the rocking chairs were unpacked and in place on the wrap around deck. I'd been mulling over an idea for some time. Maybe now was the moment to spring it on Cole.

"Let's get married."

Cole's thoughts must have been elsewhere as he looked at me with surprise.

"What did you just say?"

"I said, let's get married. We need a test run to be sure everything works and everyone knows their jobs, so why not get married right here. We've plenty of room for overnight guests. We could invite both families, all our friends, and hold a wonderful weekend wedding party here."

"Hold on a minute, are you taking about a wedding or a shakedown cruise."

"I didn't mean it to sound that way. I just think this is the perfect place to hold our wedding."

"I'd imagined you of all people would want all the trappings of a fancy church wedding in New York."

"That's the last thing I want. I belong here now, not in New York. Don't you see how special it would be to be married here?" What this place means to both of us.

"Hold on, Julia. What you're suggesting, this big bash you have in mind could cost a bundle."

"I know, but it won't be a problem. The father of the bride will pick up the cost."

Cole looked at me with surprise.

"Wait a minute, you're really serious about this."

"I've never been more serious in my life. Why wait any longer? I'm not going anywhere this is my home. The year trial run we gave ourselves has passed. I want to be Mrs. Cole Clayton as soon as we can put it together."

"You realize you've just spoiled my whole plan. The one where I get down on one knee thing and say the rights words. I've been practicing for months, but Your Highness, if you so decree, I will obey and make an honest woman out of you. Set the date. Only one thing I insist on. We don't ask your father for a penny. We foot the bill ourselves. This time I'll agree to your coming up with some money as well."

"I'm so excited I don't know whether to laugh or cry." I reached up and kissed Cole on the cheek. "It's going to be fabulous. You can meet my family and I can meet yours. We can invite Billy and Charlene and all the rest of your friends. Everything will be perfect. We'll have the best wedding celebration ever"

"You're sure we can afford this. Wouldn't you rather spend the money on a honeymoon? I'm fine with just you and me and a justice of the peace."

"I'm sure, but you could change your mind and let my dad give us the wedding. He paid for a spectacular event when my sister got married and I know he won't be happy until we're finally husband and wife. We're not getting any younger and we wouldn't want our children to be bastards."

"Whoa. Slow down. We need to get a wedding out of the way before we talk about children. Your dad's a great guy, but let's leave him out of this. Just one question?"

Cole looked at me with that boyish grin I loved. "I want you to explain what is it with you gals now a days. You're the second woman who's proposed to me. Cole swept me up and held me close. "Though I can't understand what took you so long."

"Honestly, Cowboy. When will you learn to leave well enough alone?"

I took Cole's hand and started walking toward the parking lot. "Let's go home. We've got to check the calendar and set a date. Then I'll phone my father with the news that you want to make an honest woman out of me. We have so many details to get out of the way and I don't want to waste a minute."

"Lead the way, but the details can wait. I have a great idea for an engagement celebration."

Chapter 39

My dad responded saying how glad he was we were finally doing the right thing, telling Cole as the father of the bride he expected to pick up the cost. Cole thanked him politely, but said no thanks.

Invitations had gone out. Both our families were coming. Dad called to request an invitation for a mysterious individual he wanted added to the guest list.

Shortly after we firmed up the date Cole started leaving the house one night a week after dinner on some sort of a secret project. He promised to explain later. I didn't ask even though he came home well after midnight with the smell of beer on his breath. I'd learned my lesson, I trusted him. The Cynthia thing had been resolved. Cole had been right. She'd never been granted alimony. The whole thing was a farce.

The new Chef and I were busy working out the details for the dinner before the wedding and the brunch after the service. Trying to duplicate, more or less, what would be happen when the May conference began. The small housekeeping staff was getting rooms ready. The place was a buzz with activity. My excitement level was on a sugar high, excited to see the center come alive as our wedding day drew closer.

My whole family, as well as Cole's brother and sister-in-law, would be arriving by mini-van from the airport in Billings around four o'clock Saturday afternoon. Cole's sister and her husband were driving from Boise. I knew my family would love Cole. I only hoped his family would accept me.

The plan was to have cocktails in the bar before dinner giving everyone a chance to get acquainted then serves dinner in the dining room. I'd decorated the table with an abundance of fresh flowers from a florist in Billings, not caring what they charged me for delivery. White candles in hurricane glasses graced the table and place cards were at every setting. Everything looked so festive. This was a first for me. I'd never been responsible for a large dinner party before. I'd fretted over every small detail, afraid I might forget something. I wanted everything to be perfect.

April brought with it an early spring with mother nature abounding in all her glory. The pastures were starting to turn green with new grass. An abundance of wildflowers covered the ground as far as the eye could see -- bright yellow buttercups, purple shooting stars, Indian paintbrush. This was as different from the concrete streets of New York as night was from day. Birds were singing as they went about building nests on the top branches of the mature trees. The landscaping surrounding the center was complete, the young trees beginning to show signs of new leaves.

Up until today, I'd handled all the details as if the event was for someone else, feeling detached for the most part from the idea that all the planning was about our wedding. The realization had finally sunk in and I knew I was ready for the most important two days of our lives to date. Hoping and praying nothing would go wrong.

I rolled over and snuggled up against Cole, listening to the rhythmic sound of his breathing, feeling the beat of his heart knowing whatever fate handed us we could handle, as long as we had each other.

I don't know how long I lay there waiting for him to stir before he groaned and rolled over on his back.

"What are you doing awake so early? I'm usually the first one up."

"I guess I'm just to nervous to sleep."

"Well, you can't change your mind, now. Remember you're the one who proposed."

Cole sat up, rubbed his eyes and stretched. "Seriously, what's to be nervous about?"

"I just want everything to be perfect. I want your family to like me."

"Don't be silly. They'll love you. It would be nice if everybody managed to get along, but I really don't care. The only one I care about is you."

Kissing him, I jumped out of bed. "Bet I beat you to the shower."

By early afternoon, everything was in place. We were ready and waiting as the van drove up. Cole's sister, Elizabeth, and her husband Harry, had arrived a few hours earlier giving me an opportunity to get to know them. It didn't take long before it felt as if we'd been friends for years. Elizabeth was as pretty as Cole was handsome, down to earth with no false pretenses Harry was easy going with a quick wit and disarming smile.

Eager to show her husband around the ranch before the rest of the guests arrived,

The mini-bus arrived on schedule. Cole and I rushed out to meet everyone. While our families spent time together on the long ride from the airport, they had little time to really get acquainted. It was mass confusion as all the introductions were made. Dad was the last in line, accompanied by a handsome woman near his age.

"Julia, I'd like you to meet Mary Sinclair."

"I'm delighted to meet you at last, Julia," she smiled and took my hand. "And on such a happy occasion. I'm so pleased you extended the invitation. It gave me a wonderful opportunity to meet your remarkable family."

As we moved inside, Mary Sinclair was an unanswered puzzle. Why had my father asked that she be included in a family affair? I'd check with my sister later.

The luggage had been sorted out and everyone shown to their rooms. I'd allotted plenty of time to get settled before we meet at six for cocktails.

I looked for Cole, but he'd disappeared. Probably giving a tour. Having completed a last minute check with the chef I was about to go upstairs and change clothes when Dad pulled me aside.

"If you have a minute, Julia I'd like to speak to you."

"Of course, Dad."

I led the way to the lobby and pointed toward a sofa. "What's up? Stop right now if you're going to suggest a prenuptial agreement."

"No. I wanted a chance to talk to you in private about Mary Sinclair."

I could hardly wait to hear what she was all about.

"As you might suspect, I've been terribly lonely since your mother died. I was fortunate enough to meet Mary some time ago at a dinner party and we've been seeing a lot of each other since I moved to New York." He paused. Much to my surprise my dad seemed uncomfortable, at a loss for words.

"Yes, go on. Are you about to get married?"

"No, not exactly. You see we're not young like you and Cole. We're both set in our ways and it might be difficult to change, to adjust, so to speak, and there are complicated financial considerations."

It seemed strange for my father to be having trouble coming to the point. "So go on, Dad, where is this heading?"

"Well, the last time I was here I had a long talk with your Aunt Sarah. It started out about you two and ended up being about Mary and me."

"Please, out with it. What is it you're trying to say?"

"I'm trying to say Mary and I have moved in together."

I couldn't help myself. I burst out laughing. "Why you sly old fox. Welcome to the modern world of romance. You two are actually living together? Is she fine with that?"

"To tell the truth, my dear, it was her idea. I've given up my apartment and moved into her townhouse in Brooklyn Heights. So far, it's working out very well. We could get married someday, but right now it isn't important."

"Are you happy, Dad?"

"Happier than I've been in years. Just look at her. How could I help but be happy? Imagine being with such a beautiful talented woman at my age."

"Then I'm happy for you. I can hardly wait to get to know her. How are my siblings handling this?"

"They seemed shocked at first, but I'm sure she'll win them over. I'm counting on you to welcome her into the family."

"Of course, Dad. Tell Mary I'm happy for the both of you. I've got to run and get changed before dinner. You know she looks familiar, but I can't place her or the name.

"You might know her by her pen name, Sandra Burroughs."

"The author?"

Dad nodded, looking very proud of himself, as if he'd caught the gold ring at the merry-go-round.

"I've read a few of her novels. Now I really want a chance to get to know her."

As we went our separate ways, I could hardly wait to tell Cole the news. My uptight dad had met his match and her name was Mary Sinclair.

I rushed upstairs and slipped into a pale green ankle length linen dress. The slits on the side made it possible to move as it hugged my body. The color was a perfect match for the earrings Cole had given me.

Cole looked his usual handsome self in starched jeans, a white shirt, wide leather belt with its large silver award buckle, and his best dress boots. Everyone was told in advance tonight would be casual as we'd planned a western style barbeque.

This was not New York. My East Coast family was about to meet Big Sky country with its unique western style of living.

The bar was beginning to fill with our guests. Billy and Charlene were among the group of Cole's friends who had arrived earlier.

Cole seemed to be getting along well with my brothers. My sister kept telling me how handsome and charming he was.

Cole's brother, Cody, was a lot like Cole, not quite as good looking, but easy going and fun to talk to. He and his wife seemed pleased Cole was settling down. His family was impressed with what he'd built on the ranch. Hoping the center would allow the ranch to remain in the family.

His sister and I had hit it off at once. We had Charger in common, after all. She'd driven down to the barn to see him, delighted to see the old horse doing so well. She too seemed thrilled to see Cole so happy and loved what I'd done to the old house.

I had a chance to talk with Mary Sinclair and liked her at once. I could see why my dad was attracted to her. Not only was she a striking looking woman, she exuded charm and self-confidence. I recognized all the signs, as my father couldn't conceal the gleam in his eye, nor could he keep his hands off her. I guess you're never too old to fall head over heels in love.

So far, the evening was going well. The men had wandered out on the back deck to watch the barbeque. The exterior lighting shone warm rays on the lake, making the whole outdoors look magical. When Cole proclaimed the meat was done, dinner was announced, and we all gathered in the dining room. The table had been arranged in the shape of a large horseshoe allowing everyone to view of everyone else. Making conversation easy.

Dinner couldn't have gone better. The food couldn't have been tastier. The chef did himself proud. Dessert had been served and the coffee poured when Cole stood attracting everyone's attention as he said, "I have a little surprise in store for you all.

"Ladies and gentlemen." He winked in Billy's direction. "The word gentleman excludes my dear friend Billy of course. Julia and I are so happy you could all be here tonight. So far, I'm glad to let you know that I've heard no unkind words. The families seem to be getting along. It would appear it won't be a replay of the Hatfield's and the McCoy's.

So, in honor of this evening, I'm happy to announce "The Big Sky Quartet" has been brought out of retirement for one night only, and will be performing shortly for your enjoyment. Please refrain from throwing food or bottles at the musicians. Applause will be appreciated, and we will not be passing our Stetson's for your donations. Just keep in mind we haven't performed since our college days." "

I had no idea what was going on as Cole, his brother Cody, Billy, and John our contractor left the room returning a few minutes later with their instruments.

Cody walked in first taking a harmonica from his pocket, Billy followed carrying a big bass fiddle, John, behind him with a fiddle. Last in line was Cole holding a guitar, the strap slung over his shoulder.

Cole winked at me as he said, "Okay boys, on three, and no booing from the audience. I dedicate this one to the love of my life Miss Julia, ready boys. Cole tapped his foot, one, two, three."

Cody began to play a few notes on his harmonica, then the bass picked up the beat as Billy began to pick at the strings, then Cole began to strum his guitar. Cole smiled at me and began to sing, "Hey, Good Lookin, what you got cookin'" as the fiddle joined in.

I had no idea when Cole planned any of this, but it might explain the late nights of unexplained absence. They were really quite good and having a lot of fun. Cole could definitely carry a tune and he was great on the guitar. Was there no end to his talents?

An energetic round of applause and shouts erupted when the song ended.

"Thank you, folks. Seeing as we all survived the first tune, we'd like to try a second number for your pleasure. Is everyone having fun?"

More shouts and applause brought smiles from the band. Much to everyone's delight, they played their own rendition of, "My Heroes Have Always Been Cowboys," with special lyrics poking fun at Cole's friends. The longer they played the better they got.

They were having as much fun playing as we were listening. When the many verses ended, Cole nodded to the server, "Dim the lights, please." He turned to our guests, "We're about to play our last number before we go back into retirement. Ready boys. You can all join in if you want."

With the strains of "Goodnight, Irene," one-by-one everybody started to sing along. Everyone seemed be having a good time. After the second chorus, at Cole's direction, they began to stand and follow the band, everyone singing at the top of their lungs as they left the dining room heading for the bar. The perfect end to a wonderful evening and it was all Cole's doing.

We ended the night with after dinner drinks in the bar. After about any hour, the only ones left in the bar were Cole, Billy, John and Cody. The boys were having so much fun they were in no hurry to call it a night. Their wives having already called it a night, I decided I wouldn't be missed either. Cole was strumming his guitar as I left, a large pitcher of beer resting on the bar. It was a good thing they didn't have drive home.

Chapter 40

I stirred as Cole climbed into bed. I had no idea what time it was only that it was late. He fell asleep almost as soon his head hit the pillow. The sounds of deep loud snores filled the room.

I awoke early and let him sleep in. The wedding ceremony wasn't until ten. I needed a time to myself. This was the most important day of my life and I wanted to let the experience sink in, thinking about how close I came to being in a different place a different time. Was it fate? Was I meant to be here with Cole? But for the accident I'd be Roger's wife by now." I stepped into the shower and let the hot water relax my body. I wanted to take my time getting ready.

I heard Cole's voice from the other room just as I stepped out of the shower. "What time is it, Babe?"

"Time to get up."

"Right. A guy doesn't want to be late to his own wedding. I could use a couple of aspirins and a long hot shower."

I saw Cole, as I walked into the bedroom, sitting on the edge of the bed his head resting on his knee, a hand rubbing the back of his neck. "The boys and I had a few too many last night."

"Drinking to the end of the wonderful world of bachelorhood?"

"No way. Just a few toasts to the good old days, remembering our lost and wasted youth, the fun we had playing together as a band, and last night's performance."

"You're not having second thoughts, are you?"

"You're kidding. The good old days were kid's stuff. I couldn't imagine life without you, my sweet. A guitar makes a damn lonely bed partner. Much better to have a sweet young thing like you standing by her man."

"I'll let that one pass, but tell me how come we've been together over a year and I've never heard you play your guitar even once?"

"For one thing, my old guitar went by the wayside a long time ago. I sold it when I left for grad school. I needed the money for bus fare. The one I used last night belongs to a friend."

"You were really great. How come you never mentioned the band or how talented you are?"

"There lots of things you don't know about me, pretty lady. Fireside stories I'm saving for cold winter nights when the snow is piled high against the doors."

"Everyone loved the performance, me most of all. Coffee is ready. I'm going next door to Sassy's room to get dressed. The grooms not supposed to see the bride before the wedding, remember?"

Cole gave me that silly boyish grin, "Understood, your highness, Sleeping with the bride is okay, it's just looking that's taboo."

Sassy answered my knock. I could see my dress hanging on the back of her closet door as she let me in.

"You ready for your big day, my dear?"

"I was just remembering how excited I was at my sister's wedding, it was that year's event of the summer -- bridesmaids in elegant gowns, groomsmen in tuxedos, a flower girl, and my sister in a spectacular satin gown with a train yards long. You should have seen it, Sassy. The church had been decorated with large bouquets of flowers on either side of the altar, the pews with huge white bows attached. The ceremony was followed by a sit-down dinner for hundreds at the Club. A full band played dance music."

"From what you say, Julia, it does seem like quite an event," Sassy said, as she removed my dress from its hanger. "Sorry I missed it."

"I tried to duplicate or even best the event, spending weeks with a wedding planner, going over minute details for my wedding to Roger, trying to achieve what I thought a wedding should look like.

It consumed my every thought, Sassy. As I think back, everything was about the wedding, never about Roger or our life together."

I slipped the dress over my head, feeling the silkiness of the satin as it touched my body. "I don't feel that way any longer. I'd have been just as happy with a civil ceremony if it wasn't for the families."

"Ah, yes, families. I, too, had a fancy wedding, the only daughter in the family, and of course I was marrying a prominent figure in American politics I soon learned there was life after the ceremony --one day of unrealistic romanticizing in a long life of reality."

I heard a long sigh, then silence as Sassy seemed lost in thought.

"Will you please fasten the back, I can't reach the buttons."

I glanced at my reflection in the mirror, the ankle length ecru satin gown fit perfectly. A simple elegant gown without any frills. I thought I'd be nervous, but I wasn't. I felt only excitement and joy. I'd come a long way since Sassy arranged for my stay at the ranch. I'd grown up step-by-step, day-by-day, with a few bumps along the way, one named Cynthia. But today I knew who I was and what I wanted out of life, convinced Cole and I would beat the odds. I'd stepped outside my comfort zone, took a chance, and found love.

"You've been right about so many things, Sassy. I have you to thank for putting me on the right path."

"I might have planted your feet in the right direction, but you took the journey all on your own."

"It's funny, Cole rarely says I love you, but there's no need to, I see it in his eyes, his need to have his arm tight around me as he sleeps, the way he tries to protect me. No matter what life hands us, I know we'll be okay. We have each other."

As Sassy did up the last of the tiny seed pearl buttons, she gave me a warm embrace. "If I'd been fortunate enough to have a daughter, I'd want her to be just like you.

I started to wipe a tear from my eye. I loved Sassy the way I'd loved my mother.

"Now don't start crying, Julia. Let me have a look at you. Turn slowly, so I can see the whole picture. Yes. You're what every bride wished she looked like on her wedding day. You two make a very handsome couple. There will be handsome children for me to spoil, soon, I hope. Now, go finish your makeup. Its good form to be on time for your wedding."

I took extra care getting ready. Fastening a single strand of pearls around my neck I stepped back into the bedroom.

"I'm ready if you are, Julia, let's check with your father."

He and Mary were dressed and ready as we entered their room. I admit being taken aback to see only one of the beds had been slept in.

"You look quite beautiful, Julia. Don't you think so, Mary?"

"Yes, my dear, quite beautiful."

"I still can't see why you'd want to be stuck in this God forsaken place."

"Love is where you find it, Jordan. Don't you agree, Julia?"

"That's true, but I've learned to love this part of the country. There's a certain majesty about the land that overwhelms you and spoils you for anywhere else."

"You needn't worry about her Jordan. She's found her place and her man."

It seemed strange to hear my father called by his given name. My siblings and I called him Dad, of course, my mother referred to him as Father or Dear. I'd never heard him called Jordan before.

Sassy checked her watch. "I think it's time. I'll go ahead and make sure everything is ready. Give me a few minutes. If I don't come back its time to start.

We more or less had a plan for the ceremony though there hadn't been time for a real rehearsal. Dad and I waited at the head of the stairs as the sound system began to air the wedding march. As we entered the lobby, I could see Cole waiting in front of the window wall, standing beside him was his brother Cody, his best man. Sassy, my matron of honor was waiting as well, all smiles.

Some family and friends were seated, others standing, as my father and I walked toward the minister, his back to the window.

The minister was the spiritual leader of the church in Silverton where Cole's mother had worshiped. He looked austere as he waited to preside over the service we'd designed. He'd already made it known he thought wedding vows should take place in a church and scolded Cole for his lack of church attendance. He wasn't happy that we'd streamlined the ceremony pairing it down to the essentials and adding a few words of our own.

As my dad turned away, Cole took my hand in his, drew it to his lips, gently placing a kiss. "You've never looked more beautiful. I'm one lucky guy."

The minister gave us both a stern look and began the ceremony, but I barely heard his words. I knew I'd already committed to spend my life loving and honoring my husband to be. The minister's words as far as I was concerned were for the benefit of family.

As Cole placed a wide gold band on my finger, I turned toward Sassy to retrieve Cole's wedding band and saw the tears running down her cheeks. I knew what she must have been thinking.

Congratulations began as we walked toward our guests. Cole held tight to my hand as we received hugs and kisses, and best wishes from family and friends.

"I'll be glad," he whispered, "when this part is over and everyone goes home, Mrs. Clayton."

I smiled. "Say Mrs. Clayton again. I love the sound."

"I could use a drink about now, how about you, Mrs. Clayton?"

I smiled and nodded at the guests, whispering "Hopefully the champagne will be served any minute."

After everyone had their chance to congratulate us, and second glasses of champagne had been poured, time for brunch was at hand. Everything was going as planned. The chef had prepared an elaborate buffet. It didn't take much coaxing for the happy and hungry guests to begin to mill around the buffet table.

We sat through the usual round of toasts, some serious, and some humorous musings from Cole's friends. A very nice speech from my father wishing us well and accepting Cole into the family, a warm welcoming from Cody, as well, he being the senior member of the Clayton family. With the toasts over, being sure everyone had had their say and their fill of the buffet, time was drawing near to end the festivities, when Cole arose and smiled at me.

"I have a special toast for my lady love, but before I go any further, I have a surprise to share with her. This will be the first Julia's heard that thanks to a generous wedding present from her father we are leaving tomorrow mornings on a flight for a week in Hawaii."

I was taken aback. "Really, we're actually going to have a honeymoon, and in Hawaii?"

Everyone was clapping as Cole assured me it was true. Reaching under the table he retrieved the guitar from its hiding place and placed the strap around his neck.

"This is especially for you, Your Highness, my toast to the love of my life."

The only sound in the room was Billy on the bass that had been resting in the corner of the room as Cole began to strum the guitar. After a chord or two he said, "This is called, The Hawaiian Wedding Song, made famous by Elvis Presley. If you remember, Julia, it was old Elvis who sang the words I couldn't quite speak the first time I tried to say I love you."

A few more chords and Cole began to sing.

This is the moment
I've waited for
I can hear my heart singing
Soon bells will be ringing.

This is the moment
Of sweet Aloha
I will love you longer than forever
Promise me that you will leave me never

Here and now dear
All my love
I vow dear
Promise me that you will leave me never
I will love you longer than forever

Now that we are one
Clouds won't hide the sun
Blue skies of Hawaii smile
On this our wedding day
On this our wedding day

"I do love you with all my heart, Julia."

Brides aren't supposed to cry on their wedding day, but the tears of joy wouldn't stop. Cole put down his guitar and I pressed up against him as he held me tight. How could I be so lucky? How could I have ever thought of life without him. As I looked around, every female in the room was wiping tears from her eyes.

Cole had a huge grin on his face as he whispered in my ear,

"Your dad's check was generous enough that it will allow John and his crew to begin remodeling the bathroom while were gone. With any luck it should be finished by the time we come home...a shower big enough for two and double sinks. Your wish come true."

"God, I love you, Cole."

"For me or for the new shower?"

"For you and all your boyish charm." I knew a guitar had to be my birthday gift to Cole, so he could sing love songs to me from now until eternity.

Time fast approached for everyone to pack and get ready to leave. The mini-bus arrived at three, right on scheduled for the trip back to the airport.

There was a rush of goodbyes, congratulations for a wonderful event, best wishes for the bride and groom, words of praise regarding the center, wishes for a successful opening, as one-by-one the family began to board.

Sassy was the last to leave. She drew us close, ignoring the incessant honking of the horn in the distance, "I love watching you two together. Cole reminds me so much of his father, better educated and possibly better looking, but the same warm heart and ability to show his love. Treat each other kindly and with respect, as I know you will, and realize just how lucky you are. People search their whole lives for the kind of love you have for each other. I know Hank is watching from above, so pleased at what took place today. I will be checking on you, too. Cherish what you have if not for you, do it for us."

The horn continued to blare as Sassy gave each of us a hug and walked out the door recalling, I'm sure, the time she had with the man she'd loved.

Cole took my hand in his, "Well done, Mrs. Clayton, the wedding weekend was flawless. It all went off without a hitch. When your talents are incorporated into the center's meetings, we are bound to be successful. You continue to amaze me."

"It wasn't only me, Mr. Clayton. The center you designed was the key to the success. We're at the beginning of our perfect partnership. I know we'll pull it off."

"Well, my love, if we're lucky, we'll grow old together, and I promise I'll love you as much on our last day together, as I do today."

He put his arm around me and gave me a gentle kiss. "What say we finish off the last of the champagne before we start packing."

"True love stories never have endings."
~Richard Bach

Lightning Source UK Ltd.
Milton Keynes UK
UKHW040728290322
400721UK00012B/665